The Goddess Letters

The Goddess Letters

by

CAROL ORLOCK

St. Martin's Press
New York

For Peggy, for everything

This work was made possible in part by the King County Publication Project, and is jointly sponsored, in part, by a grant from the Washington State Arts Commission and the National Endowment for the Arts in Washington, D.C., a federal agency.

 For information, address St. Martin's Press, 175 Fifth Avenue, New York, N.Y. 10010.

Library of Congress Cataloging-in-Publication Data

Orlock, Carol.
The goddess letters.

1. Demeter (Greek deity)—Fiction. 2. Persephone (Greek deity)—Fiction. I. Title.
PS3565.R579G6 1987 813'.54 87-4399
ISBN 0-312-00601-2

First U.S. Edition

10 9 8 7 6 5 4 3 2 1

PART ONE

The First Winter

Approximately 1500 years before the birth of Christ

Now I sing of rich-haired Demeter, most powerful goddess, and of her trim-ankled daughter. Aïdoneus stole that child away, a gift to him from loud-thundering and all-seeing Zeus.

Homer
"Hymn to Demeter"

I

RAPE.

My child, Persephone, a virgin.

Persephone raped. Persephone fuerza. Persephone viol. Attikan. Seletza. Persephone puere. Persephone vete.

Sea people say it sykne. The ones hanging on cliffs over water say bast. The gravelly tongues of humans who walk over deserts and who swallow sand like air say druta. The band that lives in trees says ret. Often ret-ret.

More peoples, different tongues, more sounds. Thousands of peoples and their words and I know them all, but this rock I sit by would break to sand before I remembered them all. I've learned that word in every human tongue. It echoes, loud and soft, in voices of creeks and trees and mountainsides.

I can't write in words how a sea wave says rape, but I, and maybe Persephone, can hear it. I grow impatient with the thick gray voices of rocks, their stammering and how they clear their throats between each sound, speaking slowly because they have little to talk about. Today each stone makes only a single sound, and the olive trees, high and whining. These past four days every being says

Rape.

I'm writing this letter, but who is it for? Persephone? I can't find her.

I heard her four days ago when I lay with Dionysus, stretched out beside him after we had loved. All the others, the goddesses and gods, had been called together for some great decision. Dionysus and I would not go. Let them talk of me, let them talk of my daughter. I would not dignify it. I chose this way to prepare love for my daughter.

I leaned closed to Dionysus and touched him slowly. A new sound pulled me back. I heard her cry, rape, and her father's name.

I took beak and wings and cold blood, and I became a wild white bird and rose straight into the air. I wheeled, listening and saw Dionysus below me, gaping upward. Then I heard her cry again.

I screamed, flying into the wind. I skimmed over water and hillsides and fields to the place they call Nysa.

Nysa—that beautiful meadow—bloomed with hyacinths, roses, irises, violets, crocuses. Oceanus' daughters had invited Persephone there to pick flowers. Around me the rippling grasses tried, with their too long tongues, to speak as surf.

A patch of ground ahead of me lay torn and trampled. I supposed two horses, rutting there, had stamped it down. I saw the broken stems and blossoms of flowers beaten into mudcake. Beyond them lay a basket. I smelled the sweat of horses, the black breath of fire, and a stench—female fear. I smelled the trampled earth, its scent of loam, moist and sweet.

I love that smell. No matter if I'm singing or laughing or teaching my daughter, when I smell fresh earth I lose myself. In this sweet, fresh earth I enjoy my power to grow things, to give humans the gift of food, the gift of grain. And when the earth is turned over, brown and crumbly, the green shoots begin to grow, both in my thoughts and underground. Humans worship me for that. I am goddess of the growing and the grain, as Persephone is goddess of the flowers.

I stopped and stood. My feet straddled split earth. Hoofprints stood along it like a slender seam where one thread had pulled too tight on the loom. I stooped down to touch. It felt dry and warm, like ash buried in a furrow.

Then I saw the flower. Only its stem remained. It was bent and wilted, the blossom gone. Not gone, but caught. The seam of earth held its petals.

I pulled. The stem stretched and my heels sank into the mud. I tightened my belly and I yanked. The stem stretched green as the shallows of the Aegean sea, but the head wouldn't come free. The stem wouldn't break.

No stones, no sticks lay nearby, but I wanted to break the stem. I tore at the crown I wore, then threw it. It struck, and the stem screamed

Rape.

It echoed. Rape. Fuerza. Viol. Attikan. Seletza. Every flower, every tree, every stone is a fury tormenting me. Puere. Vete. Sykne. Their voices have followed me these past four days.

The voices chased me from that field. They followed, making shadows beside riverbanks, drifting mists over mountain slopes, all around me like sunlight. The sky shone and stony wastes crackled and stuttered with those voices. Below me, by day, crimped coastlines shaped the sound; above me, at night, the loom of stars moved, bright shuttles weaving a dense black cloth, a cloak I pulled over my shoulders. Cold night currents enfolded me. I stepped down to the sea, and when I dove, the deep undersea flow made the loss of her a touch, a cold, probing caress.

I searched Oceanus' caverns. I looked for his daughters, the girls of Oceanus and Thetys. Oceanus their father. Put a Titan with a Titan and what can one expect? They have three thousand daughters, a ripe supply in all the large sizes. "Deep-bosomed," poets call them, kindly.

Sprawled in Oceanus' caverns, the girls were busy at work exercising their ankles, six thousand legs stretched in the air, turning their feet madly to work off the flesh. Curse to triviality the poet who first called a goddess trim-ankled. All the poets keep using it now, and every goddess on Olympus, even knobby-boned Hera, must have the slenderest stalks.

I paused before the spectacle and listened for the howls of the young Charites. That led me to Eurynome, who sat turning her foot while practicing her singing. Even so occupied, she was suckling the little Charites, nursing all three, the one off teat having to make do with a toe. And a toe on the foot whose ankle was not turning.

I'd brought Persephone's basket, and I threw it at Eury's feet. To ask for Persephone, I had to shout over the singing and cracking of ankle joints.

Eury cringed at my anger, then pretended nonchalance and exchanged the toe child and a teat child. Then she suggested, since I wasn't busy, would I mind?

The Charite she offered, Mirth I think, mouthed like a fish toward my nipple.

I declined quietly, turning away. "Suckling improves your ankle structure," I said.

I waded through half the deep-bosomed herd before Eury remembered how to speak aloud. "Does it really?"

I looked over my shoulder. "The Great Demeter makes it so."

At the cavern's arch, I turned. Eury's eyes had gone wide as her nipples, and a nearby brood of her deep-bosomed sisters had bared their breasts to entice the child.

Titans. And that we should have the same mother. No wonder Zeus placed them in chains ages ago.

I thought of going to Olympus and asking Zeus himself. Olympus is my home, after all, the home of all the immortals, and whatever happens must begin there. I thought of pushing into my brother Zeus' rooms and demanding answers, but my anger had begun to sour. I couldn't bear to hear soft music playing on the lyre, to smell the sweet ambrosia set out for all to eat. Demeter on Olympus without Persephone—the thought stopped me. It holds me back now, even though I must go soon.

I told myself it was better, for then, to disguise myself and go among the humans. Humans are as pitiful as Demeter is now, I thought. Go to the women, they lose children and they should understand and help. I've wandered four days among the humans. I never have understood them but I know them better than I did.

Life was simpler before humans arrived. There were Titans, of course, gorgons, many-headed monsters, but back then one could imagine, day-to-day, what might happen. Kronos would eat his children. Zeus would save us. Battles, battles. The Titans would be condemned to chains. More of the same.

But then these humans appeared, creatures so ignorant, so simple-minded and down-to-earth that they doubt the future. Not to even have the gift of future-knowing, of all things. I have difficulty imagining how they live like that.

Oh, I don't know all. For example, where is Persephone? Who raped her? Who am I writing to? That doesn't mean I don't know the future. A human knows the past when she forgets the painful parts, and I know the future, most of it.

But these humans. They stare at the sky wondering where they came from and where they're going. We immortals stare at earth and know the future perfectly well. We're just not sure how these humans got here.

It's a truth and there's no help for it. We're left with these peculiar, shadow-casting creatures populating the earth, and who knows where they came from? We make myths to explain them, all speculation. Perhaps it's too painful for any of us to remember.

They're interesting, as creatures go, but if only they weren't so pathetically concrete. Perhaps they're flawed by living on earth, made dense as Ge, the very earth herself. Maybe Ge formed them herself, as she claims, from earthly dust. But then everyone claims them. And disowns them, alternately.

I do know one thing, having met so many—humans with skin like leather and others with skin like milk, some you'd swear were children of dark obsidian and others the pale offspring of quartz, those with eyes round as the Hekate's moon in a night sky and others whose eyes are slits like shining Helios rising on the horizon. Yes, I'm sure, since I became one temporarily—I frightened the first human woman and couldn't get a word out of her—since I've sat on their hearths and laughed at their riddles and learned one word in every one of their languages, after all this, I know one thing. We're bound to them.

I knew before, but never cared. Now I know the terrible sadness of being one, and I know they're going to matter. I know how it will happen too, like a scene somewhere far into the future—a night awake with fire and. . . .

No, not that. My future-knowing eludes me. But I know that I know, and I'll foresee it some other time.

I learned enough from being among humans to sense their sadness and feel it gather inside my own. For these past four days I have gone with my shoulders covered by a dark cloak, resolved to take no comfort, not even sleep. I carried torches to move at night. I placed each step ahead of my last, as slow-footed humans do, and I went to huts and houses, to markets. I climbed ladders to tree platforms, scraped down tunnels into caves, swayed on the decks of boats following rivers—the Nile, the Euphrates, the Niger, the Ganges. To each human band I put my question, I said, "Have you seen Demeter's daughter, Persephone?"

And simple as they are, they'd look side to side, up and down, and shrug. I'd gesture to learn their word for rape. At first the women laughed, talking of sex, but when they understood me, their skins went gray as ash, and the men would slink out the doorways, or fold themselves to shadow in corners.

At that the women would want me gone. A goddess raped? All at once, I was a mad old woman who wandered and told dirty stories. Soon I'd back away from the hearth and move on.

The last place I visited is only a dark spot on the plain below me now. I stayed too long. The woman was a good one and her mate, unlike most of the men, wasn't a groveller. Perhaps being human has affected me a little. I wander with no crown, I seem to feel the loneliness of having a skin, the uncertainty of knowing that you can die. The woman saw this and forgave my staying.

Mud crumbled from the stone fittings on the walls, and her hearth reeked of fat spittings from meat. I'd asked my question and learned their word for it easily, its name always a slice torn from the tongue, common and short as the name of a body part. The woman had stared from her door. Her fields were empty and her cattle thin. She shook her head. The goddesses withheld their gifts lately, she said. No grain grew, and flowers seemed to have stopped blooming.

"Mother and daughter avoid us." She averted her eyes. "Four days now."

Then I heard a noise like a puppy's growl. The man shoved his elbow into his gut to quiet it. These two were hungry and had only enough grain for themselves, so they wouldn't eat until I left. I rose to go and perhaps because I was tired, I made my mistake.

They'll never know, I thought. They'll never guess who sat on their hearth and talked with them. There's no harm, I decided, because I wanted to feed them. Even more, I felt the sorrow of these four days. The fields all over the earth were bare, and I longed to give food again, as I always have given, as I've enjoyed from my very beginning, pouring out plenty. To feed them was my nature and my realm, yet I'd been so busy searching for her over these four days, I'd given nothing.

I stood in the doorway. Beside the hut, a starving calf scratched the dirt with its hoof. As I passed over the threshold, I left a gift.

Night was falling when I climbed this hill. After seeing me off, the woman turned to find a basket of grain, good winnowed stock, set firmly on her doorstep. But I see now, looking down, that they're not eating it.

Both stand and stare. Either they suppose it's poison, or they're afraid of magic. Either way, they won't eat. I should have sown the field and made them work for it.

How could I have been so simple? They stand away from the basket, and now the woman goes down on her knees, I can almost hear her knee joints crack. The man crouches, his head lower than hers. His wife's lips move in a prayer, Generous Demeter, Mother of Life, Loving Mother.

How ignorant humans are. They lack the knowledge of their hearts. They should have known while I sat with them that a goddess visited, yet they believe in only what they can see.

She's turned this way now, and he turns too. They must see the fire of my torches halfway up the hillside.

Oh for pity's sake, she's pressed her face to the dirt, and he writhes alongside, degrading himself to outdo her. Oh, curse them, curse them all, the humans, but curse these two especially, with a case of the shakes, with a palsy. How ignorant can beings be to believe only in what they see and hear and touch? I've half a mind to upset one of these torches and set the hillside on fire. That would cure them. Their field is dry as sun-bleached bone. Fire would feed well there.

I'll do it. I'll put my torch to one dead root. I foresee flames. They leap and sputter. I imagine it and can almost see the man and the woman run toward their hut. Flame licks the earth behind them.

Let them burn. What's the use of my kindness and my pity? Persephone's taken and raped. My crown tossed down into the earth. I can't bear to think of my beautiful home on Olympus.

I imagine that woman's prayer. Loving Demeter. Generous Demeter. Mother of Life. Grain Mother.

I'll be Mother, Mother of Flame. They fattened on my gifts before, let them eat ash awhile. My grain strengthened their sheep and their pigs, and what did they do but kill them? For sacrifices.

And the Olympians, the other immortals enjoying immortal life on that mountaintop, how pleased they'll be to see the fire. They'll rejoice and think the whole earth is an altar for some new sacrifice. Proud Zeus. And vicious Ares. And Athena, her smile a cool spring breaking free of rock. And Aphrodite. Poseidon too. Curse every one of them. They'll only wonder when the scent of sacrifices stops rising to their nostrils.

Curse them every one.

But Rhea. My own mother Rhea will foresee. She would know Demeter's done this, and only Demeter can call down rain. And Demeter won't.

Let them burn. Let flame spread around me, over me. My hair seared, my skull gleams like a torch. I feel it on my face and on my neck, deep pain, terrible. It consumes me and hurts and I am glad, glad for pain. How pleasing to burn as a field, a torching pine, a bush that gulps upward. I can hurt from one single beautiful pain and it pleases me better than my grief. I would let it burn, let the fields and the trees, the woman and the man and their hut burn. The pain will grow rich with all the temperatures of fire, and I can bear it, a single agony. I can endure it better, Persephone, than this chorus of tongues, all speaking one word.

I hold the torch. My fingers tremble. The woman and man look up. What do they see? A dark lump crouched against the sky, I shake and the torch flickers. I feel hesitant as a pathetic human.

Persephone, if you read this, see me—a crouching spirit in a dark cloak, see her bent double like a stone. She sits by a stone, a silhouette by moonlight and torchlight, double-humped like a camel's back. The people call this place Arcadia. A name, a word. I can destroy this place.

Do you see an old woman muttering in a field at night? Persephone? I think it is you I'm writing to after all.

Can't find her.

Persephone. If ever some day you read this, then know . . .
how is it I write what I feel and I still feel it so strongly?

Then if you read this, know

I set down the torch.

II

WHERE are the soft winds of spring, the gentle zephyrs? Are they blowing? I sleep in this dark, closed-up place, but I dream about hotness and warm winds. Maybe wind off a fire. I have felt cold ever since I left earth. This can't be earth. Or Mount Olympus either. I'm not sure where I am any more, if I'm anywhere at all, or even if I'm Persephone any more. I dream of warm wind and fire, then I wake up all cold and shivering.

I tell him he keeps it too cold. He smiles and says I'll get accustomed. I won't. I've decided.

When zephyrs blow, flowers wave. I want to go back to the flowers. He says I can't. He says he'll make a flower for me.

I think he made the flower that I wanted to pick in the field at Nysa. No, it was pretty, so he couldn't have made it. But the flower was the trap that took me in. Ge makes the flowers, but she wouldn't have made this one, not her.

Could she? No, she wouldn't make a flower to trick me.

But what if she did. Then who else was in on the trick? Oceanus' girls? Eurynome? What big breasts Eury has. I want breasts like hers some day, but then everybody says

Mother Demeter is perfectly formed. One day I'll be like her.

Today I miss her. He says Mother Demeter gave permission for me to be here, but I don't understand why she didn't tell me. She'll be coming, so I wait.

I don't feel well. I don't like it here. I feel so, so what? So tricked. What have I done to make anyone spiteful?

Maybe we should have invited Mother to go with us to Nysa, but Eury and Clymene agreed we could go by ourselves, and they are my friends after all. I'm not a child any more and shouldn't have Mother Da everywhere I go. Yes, Mother likes flowers, but I like flowers too and have a right to look for my own. As I did. And saw one, only one like it. And wasn't it the most beautiful? Oh, but that's why I'm here. And chilly.

I felt afraid even before I saw that flower growing all by itself. Eury and Clymene wanted to stay up the field a ways, near Mount Olympus, but I saw no reason to chase their leavings, half-wilted ones, several with crumpled petals and twisty stems, so I went on by myself. I felt afraid, but of course I would, first time out by myself, and of all places in a field where they grow grapes for wine belonging to Dionysus. The stories they tell about Dionysus, so handsome, a god who brings wine and makes women go mad! I felt afraid and I looked back.

I had gone so far that Oceanus' girls, big as they are, looked as small as little nymphs. Was Dionysus near? I wondered off and on. Anyway, I told myself, he plays tricks —Dionysus, the gaping one—he plays his tricks on women especially. But nobody says he's cruel. And besides, if I was going to let a little fear send me running back to my friends . . .

Well, maybe more than a little. All over me I felt thin sweat and my wrist shook until I dropped my basket. And then when I stooped to pick up the flowers, I saw that special one. He came right after that.

I wonder. Feeling afraid like that. Mother says I'll know the future when I get older. I am growing. Everybody agrees I am. Maybe I knew a little future.

Now I'm stuck. What was I thinking? Oh, the flower. So then I knew if I was going to let a little fear send me running for the others, I would never grow up. Oceanus' girls would laugh at me—when they laugh their breasts jiggle. I wonder how that feels? So then I knelt to get my flowers, and wasn't it lucky having them drop right there? Just a reach away from that one flower?

No, I think again now. Maybe it was unlucky. I feel so tricked.

But what a flower. Its stem was a fat fertile tube, bright as the rind of a lime. Its two leaves arched, pale and slender, and they looked so soft, lined by a furry, funny down of hairs. And then the flower, right in the middle of those pale leaves, a hundred blossoms. The outer ones burst pale pink, but their lips folded, lapping like rose petals, layer and layer of pink and then purple and then red. Each petal was outlined with moisture, the way a valley can be by fog. Wet silver dew circled every petal as if a snail had traced its edge and left silver filaments, frothy and moist.

Then, just at the center, I saw the tiniest, most hidden bud—a ruby-colored thing, single and small. I smelled a fragrance, not too sweet, but fertile as sea water trapped in a tide pool, and it promised the sweetest sleep.

And I had to have it. That flower was mine—Persephone's alone. I'd discovered it. I didn't need Mother or Clymene or Eury to point it out to me. My hand got moist, wanting it. Will it wilt, I wondered. But somehow, perhaps already knowing the future, I knew it wouldn't. It seemed that at my touch, just like at Mother's touch, this thing would grow. Everything grows and becomes beautiful when Mother touches it. It would swell, becoming large and its blossoms redder, and when the moment came maybe burst—yes, burst spraying pollen all pink and purple-silver and red.

Oh damn.

Aren't I getting a temper, just like a goddess?

I never even touched it. And, of all things, when I'm thinking of it again, here he himself comes. To interrupt me.

* * *

I must think it through again. I must remember it all from the beginning. I must be calm. He's left now, and I should be calm. But how can I when I feel so empty? I was thinking of something when he came. The flower, yes. And he came in, that's it.

I asked him something, what was it? I asked, what does he do when he's away from me.

I make decisions, he said.

I remember now. I could see he wouldn't lie, but he didn't want to tell me the truth either.

I said that sounded just like a human, taking ages to make a decision.

I carry out decisions others make, he said then.

Like a slave, I asked, afraid to think for yourself? That really upset him, but he wouldn't show it. He just said I knew perfectly well that he wasn't human, that he was a god.

So I started playing. I said, if you're immortal, prove it, change your shape and turn into something.

He couldn't decide, probably wanted to impress me. He took so long, I made suggestions.

But the oddest—no, the saddest thing was: they were all him. First I asked him to turn into a valley and try as he might, the closest he came was a chasm. Then I switched and said I wanted a mountain, not a jagged one like he first made, something soft and rolling, a big ball of hills. But for all my explaining I couldn't get anything from him but a cliff. So I switched to animals.

His monkey looked more like a gorilla, his mouse had the sharpest teeth and wasn't any good to pet. Likewise his cat—and did it spit! His dog was a cur, almost a wolf. His bird was nothing but a starving nighthawk.

I'm sure he saw my disgust, so he changed right out of it

and became himself again.

He is dark and tall, like a wort, a long mandrake root. I'm sure I never met him. Especially I don't like his eyes. They look as sharp as a thunderbolt order from Zeus.

Then he began to talk, very fast as if he knew how bad he'd been at the changing game. He walked around this place that I'm in, and while I hadn't bothered noticing it before, as he pointed out its traits to me, which he called its qualities, I saw it.

How like his changing game it was! Each thing as he praised it was nice-as-nice to him, but I only saw pale copies of actual things.

"You have space to move here," he said, showing how wide the walls spread around us. I saw walls. This was a place, only one place and no other. It wasn't everywhere, like I'm used to.

"Over there," he said, "your bath." A lukewarm pool, with alabaster sides that should be marble. "There you'll refresh yourself." It's filled up with a liquid that pretends to be water, but I knew already it wasn't.

I might have said, "I bathe in rivers and waterfalls, not your brackish seepings from the sea," but what was the use? According to him, it would make me feel clean, but I'd already tried it, and I didn't feel clean. I still felt the film of his breath all over myself.

"A couch. For your rest." He pointed out this place where I'm lying now, a long smooth stone, curved over at the edges and lined with a fur of moss. It's pretty to look at, but when I lie down it always gives the thinnest edge of pain wherever I touch it.

"And ambrosia, of course."

Here I should have disagreed. We eat ambrosia on Mount Olympus and it has the sweetest flavor, tart as good stinging rain but gentle as a spring wind. His ambrosia had none of that, only the ghost of its smell. Everything here, now that I think of it, reminds me of the drawings humans make—of the sea, for instance, which isn't the sea at all, and much worse for trying to look like it.

I could have objected on the ambrosia, and won my point by insisting we go to Olympus to compare. Assuming he was, in fact, immortal. Only goddesses and gods are allowed on Mount Olympus. But then he does seem to be a god, what with the changing. I could have objected, but I didn't.

First, I expected him to say I wasn't allowed to go to Olympus. I'm not sure why I thought that, but I didn't want to ask since then I'd know. But most of all, there was his way, his telling me how nice-as-nice his place could be, his wanting me to like it, then to owe him so I'd give him something in return. I couldn't figure what I was supposed to give.

Then I had a thought. "I'll change for you."

"No!" He turned red, angry like that, but I kept on.

"I could be a green shoot, a bird—I've never been good at birds. I could be a stream, a brook . . . "

He cut me off.

"You're lovely now, Persephone." That was the first time he used my name. He didn't speak it, he handled it the way a human lifts a seed puff, afraid she might break it. "No," he said. "I don't want you to be other than you are. And please stay just as you are, I must be sure of that."

I asked why, of course. He started to answer, then stopped and thought before going on. "Mother Demeter asked me to be sure you did not change," he said.

Now that subject interested me. I didn't believe him and he saw my doubt. "I had to bring you here," he said. "It was a decision made in a Boule. That's why I looked for you at Nysa."

A Boule! I almost laughed. Think of it—little me, maid Persephone—for me well-counseled Zeus, the mighty god of the sky, made a Boule decision. I mean, the inevitability of it! All the goddesses and gods sat down together and argued it out, and then the great Zeus made a decision, about me! Whatever comes out of a Boule becomes so, which meant this was decided for me.

"Demeter let you bring me here?" I asked. Everyone has

to be invited to a Boule, except Eros and me, of course, we're too young. But I know, whether by nodding or by absenting so as not to disagree, all immortals, everybody—Mother Da included—must vote in Boule. I know about Boules.

I know most of the rules. I'm quicker than Eros at naming my relatives. I name them—Ge is the earth and makes the firmness of things. She is earth, but she can be shaken. There's Poseidon, earth-shaker who is also the sea. He loves horses. Mother likes him.

Once long ago the immortals threw stones to decide who got what, and Poseidon won the sea. Mother got the fertility on earth—definitely best. And Zeus got sky. Zeus is my father—but he's married to Hera. I never actually met her, but I don't like her.

There are so many, I can't remember them all. Another one was there when they threw the stones, too. Sounds like Helios. Or like Hekate. Not the sun, though, not the moon. What was it?

And where was I before I thought of my relatives? And who's he? That's it. He said my coming here was decided in a Boule and I asked him then if Mother Da agreed too.

He's strange. He didn't say yes right out. He stood thinking. He looks like a mandrake root that got up on its two legs and just walked. Then instead of saying yes right out, he asked why Mother wasn't with us at Nysa.

"We didn't invite her," I replied.

But then, he said, wasn't Mother Demeter with Persephone always? Until that very afternoon?

He was right, of course, but I didn't nod. I was beginning to feel, with all his questions, like some human that Doubt has taken hold of. Doubt flusters them so completely with his questioning, questioning—all of it silly—until they're upset enough to admit Ge herself didn't even exist—they've never in their lives stood on firm earth. That's how I felt. But it got worse with what he asked next.

"You were at Nysa. Where was Demeter?"

Think of it. I hadn't thought of it. I didn't know where

Mother was and that was strange. Mother and I are always together, like twins in the sac, neither one moving, not dreaming, not thinking without the other one part of it. If Mother takes ambrosia, sweetness fills me. If I swirl underwater, Mother feels refreshed.

That's how things go. They've always . . . but no. Not now. I feel different. I felt it at Nysa but never noticed, never thought about it. I was alone at Nysa, finding flowers for myself and I didn't know where she was. But I only realized it when he asked me.

I looked at him and he stared. His dark eyes stared hard, hard at me, as if he hated asking.

I felt awful, split open and empty like a seed husk. I felt all set apart and afraid.

So then I asked who first came up with the idea of bringing me here, who asked for this Boule of goddesses and gods that decided it.

He didn't answer. He didn't have to answer because I knew. I knew what frightened me, too.

He could come over me, come into me. He could take me over, invade this half-me left without Mother Da, change me somehow, like lightning changes the shape of a tree, the way earthquakes change mountaintops, like that—I was scared.

I thought maybe the changing game could help. I might change to a river. Then I saw that if I did, he'd turn into a huge gray ocean. If I were a rock, he'd be a landslide. If I'm a tree, he's the wind. He'd come over me as a storm takes over a field and flattens it. I started to shiver with how he looked at me.

I wanted him to leave and I said so, but before he went out, he turned. "I'll make you a Queen," he said. Just that.

* * *

Not sure, but I think so. Yes sure. My being here is serious. Maybe a Boule was called and a decision was made. I'm sure it's serious because of how I've changed. It is serious—my very first serious experience—and I must—

must—experience it seriously.

That's all wrong.

Words are pretty hopeless. But they're something to do.

Here goes: the serious is serious and this is serious because I saw my reflection. I've changed.

Everybody's always said I'm the loveliest, I'm the perfect ripening maiden, as they say, beautiful and all. I have a right to enjoy such beauty, don't I? That's not all of why I looked though. More, I looked because of the crown, my very own crown and my first.

Not because he gave it to me. I would never wear a crown of his. But I have a crown because. . . .

. . .to explain with words takes forever!

So I was at Nysa. I saw that flower. It stunned me for an instant when I first looked, but then I reached for it. I stretched to get a hold on it, but I never even touched it. Instead, below my arm, the earth began to shake and it split open, a mouth showing deep black rock and giving off a smell—a smell of burning. Shapes appeared out of the rock—heads and hooves and six steaming bodies. Six huge black horses came up, thick and sweating, and they rushed up at me. I felt hot wind off their flanks and smelled earth and horse and him.

His chariot rose behind them. The shadow of the horses and the chariot and of him fell over me. A shadow. I'll remember that. Helios' sun must have been shining and seen it.

My arm still reached, frozen by fear at his hugeness over me. Even with the sunlight behind him—surely then Helios saw!—he was deep purple-red color, nearly black with rage.

I thought it was my father. I thought Father Zeus was angry at me, maybe for wanting that flower, and I was surprised. I said Zeus' name, but just at that word the darkness—not him but the darkness—gripped my wrist and pulled me in.

Rape, I cried, but I'd already been pulled, pinned on the seat of the chariot. In front of me the horses' haunches were slick, shining with sweat, and we whirled from Nysa's beautiful fields. Hoofbeats pounded not just ahead, but inside of me, and we moved so fast, like a bolt of black lightning. Very suddenly, we'd gone once around the entire earth. There must have been things to see, but I won't think of them now. Then we were back at Nysa again.

It must have been Nysa, I remember seeing where the earth had split where he came up through it. I caught a glimpse of the flower, and its stem had been stretched, as if someone came along while we were gone and had pulled it, but its head was caught. Then that earth-mouth opened again to swallow us—the horses, the chariot, him furled totally black, and me, part of all this. And one more thing.

A glimmer of light seemed to be trapped with us under the ground. My one wrist was still held tightly, but he was holding the reins of the horses with his other hand, so I reached with my other hand, grabbed that glimmer and tucked it into my skirts before he could see.

Now, finally, I get to the part about the crown.

I don't remember what happened after that. I woke up and I was here in this cold, strange place, but I still clutched my skirt. I was alone, so I untangled it. What I found, what had fallen under the earth with us, was a crown.

I don't know whose crown it is. It's an ordinary one, I've seen goddesses wearing hundreds like it. Mother Da always says I'll have my own crown soon, so I've decided this one's mine.

I tried it on once or twice, secretly when he wasn't around. The feel of it, tangled into my hair, cheered me up when I walked around the four walls of this place.

Why didn't I look into the bath's water before? I don't know, unless maybe I do start to sense the future coming. Anyway, I just now looked.

Feeling the crown in my hair no longer pleased me as much as at first. I needed something because I felt awful, that's all. It's been getting worse. Partly it's being here, and not knowing where here is. If here is where I am, I don't know where I am then, do I? I've lost Mother Da. It's like losing myself. Whenever he comes I smell the burning still on him from out there, wherever out there is, and I hear cries, of night birds I think, and once in a while I hear a low moan. I can't be sure what I hear and even that adds to the awfulness.

That's why I looked into the water of my bath, but telling it is less than feeling it. I only wanted a little happiness, so I put on the crown and walked, balancing so it wouldn't slip—it's slightly too big yet—and I went to the bath and looked in.

Maiden Persephone, ripening Persephone wasn't there. Where was she? She didn't look back at me. I only saw someone who looked like a little death, just that, a little death wearing a crown.

This is serious.

III

DRAW myself out little by little. Draw myself back bit by bit. As I always do. As goddesses and women do everywhere. I became a sea wave, a wall of Poseidon's surf. I crashed against the sand, and my froth still tumbles. I'm a confused spraying mist and soak into air and stone and sand. I seep into each thing I approach.

Then the drawing back. The wave curls and then tumbles and spatters. Then it gathers its spent self, separates from sand, from stone, from air. Its tide turns and it pulls back out to sea.

I must divide up this whirl—these past three days, my present, my future. I must gather myself now. I'll take back the gift I gave, gave gladly in the crash and tumble beneath Poseidon's thighs and return to myself now.

He's left and it begins. I come back slowly, I have only loneliness to take back. I'll reclaim myself gradually this time.

First a memory. Fire. My torches. I wanted to set the hillside on fire. I thought of how Zeus torments humans to amuse himself, and thought perhaps fire and killing could appease me for Persephone's loss.

And perhaps they would have. I watched that woman and her man, and knew they'd stand and stare as long as I sat on the hill, so I put my torches out and left, sneaking off in the dark. Sorrow returned, heavier after a moment's rest.

As, bit by bit, I return now. My self, my memory, my future-knowing.

I thought of Sisyphus' story. All through eternity he lays his huge shoulder against the more huge stone, pushing it up the hill only to watch it roll from his hands and down again. I thought of his strength and I managed to rise like a bird over the countryside of Arcadia. I knew what I had to do. I'd put it off too long. I went to Olympus.

My belly spasms. I laugh, and Poseidon's froth, still hot as my womb kept it, leaks and trickles down my thigh. I won't wipe it off. Let it cool and bead, I want it to dry slowly. Then I can laugh and remember. What words are right for Olympus? Slippery, sliding sounds? Salacious? Succulent? I arrived on the dark side of the mountain, near the doorway of Dusk, that old sneak.

Dusk holds himself aloof to appear mysterious. He is so shadowy he'd like to hide even from the moonlight of Hekate, but she moon-roams over him. Yet try keeping a secret from him and see if the shadows won't creep in and discover it. To the left of Dusk's doorway, I heard his breathing and followed the sound around a rock wall. I saw the shadows folded on his back where he'd crouched to peep between two clouds, and tiptoed nearer to have a better look.

On the bright side, beyond the shadows, I saw why Dusk was panting. Pan stood there, stuffing himself into Eros' small parts. I laugh, remembering. Thinking he was alone, Dusk had crouched down on his knees to draw his huge hands in and fondle himself. I waited. When his stroke sped and his sweat began to sparkle, I spoke.

"How dark it is," I said softly, "but small."

He turned and looked, then looked back down at himself, then at me again.

I didn't want to anger him, so pretended I meant Pan and

Eros, and nodded toward Pan. Pan's small pipe chucked under Eros' cheeks now.

"You see so much," I told Dusk. "You've probably seen my daughter, Persephone."

He nearly wilted.

"Daughter?" he stuttered and tucked his hands beneath his cloaks. "You have a daughter? Persephone. Lovely name."

Dark eyes shifted, this way, that way. I could tell he knew the secret, but he would be the last to betray it.

Eros' giggles came through the shadows, muffled but high, and Dusk pressed his spiralled ear to the crevice. Another time I would have stayed for the fun of it.

Another time, but not now. I gather to myself now, though not too quickly. First I'll remember them and laugh a little.

I left him and climbed higher over outcroppings and rocks, each stone cliff dressed up with a necklace of clouds. I climbed upward and upward, and as I went I saw them all. I saw Artemis, talented, titillating, inside the door of Oceanus' chambers. She cock-teased Oceanus in a wet dream. I saw Aphrodite. She soaks too long in her goat's milk baths, one day she'll wake up in cheese. I caught Hephaestus, laboring over Rhea's forge. Not forge, gorge, a caldron where Hep's hammer pounds to make pretty squeals.

He paused anyway, long enough to shrug an answer to me. Innocent as Persephone. No, ignorant as Oedipus.

I saw the furies, bickering as usual. I don't mind perversity, but they could assign orderly turns, last one underneath gets to be on the top next time, or something like that. Anyway, the sight of me froze them in their twisted and humped postures and stilled the slapping of their parts.

But my happiness drains, drop by drop. I return to myself. I asked my question, and each wide stare, every shrug stabbed deeper into me.

Not one, not even Athena—Sweet Objectivity herself, offering to lend me a crown—not one admitted seeing my daughter. No one recalled a flower like the flower I described, not one. I heard the echo, her cry of rape, even on Olympus, but they heard nothing. I named rape, and brows furrowed, but not one spoke up. Not on Olympus. To learn the truth, I would have to go elsewhere.

I won't think his name yet. I won't imagine her there with him. No, not yet. But later.

For now, let me gather gradually, my mist collecting into drops, drops combining into rivulets. My memory, my future-knowing, my weight warming the stone by this pool. And the sorrow, that returns too.

I climbed all the way up to the pinnacle on foot. My all-knowing brother, Zeus, would be posturing there, standing huge among cloud banks and whipping them from side to side with his breath. I used to think he'd eventually get over having his wish and winning the sky. Never mind that it's empty, he only sees that it's high and large.

Take Poseidon, for instance—my breasts shudder, another drop soaks the stone. Poseidon's sea holds kingdoms worth ruling, but Zeus, he's so bored with his sky he's reduced to toying with humans.

From far off I could see him, leaning lightly on his jagged cane. When I got closer he shifted position, propped his thunderbolt behind him and leaned backward on it. That told me something was wrong, since he's always shown it off before.

"About time, Sister. Where have you been?" He winked. "And what have you been up to?"

I saw no point in playing. Zeus only wants to win, and pouts if he loses.

"I've been on earth," I said. "Looking for my daughter. Our daughter, one of those you forget fathering."

He glanced over his shoulder, but that jealous mate of his, Hera, was nowhere nearby, so he stood straight again.

"I was about to mention that child," he said. "Everyone says Persephone's growing. A girl her age wants privacy."

"Privacy is one thing," I said. "Rape's another."

He cringed, cringed so deeply I thought he'd done it himself.

"Persephone raped? Impossible." He paused. "By the way, I called a Boule. Hardly anyone came. Where were you?"

"Don't answer a question with a question. Where's Persephone?"

"But you just answered my question with yours." He smiled. He wanted us to fall into a simple bicker, but he wouldn't get it from me.

"Ah, Demeter," he continued. "I like you. Not just as my little girl's mother, but as my sister too." Slyness strains him, yet he went on, repeating himself when he got confused. He gave off the usual euphony—goddesses and gods admire me, humans worship me rightly, trees and fields would simply die if I left them.

"That story is as old as our mother," I interrupted. "Tell me about Persephone."

"My compliments, dear one, were sincere. Since you won't accept them, take this." He shifted and looked up, as if struggling to recall something. "Where was I? Ah, yes. Not long ago, but long enough ago, which is to say in recent memory, but . . . but never mind. I thought it over and I've penetrated the problem."

He squared those cliffs he calls shoulders and drew in a cloud with a breath. "Now. If a mother, so-to-speak, of course, if this mother had a daughter, and this so-to-speak daughter were a virgin. . . . Of course, speaking technically, a mother couldn't be a virgin or our argument would be circular, wouldn't it. See my point?"

"If that's a point, Pan's got a bull-prong," I said.

"Now listen." Squaring his shoulders again. "I mean to say, quite frankly, Sister, you can't stay young forever. Keeping your child innocent won't help. If you think her innocence preserves your. . . . How did that go? If you think that—oh yes—my dear Mother-Lover-Sister Demeter. . . ." Here he paused and shifted the thunderbolt to his side again. "If you think that, well. . . ."

He realized his mistake. I'd seen what his hand held so tightly—a new, freshly crafted gold cane—just the thing to frighten humans and make them sweat.

"If you thought that," he stopped, coughed and cleared his throat. His mind hadn't caught up with his tongue.

"If I thought that, I'd be a cow-wit," I said. "Which we both know I'm not. Not blind either. Why not flash it in front of me?"

He blinked, bewildered.

"Why not twirl it? I see the bribe you took for your daughter's body. Why not toss it in the air and catch it? Better yet, break it over your knee right now. If you can." I looked hard at him. "Because no matter where you got it, no matter what it's made of . . ."

"Gold," he said. "Pure gold. Why the quality. . . ."

"It will decompose. It will be dust. Wind will scatter it, and it will mix with dirt before I speak here again. Or I step here again. Before my tongue melts a drop of ambrosia. Or my body sways to the lyre."

He began to get my meaning. And his bolt sagged and he sagged onto it.

"Take Olympus," I said, turning. "But without Demeter."

I spun and left. Let him work out the politics of it. It'll take him days.

Ages, more likely. Long after I've left him, long after Poseidon has seeped from my channel, then Zeus will grasp his dilemma. If I wander earth, separate from the immortals, refusing to go near Olympus, great Zeus cannot call the immortals together. He can hold no Boule if I will not visit Olympus, no human can be ennobled or punished. And when the humans catch on to that, who will Zeus be then?

"Zeus?" they'll ask. "Wasn't Zeus one of the old gods?"

The rivulets run to a river, the wave withdraws to the sea. I dry. I harden. I feel my anger returning, but it comes too quickly. Why did I think of Zeus? Stupid brother, what good is your new bolt now?

And your boasting, as usual, betrayed you. Pure gold,

you said, as if I did not know such gold grows only below ground. From that I knew how you had gotten it, and suspected the name even then, but wouldn't think of it.

I feared knowing the truth in full daylight and I turned away. I climbed down those hillsides, kept to the shadows and darkness. I emerged into a field to find the moon.

I had been looking for Hekate. I wanted her moon's dim glow to reveal by halves what I already knew. Graciously she kept her face half-covered by clouds, showed me the shadow, and hid the shape. She spoke in moving light to tell me what she'd heard. She knew of hooves pounding and my daughter's cry, but she herself had seen nothing.

I crossed the foothills, moving further and further away from the shadows. I knew enough and I wanted sunlight to show, solid and rude as a rock at noon, the certainty of what I already knew. I went to Helios.

I crossed the long trails belonging to Dawn and entered the valleys where sunlight clatters on waterfalls. Around a bend I stepped into the bright sunlight, the full light of Helios, light which can see everything. I faced him and spoke my question. He named the name.

He spoke that unearthly sound. Even humans fear to speak it. Sun of Darkness, Host of Many, Unseen Ruler. Giver of Invisibility. Even I avoid speaking that name. Grim Smiler. Dreadful Host. Hades.

Before Helios spoke, I knew it. Even on Olympus' slopes, I'd suspected.

Thinking back now, after that name had been spoken, I saw how even my brother Zeus' words betrayed the Dark King's cunning. Surely Zeus had rehearsed with that rapist the oily talk he tried to give me. My brother should have tested his words on Hera first, or on any female, on any nymph. Or perhaps he feared being laughed at. Probably that. Zeus may be cow-witted, but he's practical. He knew he'd sold his daughter's pleasure for a gold cane, but even he couldn't have believed such stupidity as the Dark One taught him.

I recall Zeus' words and my anger rises again. Imagine, him talking of virginity. So-to-speak virginity. So-to-speak Motherhood. Zeus so-to-speaks words without meanings. Fertility, my foot—virginity, my vulva. What goddess, what woman, cares for a hymen? What mother would delay her child's joy?

Curse those gods, and those misled men who value a hymen. Do they think a reed's no longer a reed when it enters the basket? That a woman's no longer her own without a flap of skin? Persephone's time for loving had come. All the immortals knew it. Her age gave her grace and lightness, and when I talked to her of love her eyes grew wide and soft. She saw how I grew thoughtful, deciding whose touch should bring her to bloom. She seemed to sense, too, when I had chosen her lover. She drew away from me to go by herself to pick flowers at Nysa.

Zeus asks where I was during his Boule. Participating, I might have said, by my absence.

All that afternoon while Persephone was off by herself, I lay with Dionysus. I instilled the gentlest skills in him, taught him how to hold back the reaping, how to thresh her thighs so the seed would stay. I had taught him every skill I knew, and then I told him where to find her.

She wandered in his field at Nysa. Dionysus would go and find her, carrying wine and tumbling toward her through the tall grass and narcissus. He would caress her and hold her, get that film of a hymen turned back out of her way when . . .

It returns now.

I lay with Dionysus, then I heard . . .

Her scream.

I lifted and flew. Dionysus stood gaping below me.

I'd planned it differently. That very afternoon, after they'd been together, I'd have gone to her. I remember how I intended it now, how her hair would stream away from her face and tangle into the grasses. Her little back would press the new wheat flat, warm and moist. I would find her as she lay, just as I lay now.

I would settle myself beside her, stroke her hair, untangle the twigs and stems while I talked. That was how she was to learn what every goddess and every woman knows. The very knowledge that Mother Rhea taught Demeter, Demeter would teach Persephone.

No god can understand the Mother Knowledge. What do they know of Mother Knowledge? I've been virgin time after time, and each time I have maidenhood in me. I have motherhood in me. And the greater mothering, to be grandmother—a mother of mothers. I myself am the fullest fertility.

Fertility. Virginity. Both are in us eternally. Gods discover the virgin in us time and again, and that's the true aphrodisiac, to use Aphrodite's own words. The first thrust—every separate time—delights and surprises. Later we return to ourselves and know separateness again. We take pleasure in choosing what we choose, turning back what we don't choose.

No god can understand it, so they fuss over this thing called virginity, fearing they'll be compared. I taught Dionysus the gentlest ways so that after Dionysus, perhaps for her, as for myself today, three-pronged Poseidon. Perhaps Apollo. But Poseidon surely.

I reach out and touch the stone, but it's cool now. Poseidon is gone a long time and still I lay here. How many thoughts have passed over my mind, yet I don't feel like myself again. Why do I take so long today?

I've often lain with Poseidon, and many times with others, and my strength, my virginity, has always returned before. Each time, after love, I gather to myself again as the tide of yielding recedes. I discover my separateness again, virginal as a shore at dawn. That is the Mother Knowing, and each mother gives it to her daughter. It has never failed before. I search my memory. Poseidon pleased me, as always. Today was no different. What has gone wrong to keep me from claiming myself again? I should think back over it, remember each detail and try to know it. Perhaps then I can recall my separateness, then the strength inside of me will return.

I had left Olympus, stunned by Helios' speaking that awful name. Helios spoke that name and my lips repeated it without giving it breath. I turned away from his sunlight. I turned my back on Olympus and went down its hillsides, empty of flowers now, let my steps take me back toward the earth. I walked on earth while the sun moved away from me, listening to the wind and listening to my own footsteps on the hard, caked soil. All the world seemed colorless, Zeus' sky gone gray, mountains and land the color of ashes. I listened to the hiss of the wind between the bare limbs of the trees, and then I heard another sound.

I heard hooves behind me. I turned. Half a field away, Poseidon stood posed as a horse. Zeus had sent him, I supposed, to lure me back. Poseidon reared and whinnied, wiggling that extra, unshod hoof.

I was not in the mood. I turned into a bird and threw myself into the air which felt cool and fresh around me.

I flew over the fields with, curse him, another bird behind me. This one's underfeathers were stiff. They slowed him slightly, but not enough.

We neared water, so I changed into a dolphin, diving like a warm stone into the waves, as if I didn't know my pursuer was the sea itself. I suppose even then I wanted to turn and join him. He came across the waves more slowly, his swollen prong unbalancing his swimming stroke.

I saw a marsh. My body touched reeds and I reshaped into a snake, a python. But wouldn't you know, there was a lopsided slithering right behind—slither, slap, slither, swish.

I'd had enough. I whipped into the shadow of a cave and considered my choices. What creature, I asked myself, what creature awed Poseidon above all others? What lust might out-last his own lust? Quickly I reared, shifted from a python through a cobra, and when I came down I touched earth as a mare.

There we stood. Poseidon playing steed, me as mare. Then he saw my girth, my wide haunches, the teeth I bared, and that was another matter altogether. I soon found myself the only horse in that cave.

Trying to pass for a human maid, Poseidon tucked it between his thighs. Gave me a look as if she'd just happened into the wrong cave.

Being a horse was taking its effect. I trotted to the cavern's opening and blocked it to keep him in. As I'd passed through all those other animals, they rose up in me too.

And if I sent Poseidon back blue-balled and aching, why Zeus would get a laugh out of that too. I told myself this finished the argument.

I whinnied, more softly this time. I turned my flank and pretended to graze. A waterfall near the entrance made a pool, and I'd licked most of the moss from between two rocks before my cavemate regained his composure.

How pleasant it was to feel hooves on my back again. And to snort, turning my head from side to side. But the memory pleases me less than it should. The pleasure's gone now. Poseidon's gone. The film on my thigh is cracked like clay fired too long. And I am finally . . .

Myself again?

Not quite. No, that's it exactly. Persephone's taken from me, and I can't find her. I can't find her feelings, my own maiden feeling, inside my thoughts any more. I don't grow refreshed this time. She's gone.

Curse her rapist. I've lost my skill, this skill I meant to teach her. Every goddess and every woman renews herself after love, yet I fail today. I would have sat beside her, teaching her, as Mother Rhea taught me herself on that day I first discovered love. She needed that gift, the very one I need now, and now I can't manage it. Virginity.

I would have taught her exactly as I learned it. You're every female, I would have told her, you're the moon. As the new sliver, you mother yourself. You can swell, I would say to her then, grow round and huge. Yet your shining arms still hold the cresent moon, your daughter. Persephone will understand. I'll teach her how she can wane, grandmother—

mother of a mother of a daughter—and still all three. Then when she's a pale virgin again, she'll appear . . .

She would have appeared.

I would have, would have taught her. But the gift is stolen. I came too late to give her the Virgin's Gift. That's what rape has torn away, and for what?

At last my anger is mine again. I lie on this stone where I've rested since noon. Hekate is rising again, only a pale disk moon tonight, spread through a haze of clouds. As in the inner center, I still feel diffused and lost to myself.

Persephone, raped. Her maiden part stolen. Mine, hidden from me. No woman may be her own without this, and I curse Olympus. I curse the earth. And I curse the underworld, that Host of Many, and I name his name, Hades. That Dark King steals her gift, and I, I who could have taught her how to take it back, lose even myself now.

IV

I WANT flowers. I told him that. He went away to look for flowers and he hasn't come back. It was a good trick, even if I did actually want the flowers. I'm Demeter's own daughter, thinking of a trick like that.

Considering where I am, which is in the underworld, and who he is, awful Hades himself, how can flowers grow here? If he can't bring them to me, he might have to let me go. No one ever returns from the underworld. That's supposed to be an unbreakable law and even I know that. Which means, when he has to let me return, I'll be the first he has ever let go. Humans will tell stories about me, remembering that.

I like the idea. I've never had to figure out such things before, the rules and Boules and deals, but now I'm learning. For example, I've decided I won't eat. That might make him let me go.

At first I refused to eat because I missed the earth and Mother, and I didn't want any food. Especially not what he served.

I wasn't having any of his ambrosia, so he brought in bowls and platters and baskets, but his breads were dry cakes and they had no smell. Along with the bread, he brought a slab that looked like the hide of a dead cow. It turned out to be cheese. I wouldn't touch it, so he went away and came back with fish, scaly black chunks in the middle of a gold platter. Unlike the bread and cheese, the fish did smell.

I went into a coughing fit, so he snatched up all the platters and baskets and dishes, and left. I was almost able to start breathing again when I felt him returning.

It's the strangest thing, I can feel when he's close. It's like I've swallowed a stone. Mother Da used to tell a story about great old Kronos, father of us all, and how he swallowed a stone. Now I know what Kronos felt. I get a weight at the bottom of my belly, and I feel cold and I start to tremble. Then I look up and he's there.

I was glad he didn't bring more food. He stood beside me, exactly between me and the lamp, and I thought he was angry. He just stood, so quiet I could hear the lamp sputter, and his shadow flickered over me. I sneaked a look. He wasn't watching me.

He stared at the table where the food had been. He wore the long black cloak that he always wears, and had his arms folded over his chest so I could see his wrists. On the backs of his hands, on skin the pale gray of a legume, black hairs grew out.

I looked at his face. It was dark too, and oily curls fell on his forehead, but his eyes were bright, black as lava. He seemed to be thinking. I didn't yet know his name or who he was, but if I'd thought about it, I would have guessed.

Then his chin jerked up. I heard a crack, like thunder, and I jumped. He'd clapped. "Fruit," he said and went out.

Well, when the gate swung wide again, he stood there holding another gold tray. His eyes gleamed as brightly as the gold.

"On earth, Persephone loves fruit," he said. He set the tray on the table and stood back, looking like a tall black urn with his hands on his hips for handles.

I saw orange slices, figs, apricots, pears, pomegranates, pumpkin slices—all the sweet fruits Mother and I love. I looked more closely, then I looked up at him. The handles of that tall dark urn settled slowly, slumping as if the potter had made them too heavy or wet.

The oranges, the pears, the pumpkins all were shriveled like old human skin. The figs looked like dry mud clods. The pomegranates had split open and spilled their seeds.

"They're dried," I said.

The urn looked like a plain black pot. "You're unjust," he said and took the tray and went out. I heard his steps in the hall, then a crash. Gold chips flashed through the air outside the gate, and something like an orange mouse scuttled under the gate and across the floor. It spun and stopped right at my feet.

To tell the truth, I was hungry, so I picked it up. It was a pumpkin slice. Being dried, it was hardly as heavy as a seed puff, but I tried to make myself take a bite. I imagined it was a ripe pumpkin. I pretended Eros and I were playing, and we'd found a sweet pumpkin and dropped it on a flat rock to pop it and scooped out the seeds and now we cupped our hands, Eros laughing, and we dug our nails into the soft meat. We lifted it to our mouths.

My mouth was dry and my throat felt tight. Even if I took a bite, I'd chew and chew but could never swallow.

So I decided I wouldn't eat. I set the chunk of pumpkin in the middle of the table, and decided I'd eat nothing. I would get thin, as thin as one of the ghostly lovers in his Mourning Field. But I haven't explained that part yet, have I?

Anyway, I felt awful. I still didn't know where I was, or who he was. I wore my crown sometimes to feel better, but I wouldn't look at myself wearing it. I thought of earth where I used to live, of life blooming and tumbling there, and that made me feel worse.

Thinking back, I'm sure that was the saddest I've ever been. Well, it's happened now. I'm glad it's over. I'll never be that sad again either, because here I sit, waiting, writing for something to do. He hasn't brought me any flowers, so he'll have to let me go.

I got tired of being sad, so I lay down on the couch and I fell asleep. I don't know how long I slept, but I awoke on the couch and feeling a slippery pool. My cheek felt wet. I'd been dreaming of a banquet and I probably drooled in my sleep.

The lamp sputtered. I looked up and saw him. He sat very still at the table.

"You'll get used to it," he said.

I didn't answer.

"Dreams are difficult here at first."

I wondered how he knew. I wondered how long he'd been there. Also, I wondered why he kept coming and going just as he pleased.

"When I began here," he said, "I dreamed of Olympus, nothing but Olympus."

"Why don't you leave," I said, "if you hate this place?"

"A king can't leave his kingdom. Besides, these days my dreams improve. When I'm awake I see a beautiful grain maiden. I dream that she'll be my Queen."

He smiled. I didn't see anything funny.

"Would you like to see your realm, Queen Persephone?"

Queen Persephone! At that I wanted to laugh. "I'm not a Queen," I said. Imagine, me, a Queen! Like Zeus' wife Hera, like proud human Queens, all of them with their terrible tempers. "Or then again," I said, "maybe I am one."

"You're a maid, Persephone." He laughed. He wasn't angry any more. "But I'll tell you what. I rule a huge realm, a realm too big for one god. Look it over. If you like it, I'll make you its Queen."

I thought he was playing, but he stood, curled his cloak around his ankles, and took a step toward the gate. The gate, I saw, was open. I was free! Or so I thought.

I was up and past him and out the gate—fast as a woman crazy with wine. I flew along the hall, but I only remember a flashing tunnel. I saw two enormous gold gates and I pushed faster and got my weight ready—like a lion about to bring down an antelope—and I threw myself. The gates gave way. The gold hinges squealed. I tumbled down steps and rolled.

The cloth of my gown tangled around me. My arms felt prickled and poked and hurt.

I rolled until I stopped. I lay, heaving to catch my breath, but when I looked up—oh damn—I lost my breath again.

I don't know what I expected to see, green hills maybe, sunlight and waterfalls. Maybe I was wrong to expect that, but I'm not sorry because for that tiny space of running I was glad, very glad, so what did it matter?

I landed in thistles, not green or gold ones, but black shiny thistles. The ground wasn't colored correctly either because instead of being dirty my hands came up pasty with ashes.

I heard water slapping. I expected to see the clear line of horizon, but I saw only fog that rolled and gathered in bunches, which was odd. I didn't feel any wind.

I heard high yelping, like dogs. I thought a pack had been set after me, but I couldn't see them and the barking stayed far off.

I turned, looking for Helios but he wasn't shining, and behind me, the pale battlements of the palace gave the only light. This palace must be made of good gold, I realize now, the rare best kind of gold that shines of its own power, because nothing else in this place has light. Especially not the dark spot I saw then, getting larger, with his cloak pulled above his ankles to avoid the thistles.

"You tricked me," I said. I was standing up now, pulling thistles out of my knees and especially one that had worked into my elbow.

He looked surprised. I'd run quite fast.

"Don't say that Persephone," he said. "That's unjust."

"That flower was a trick." I was really angry.

He shook his head. "Ge made it, not me." He acted as if I should have known. "I don't play tricks."

I thought his story was peculiar. Mother and I usually make flowers.

"Zeus commanded it," he added.

That sounded a lot like Zeus, tricks and Boules and

deals. Naturally, I didn't say that.

"You don't trust me," he said. "Have I deceived you?"

I didn't answer.

"I haven't deceived you even once. You'll be surprised at my kingdom. You'll see things differently."

"I can see," I said. All around me, fields of those spiny black thistles lay, but not a single blossom, not even a spiny clump of sage. And sage can even root in rocks.

He saw my disappointment. This, he insisted, was only the palace grounds, and he went on about how large his realm was. "Look it over. There's proof I wouldn't deceive you."

So I went with him. What I saw didn't prove anything, but at least I discovered where I am. I'd begun to suspect it, back in that field, but the Mourning Field was where I became certain.

We didn't go there right away. First he said I must meet the Judges. We took a road that began by the palace and led up a hill past black fields. I saw the water of a river, but it wasn't clear or dancing, only slow-moving mud. No marsh marigolds grew by it, and river fog moved around us. I saw figures mixed up in it, but when I looked hard they were gone. That's why, when we got to the clearing, I wasn't sure what I had seen.

"Minos," he called. "Aeacus. Rhadamanthus."

They weren't fog. I saw three creatures nearly as tall as he is. Each of them wore a dark cloak like his. Each raised his hand—more like a claw—and their hoods fell back. I only saw the face of the closest one, which was enough. They weren't humans, but they weren't immortals either. The nearby one had no beauty. His forehead was dark and wrinkled, and his cheeks made deep caves on his face. Worst, his eyes—big as an owl's but not soft or wet—gave cold glimmers with no glow of their own.

"Now watch, Persephone," he whispered. "I'll try to play a trick." He spoke out. "Judges, bow to your Queen!"

The nearest, the one with awful eyes, stared. "Minos judges," he said in a voice like howling wind. "This is no

Queen. But she will be."

Then fog fell over him, and I saw the face of the second one. This one had no eyes at all, only blank holes where eyes ought to be, but his ears were as big as abalone shells.

"Aeacus sentences," he said. "She's not a Queen. We won't bow."

Once again the fog fell. It cleared just in time for me to see the third creature turning away. With his back turned to us, he just stood until the fog fell again.

"That's Rhadamanthus, Persephone," he was whispering. "Rhadamanthus executes and never speaks. Aren't they excellent?"

I swear by the River Styx that's what he said.

"See what happens when I try a trick? I rule here, but I can't bribe them. They speak only the truth. But I'm sure Minos' eyes told you that."

"I tell the truth too," I said. "They're ugly."

"Persephone, they're just!" He looked simply amazed and stood there with his mouth open. When he recovered his voice, he started praising them, their truthfulness, how quickly they worked, how little food they ate. I could understand that last.

He said his three Judges were in charge of dead humans, figuring out what was to happen to them now that they were dead. The Judges gave exactly what was due, he insisted—good for good, evil for evil. I stared at him.

"I'll show you," he said, turning to go.

He strode away along a path. I didn't want to stay in that clearing alone, especially with his ugly friends, so I followed. He hurried and I had to run to keep up so I couldn't hear half of what he said. I think I was supposed to see how just the Judges were.

We went back toward the palace crossing thistley paths and brambled walkways. Opposite the thistle field, I saw a field I hadn't noticed before, but when I asked about it he said we were almost to Elysion.

"You say this realm is worth seeing, let me look where I

want." I refused to take another step.

He insisted that I'd understand when we got to Elysion, but I wouldn't budge. He looked perplexed, but finally shrugged. "Look where you want. You won't find deceitfulness."

We stepped from the road that I had been chasing him along, and suddenly—so quickly I was amazed—we were standing inside a dawn. In the pale wolf-light, mists floated over slim leaning grasses. The rocks were gentle sloping boulders, good for lying on if there were sun, but it was dawn here, tender and uncertain like on earth.

I looked for flowers. This was the moment they'd start opening. Then I felt something chilly touch my cheek, like wind but firmer. I jumped.

He smiled. "That was the hand," he said, "of some lover. He hoped you were his maiden."

I looked. I saw mist and grasses and rocks. "Where?"

"He's here."

We heard whimpering, like a kicked dog. I spun, but saw nothing.

Then I knew where I was. What told me? Maybe that weeping, a ghost's. Maybe the Judges, the river, the cold glowing palace. Maybe I just knew, as goddesses and gods know where humans came from, but won't think of it. Never mind, I knew.

I looked at him and I saw Hades, Dis, the one humans don't speak of. He was the other brother who was with Mother, Zeus and Poseidon when they tossed the stones to decide who got what kingdom. He was the one I'd forgotten, but I knew him. He'd won the underworld. Even immortals would rather not mention him or his kingdom. Now he saw me know him and his eyes grew bright.

"For you, Persephone," he said. "You will be Queen."

I stared at him.

"You'll rule all this beauty. This place, the Mourning Field, and all my other regions. The ghosts in this field, for example, they perished for love. My Judges, being just and wise, blinded them and sent them here. Now they suffer their sorrow perfectly in these misty fields, mourning eternally. They search for their beloved by touch. Eternally, Persephone."

"And?" I said, hoping for a happy ending.

"And Elysion. And Tartarus. And the Cocytus and the Phlegethon. I told you it was large. All yours. The palace too, most assuredly."

"You think I want this?" That must be what he thought.

"Only Persephone, beauty herself, could appreciate my realm. You'll share it with me, of course, but just think. No tricks, no lies, no illusions. Only truth. And justice. Absolute beauty—eternal, unchangeable, immutable. . . ."

"Beauty?" I looked at him. "This place, this place. . . ."

I was afraid to say it, but then I remembered where I was. This was the world humans came to when they died, and nobody ever went back, so what could it matter? "This place has only death."

He looked amazed. He sat down on a rock that poked out of the mist. He stared at the backs of his hands and said nothing.

"Why did you bring me here?" I finally said. It was decided in a Boule, I knew, but the Boule was his idea to begin with.

"I rule here," he said again. "There's beauty, Persephone. You must believe me."

Believe him? I couldn't even understand him.

He shook his head. "I admit you have to think about it. But surely you can see it."

"Flowers have beauty," I pointed out. "Earth and life and trees and hillsides." I went on about plenty of things. I can't remember them all. He interrupted me.

He brought up his old justice again. I admit—to myself, not to him—that I don't completely understand this justice of his, but if it's so beautiful, maybe flowers have it. I didn't say yes or no, but I did make clear, by saying it five or six times, that flowers were what I wanted.

He paused a long time. Finally he shrugged and said he'd have to think about it. He still wanted me to see the place he called Elysion, but when I asked whether flowers grew there, he changed his mind.

We came back to the palace. The gate stands open but I see no point in trying to escape. The underworld, after all, is the underworld, and I'm in it. The law says no one may ever leave it.

Yet I think he must let me go. This realm can't possibly grow flowers, I know that, so I'll be leaving soon. Actually, there's hardly any point in writing this out since I'll be returning to earth soon. I can tell all this to Mother Da. I suppose I'll keep these pages anyway because they'll make Mother Da laugh.

Think now—what, first of all before anything else, will I do on earth?

That's not a riddle. I'll eat!

* * *

Nothing. Nothing means what it should mean here. Nothing is itself here.

He tells it the other way. He says everything is itself here. He is lying.

I know he lies, but knowing it doesn't make me feel any better. A comforting thought gives me no comfort here. The sleeping-couch here gives me restless dreams. The bath water here gets me dirty. And that—that which he calls justice, which he calls love—well, it hurts. Everything is opposite here. Everything.

It's like on earth if I tried to be kind, if I fed a wild dog and it bit me.

Nothing is as it should be. He shouldn't have been able to make flowers, it should have been impossible. When he arrived, he only looked tired because it was difficult to make this gift. Difficult, he said, that's all.

He'd brought what he called flowers, I couldn't say he had to let me go. He'd made them. No sense in being cruel, I thought. How he stood, practically begging me to like his flowers. No sense in not being nice enough to look at them.

He should have been ashamed to call those things flowers. Yet that's what he called them.

He stood in front of me, looking pale, like one of those perished lovers before his Judges make them invisible, condemn them to the Mourning Fields. His hand shook and, because he held them too tightly, those ugly flowers were wilting already. Asphodels, he called them. Acting, pretending he was proud that he'd made them, but I'm sure he was laughing inside. I'm sure he was. Laying low like a dog ready to bite.

I should have seen what he was, but this place—it's all appearances, deceitfulness.

I should have hated him, not felt sorry. Not for the shortest instant. Nothing is as it should be here. It seemed unimportant whether I accepted those flowers or not. All the gifts he had brought me, I refused every one, except these. I felt sorry for him. I took them.

But when I did—that's what he means by justice. That's what he means by his beauty. He calls his Judges beautiful and they're ugly. His place he calls a kingdom and it's a poisoned well. Stinking. Stinking. Like his flowers, thrown all over in what he calls his love. Pushing me down, pushing me around until he pushed into me. Mother said it would be beautiful. My belly had a stone before. Now the stone burns all over me, a lava ball. It hurts me.

Hurting is itself here. Nothing else. Everything else is appearances, lies. I yelled rape at him, it was rape, what did he mean, his whispering, his face pushing into my hair, his saying "It's just, it's just," over and over.

I should not have been kind. I should not have pitied him. He looked tired as if he'd actually tried hard to make flowers. I should not have even touched them. How can stems be so cold?

Nothing is as it should be. I should have seen that. I'm sadder than before, yet he says I'm Queen now and he says

I'm beautiful. I've seen myself. I know. And I know how I feel. Mother said I'd feel happy, happy like never before, and what am I doing? The crying's starting. I can't stop it. Nothing is itself.

V

THE branches of the olive tree curl like burnt wicks. The sky is a low sooty ceiling. Helios makes a pale spot of sun above the smudge of sea. Earth takes up the sorrow of my thoughts and shows them back to me.

The rocky hill, a few steps from this temple, might as well be the village ash-pile. Between the rocks, a cluster of sage withers, the color of rust. Blossoms fall away before the cold wind can break them. The fields stretching out toward the sea were brown when I came, but now they're gray stubble, growing like the beard of a corpse after the spirit's gone to the underworld.

I could go to Persephone in the underworld. I know the way. I've tossed away my crown, left my home on Olympus, taken up humans' fumbling ways, yet I still have my powers. I could go.

But law is law. If I went there, both of us would remain in his realm for all eternity. So I plot. I cling to earth, wandering for nine days now, and I discover no trick to win her back. So I wait at a temple built for a goddess, yet no goddess lives here.

I thought of her as I crossed the dying fields, as I moved along the hillsides covered with frost. The earth has never been a terrible place before, but now without her I let nothing grow, and the emptiness terrifies me too. Her absence meets me everywhere.

I watched humans scrabble for the last stalks in a field, and I felt how my own gifts, the food that might have fed them, lay withered inside me. I saw humans fight over the empty skin of a goat that had starved and fallen in its steps. I saw a woman sneak out at night to slay her bull, the strong one she'd raised for sacrifice. She took its carcass home and ate it for food.

All these things I studied and I felt no pity. In the villages, the cities, the empty places, I wandered and took no rest, took no food, no drink, no love. And I gave no pity. Not until I came to this place the humans call Eleusis did I relent. Here I showed a little pity, and sit alone now regretting it.

From the new stone steps of this temple I can see Metaneira and Celeus' house, the only stone house on a plain of wood huts. I can see the Maiden's Well where mothers once brought their daughters to teach them. That was where Metaneira's girls found me. My wandering had brought me to Eleusis, and I sat by that well, remembering all I would have taught my own daughter, making my memories smooth as a shore stone.

Metaneira's girls probably came to sit alone and talk about men, but as they approached they saw a new stone at the well's side. It must have surprised them to see a bent figure there, an old woman, her gray veil drawn down, her hood clutched to keep out the wind.

Yet the girls didn't throw a single pebble to chase me off like a stranger. The three younger ones hung back, but the oldest spoke up, clearly and loud in case my senses were dull. She told me her name and whose child she was. She was sorry, she said, she didn't know me.

I invent different names in different places and then I forget. Here I said Doso.

Still she didn't throw a handful of dust to frighten me, even though I might have come to steal. She worried why I sat in the cold.

Her questions startled me. Elsewhere no one had bothered with my comfort. Since my anger had made food scarce, humans had turned against each other and driven strangers from their land.

The young girls held back, but the eldest approached. She asked where I came from, so I made up a story to test her.

I started with pirates. Young girls love pirate stories. I named Crete and a great woman's house. I said I took care of children before my capture by pirates. I described creaking boards and our moaning, old women in the belly of the pirate ship. We were to be sold as slaves to raise the children of a race more prolific than insects. I made those slave-owners sound ferocious, borrowing traits from races I'd visited. The first night in port, I said, I alone escaped. My wandering brought me here.

The younger girls had crept close. I didn't look up from my lap. Falling silent, I sighed heavily, as if I'd used up all my strength.

"Old mother, you're in Eleusis," the eldest girl said. I'd be welcome in any house. Metaneira, her own mother, would take me.

I thought a moment. What would old Doso say? "I'm good at tending babies," I whined. "My milk is dry, but I can hold a baby. I have a recipe for a mush that cures any cough."

"You don't have to beg," she interrupted. "Wait while we ask. We'll run. You'll stay?"

I nodded slowly, as if I were already falling asleep, and they hurried away. When they returned, they found Doso snorting and snoring.

So I was led to the house of Metaneira and Celeus. Along the way I studied Eleusis and found my anger hadn't spared it. All the humans crouching in their houses were thin, and Metaneira's own girls, whose age should have made them dimpled and round, moved lightly as reeds. Yet they called out and waved to others who passed. An old man stopped us to ask if Metaneira's baby felt better. The girls told him that Doso was being taken in to help.

I gathered that Metaneira and Celeus led Eleusis, perhaps they even ruled over it. Their house, although small, was of stone and they kept a sow in the yard. I had to stoop to pass the door, and the youngest girl remarked, in a whisper, that old Doso was certainly tall. Once I got inside I lifted my head and two things nearly betrayed me. My hood brushed the ceiling beam. In that instant, I saw the mother and the child.

Metaneira, the girls' mother, looked up from where she sat nursing. She stared, thunderstruck. My radiance, which I was helpless to withhold, lit the room. Their old dog, which had been lolling on the hearth licking himself, yipped and cringed.

I struggled to recover old Doso.

"It's dark in here," I complained. "Stop. Let my eyes get better."

Metaneira blinked, clutching the child. Now she saw only an aged stranger no different from any old human. I still wondered if she suspected me, and now I wish that she had.

She stood up from her chair and offered me the couch. I stammered apologies. I wasn't taking comfort from gods these days, and I wouldn't take it from humans either. By the hearth, a three-legged stool set my head just higher than the dog's. When I sat, he sniffed me once, then lay down, his eyes watchful.

Metaneira wanted to give me old woman's wine, sweet with honey, but remembering Dionysus and his wine grape field, I flapped my hands in protest. Metaneira insisted my wandering must have made me thirsty. Barley water with a broken mint leaf would be good, I said, inventing the drink. The poor like me enjoyed it on Crete, I said and called the drink kykeon. I hoped that the word meant nothing in any humans' language.

Metaneira thanked me for the recipe. The folds on her

face told me she had once been plump, but she was thin and fading now. I guessed the child she held would be her last. She sent her slave, Iambe, to make this kykeon. It wasn't nectar, I warned her, unsure how the drink would turn out. Still Metaneira thanked me.

Soon Iambe returned with cups, one for me, one for Metaneira, and a third for herself. I'd seen most human ways, but never a slave sit with the family.

I studied this serving woman. Perhaps from sickness, Iambe was round as a roof beam. Rolls collected at her waist, and the flesh of her arms quivered like milky cheese. She bent over me with the tray, and her eyes, dark and merry, peeped under my veil.

"Old Mama Doso looks sad," she told Metaneira. "On Crete, does Baubo visit the threshing floor?"

I pretended I'd never heard of a ritual like that and shook my head. Patiently, between them, they explained the very festival I'd created, the Women's Day, when I bless grain on the threshing floor. "Queen Demeter appears as Baubo," the oldest girl added. "Baubo. Fatness. You know the word?"

I nodded.

Old Doso shouldn't sit grieving, Metaneira insisted. Iambe must play Baubo to cheer me up.

"We're all women here," Iambe said. "Cover the baby's eyes."

The girls giggled.

Iambe set down the tray. "To be Baubo, I need a belly." She surveyed herself. "Oh! I've got one."

She poked a roll of herself and her thumb sank like a ladle going into a porridge pot. I smiled, only pretending, but she saw that. Her eyes sparkling, her full cheeks flushed, she crimped her arms and elbows up to force her belly rolls higher. Her breasts, healthy loaves, swelled to fat melons. Pushing their lumps forward, she minced to show us Demeter, fat after reaping and now hungry for lust.

Metaneira giggled. I smiled and patted my knee.

Iambe warmed to playing Baubo. She tossed her melons

side to side and tiptoed toward me. Then her mouth dropped open.

"Baubo sees Poseidon," the girls whispered.

Baubo gawked at a spot beside me. Delighted, she threw her arms into the air, and the melons splattered to her waist.

Baubo, crestfallen, elbowed herself back up. She tiptoed again, each step as heavy as a boulder. Soon she approached, her tongue wetting her lips, her gaze ogling the empty air beside me. She pretended to be fat lusty Demeter seeing Poseidon and getting ready to sneak up behind him.

The girls squealed, "He's grazing! He's grazing!" And so Poseidon would be grazing, with his flanks turned and too busy eating to notice Baubo. Iambe couldn't let her breasts fall to reach out and pull his tail, so she started to shiver and shake. All her ripples quivered and slapped, going glug-glug like a pouring pitcher.

Metaneira and the girls roared, holding their sides. They knew only half of it, I thought, and I was laughing too. Here Iambe played Baubo, who was Demeter, and here Demeter played Doso, who watched Baubo. We howled then as Poseidon suddenly noticed big-bellied Baubo, fat with harvest.

Iambe leaped and turned away. She would act coy. Yet her buttocks still wiggled, their cheeks slapping so hard I thought they'd knock me from the stool.

"He comes," the girls squealed. "He's coming!"

Baubo let out gas and "Oooof!" Poseidon lurched onto her. She tumbled over onto her wide back. Her belly joggled like a bowl of mush. She hunched and quivered and shook and giggled, giving a good high whinny for Poseidon's last cry.

Iambe lay heaving. She opened one eye. She'd pleased me and she saw it. Her Baubo tossed a final twitch, then she rose, still shaking with sighs. She dusted the back of her skirt, took the tray and minced, still quivering, through the doorway.

"Baubo! Baubo!" The girls wanted her back.

Metaneira clutched her side, whimpering and wheezing. I

remembered that I was supposed to be older than she, so I coughed and let my breath rattle in my throat.

The girls called again for Baubo, Baubo.

"Baubo comes but rarely," Metaneira said between gasps. "Or we'll offend the Grain Mother."

None laughed at that, which pleased me. Nevertheless, I asked, hadn't Baubo come to them recently when they were threshing the grain?

No, Metaneira replied, there had been no threshing. She turned and told the girls to go outside. They did as they were told, and we heard them there, pretending to be Baubos, while we talked.

Metaneira and I calmed ourselves, sipping kykeon to sooth our throats. Metaneira's child had hiccups from being shaken, so she tossed it to her shoulder. She saw that I was cheered a little and she was glad. Would I stay?

I hunched down, swaying on my stool as old Doso would. "You haven't reaped," I protested, shaking my finger at her. "I've got no teeth, but I still get hungry." I turned away. "No, I'll go. Wanderers always find food or a coin."

"Who's hungry?" Metaneira laughed and bounced the child. "What's hunger to a house with Baubo?"

I smiled but still pretended to disbelieve her. I'd stay one day, I said, perhaps two. I could sleep in a chair, kykeon quieted my belly. I complained more and apologized too, leaving her no doubt that I wanted to stay. I'd wandered, I added. I had stories to tell.

Her child was falling asleep now. She stroked his hairless crown and sat patiently. I could see she would not move to disturb the child, so I began telling stories, and she let old Doso ramble without interrupting. I made Metaneira imagine she'd taken in a most tricky storyteller, one who leaves out parts and then apologizes, yet never misses a beat when she gets to the terrible details. I named the days and the places I'd wandered. My best telling was of the cries of the dying. I showed the thieves' way of smiling as they snatched the last bite. Especially, I made a vision for her of unfed children who crawled forward on their elbows like insects.

I said I'd seen these things everywhere in this barren time. Thus I brought Metaneira herself to tell me about Eleusis.

She and Celeus ruled it, as I'd guessed, but they had fewer subjects now than they once had. She hoped Eleusis might have better stories to show me. They too had seen the bare patches spread on the fields. Talking late at night, they discovered the bitterness rising between neighbors. A goddess or god blessed them with foresight, the way she told it, because when the fields were finally empty, she and Celeus had given an order and were first to obey it. For three days the experts, those who judged festival games, went to each household. They counted heads and then divided the grain from Eleusis' stores. Each family received filled baskets enough for its number.

"We're all thin," Metaneira said, "but most—it's true not all—but most behave kindly." She paused, then added. "Even if they don't feel it."

She and Celeus, she said, had made a game for the girls. "We pretend that pity is a food, that pity is something to eat and it's making us fat. At meals we say, 'Give me another pity-cake. I'm eating this one for the neighbors.' We pass the empty plate and pretend to take portions." Metaneira chewed her tongue and smacked her lips. "'That's a good one,' we say, 'Aren't I fat?'"

She laughed, and her child, fretting in its sleep, gummed the bone of her wrist. She filled its mouth with her finger, shushing him, calling him Demophoön.

How like the humans I grow, more every day. I pretend to be one, then forget I'm pretending. I become changeable and uncertain, my resolve no longer that of a goddess. I hurt to hear a human talk of pity, that thing I love to give even more than I love to laugh.

In my travels I'd met a race who, when they grieved, scarred their arms with fire. In that moment I found myself more pathetic than even that. I had yanked out my own root, my pity. I'd let it wither and dry. I longed to give it as I used to, to spill one drop of it. That drop would soak at once into the parched ground and would not be enough, yet I longed to let it fall.

Old Doso tilted her stool to reach for Demophoön. Inside I was laughing, even as the baby cried. It amused me to think that a goddess had brought herself so low that an ignorant human had to teach her. The child's cry stopped mid-breath when I pulled him toward me. It seemed he recognized the perfect comfort of my arms.

"Mama Doso has some skills," I said. "I'm old and I learned in great women's houses."

Metaneira smiled and got up from her couch. The child's care could be my lodging, she insisted. I should stay. And I shouldn't try to pretend I didn't have to eat.

As she went out, I joked, saying I'd have a double portion of pity for dinner, please. She laughed. She, herself, would ladle it out for me.

So I came to sit by their hearth. I slept in the chair and cared for the child in Metaneira and Celeus' house. The days passed quickly. Doso's stories teased and terrified the girls. I gave recipes to Metaneira and Iambe, always adding one ingredient they wouldn't have. I ate nothing myself.

The slave, Iambe, suspected me. She was too quick not to notice that I took no food, that I never fed the baby in front of the family. Metaneira, I think sadly now, should have been half as wise as her servant. Metaneira showed only delight and amazement as Demophoön flourished like a young god in my care.

We sat together afternoons in the yard, and we guessed at which fruit Demophoön's ripe cheeks most resembled. When he scrambled between us, squealing like a young pig, I laughed until my ribs hurt.

Most of all I loved the nights, when the family slept and I was alone with him. He was a man-child, and all my anger was at men and gods. Their kind has taken my daughter, tried to deceive me, defiled even the Mother Knowing, and to pity

Demophoön demanded all my heart. Tenderness found new flavor. I nourished and healed him. I helped him grow fat and blossom out of hungry listlessness. I held him at night, and I decided to give him the best gift I could offer. I would make him immortal.

Each evening I built the fire to a roar, then unwrapped him from his ragged clothes. I held him in by the embers and each evening his arms and legs grew fatter. I bathed him all over with ambrosia and I hummed the Mother Song, recalling the days when I had set Persephone in the fire, when I'd made her ageless and deathless. I said the spells and set Demophoön gently among the logs. He spit and giggled, turning over and over like a log himself. As the blaze deepened, he tired, until at dawn he slept on a pillow of ashes. Each day he grew more bronze, more beautiful. Each night I hummed and dreamed, remembering how I'd done this for Persephone, my infant maiden, myself renewed.

So it was. My heart, my love, my pity—all my care I laid open in that house. Gladness grew back as quickly as Demophoön fattened. It was new to me, fresh as Demophoön to the world, and so, like a newborn, it was easily injured.

I would have made Metaneira's child immortal, a god, and only one night of ritual remained. Hekate rose that night, a pale disk in a dark sky. As I bent over the child's bed to take him up, my sense of the future pricked me. I looked at the fire. It was right. A handful of ambrosia remained in the bowl, sufficient to oil him once. I saw nothing to fear, so I pushed my fear away, as no goddess and no human ever should.

I unwrapped and bathed him, gave the final night's promises into his ear and nestled him firmly among the logs. The blaze soared, as it does on the final night, and my joy soared with it.

Then I heard the cry, female shrieking behind me. I turned.

"Take him out—what is it? Take him out!"

Curious at her son's ripening, Metaneira had stayed

awake and hidden behind a wall. "Out, take him out," she shouted.

I snatched Demophoön from the embers, set him down and let him lie on the hearth.

"You stupid human," I shouted back at her. "You stupid, stupid human." Demophoön wailed, the sound sudden and shrill. My joy, my pity swept out of me. All I had felt turned to rage.

Metaneira took a step toward the child, then stopped, thunderstruck.

My cloak fell away. I tore my veil back. "You don't know good when you see it," I shrieked. "You don't know evil when you see it. I would have had him immortal."

My hair fell to my shoulders and radiance filled the room. Metaneira smelled the ambrosia, the immortal fragrance, and heard, in my voice, the lashing gales. She saw me, huge as I am, a goddess before her in her own house. Her knees struck the floor.

"You, you, you human," I shouted. "You think fire only burns. You talk of pity as food. You believe only in grain. You talk sweetly of goddesses and gods. You believe what you see."

She wept now and crouched, too awed even to cover her face.

"Have your mortal son then." I spat out the words. "Have a hero, I gave him that. But he'll be only mortal. A human, ignorant, thick-headed, fearful of death like the rest of you."

She wept and babbled, pleading. She had offended a goddess and she knew it. She begged for ways to appease me. My curse might fall, maiming not only her, but Demophoön, her girls, her Celeus, Eleusis itself. I felt ready to give the curse, and she knew that.

And I knew too. Spilling from my chest, my rage had filled the room. Its flood left me suddenly empty. Then I felt what it was to be human, and the knowledge stilled me. I saw this woman ready to risk my wrath, ready to crawl to her child, and yet too frightened to move. Her forehead smeared into the floor dust. Her palms cupped, upturned and helpless. She begged to appease me. What sacrifice, she cried out, what sacrifice?

I knew myself as a goddess and I knew her too, as a mother knows her child and must strike it, changing the heart's pain to only the hurt of a slap. Metaneira's shame was so great only a blow would give comfort. What sacrifice? I must demand one.

I stared, wordless. Metaneira shook and stuttered.

"Quiet yourself," I said. "For sacrifice, then, build me a temple." I drew my presence from that room. "A temple, yes. Build it on a hill."

I withdrew, my brightness fading away as she crept to the hearth. No doubt she huddled over Demophoön until dawn. I listened and heard his cries go on and on, heard how nothing could comfort that squalling child.

Each day now, from this hillside, I can see the stone house. At night, I still hear Demophoön's cries. Human care leaves him unsatisfied now.

For days, I hurt to hear his wails, so loud they carried over the thundering of stones being dug and rolled. The people of Eleusis also cried out at times, pulling the stones from the hills and heaving one block on top of another. Feet tramped continually, stamping pebbles into the temple's floor. When the workers rested at last, I took up residence in the temple. Otherwise they'd start sacrificing, and I wouldn't let them waste food.

Eleusis spreads below me now. It abides. I would not curse that family or this town for what Metaneira did. She feared my anger, so they have given me a temple.

Still, the sow is gone from Metaneira and Celeus' yard. The fields lie bare and sterile, blank as my heart. Eleusis suffers as all places suffer.

I will give no pity. I will not eat. I will take no pleasure. I will win Persephone back, I know that, know it better than I know my grief, know it better than any sense, future or past. It is more sure to me than my powers.

Yet I don't know how I'll do it. I think and plot. No trick suggests itself. Zeus has his thunderbolt, Hades has my child. I have my rage, have my grief and a view of the Maiden's Well. I'll stare a while. I'll imagine she and I sit on the stone side of it. If she were with me, the olive tree would shade us, the olive tree would have fruit.

VI

HE IS Lord Hades, Lord Dis. This is the underworld. I have to learn the ways here, must find out his tricks. Then I can escape.

If I can escape. Which isn't certain.

I won't think that. I'll think only this: I will, I will. That's how a goddess, a Queen thinks. I'm both now, goddess and Queen. I must think: I will, I will.

First: I will learn his tricks.

Second: I will learn what tells lies and what doesn't.

Third: I will escape. Or else Mother will save me.

There I go again.

What goddess or Queen would rely on her mother? I worry like a child.

I worry about the crown, for example. I made a choice and now I wonder if it was childish.

He brought me a crown of his own to prove I'm Queen, and he insisted I put it on. There's a ritual only goddesses know, I said, and I made him turn his back. I had my own crown kept in a secret place. His crown was realms better, had twice the stones set in rare gold, but I put my crown on. Then I let him look.

Hades' crown suited me perfectly, he said. How beautiful it looked. Which proves, absolutely, that either he lies or else he doesn't know beauty.

He'd be angry if he knew I tricked him, and that thought pleases me. Is this childish? I have only this trick, and he has all of his. No, it's not childish. I won't think that. I'm certain, not fearful, and I can't be weak.

To be frightened, or doubting, or even be kind—all that's useless here. It's worse than useless, what he did shows me that. He doesn't know what he's teaching me.

Every day he comes, and he tries every way of touching. Surely this way, he says, or this one will please me. The tricks he invents! He asks me not to turn my head, not to push back at him, not to cry. Every day I grow more careful, more hidden. Can't he see that? It won't work, I won't be deceived, can't be pleased. I can't eat, or feel pleasure. Doesn't he see?

Perhaps he does. Perhaps he truly doesn't care.

Oh damn, I said "perhaps." I said "perhaps" twice. He doesn't care, I'm sure of it. I'll think only I will, I will. I won't doubt myself.

And then his ghostly flowers. Because I took one, he says I'm not raped, and he calls that justice. He wants to bribe me with new rooms and calling me a Queen, and he covers the sills and benches with baskets and pots and urns, all stuffed full of his asphodels. He brings fresh ones every time he visits, and he calls this love.

This isn't love. I know. I'll believe in myself. I'll believe what I know and I won't doubt. I could tell him the truth and say they're ugly. I could say, I never liked your flowers, and all his pride would turn to shame.

But perhaps these cold blossoms, these dry blooms deadly and gray predators, are themselves a trick. Maybe he knows I hate them and maybe he thinks it's all a game. Is that why I haven't said they're ugly? I don't know why.

Again. I doubt myself. Again.

Is this what it's like being a Queen?

* * *

No, it's not.

I discovered the answer and I didn't even have to ask. The underworld itself is deceitful. Doubt, wavering, sad thoughts that change faster than the changing game—it's his realm that causes all this. Every trick is a seed, and the underworld is the furrow where it grows.

I found the answer from his ghosts, the dead humans that I went to visit. Thinking back over the deceitfulness now, I see that every creature points to it, as clearly as mountains point to the sky. I could have seen it sooner, but that's the proof, isn't it? Everything that I misunderstood before proves how this place begets lies. I doubted myself and only my certain knowledge of Mother Da made me sure.

I went outside. I wore my own crown. I carried his crown with me in case I met a creature who could distinguish beauty.

Asphodels overrun the field around the palace now. He's planted bunches and they sprout so quickly. I should have seen the lie in that. How can plants grow, not in soil, but in ash? How can they sprout without Helios' sunlight to warm them?

Helios' sun doesn't shine here, only the palace itself gives off light. It's huge, but it's not like the sun, making life grow. The palace has colonnades and battlements and, most of all, it has decorations. I never saw such confusion. Sea people's carved scrollwork lines the palace walls right next to the hard grids that desert people make. Scalloped patterns, wandering tribes' work, lie beside the busy scratching of village builders. I suppose he made it, but he didn't know which was beautiful so he used them all.

I'm not sure how this is a trick, but it may be one. I do know that the walls themselves lie. They glow by their own power, but I touched one and it was cold. I know this: bright is warm; cold is dark. So how can that be? By a trick, of course.

I passed the Mourning Field, but the thought of invisible hands made me shiver so I didn't stop. Here again, love, which should be warm, made me shiver. Now I remember the quiet dawn there. It's deceptive too. He makes those lovers believe their love approaches, coming to them across the empty field. They caress the air, looking for the one they love, but they're never satisfied. The Mourning Fields promise comfort that they never give. Another lie.

I followed the road he showed to me before, but I didn't want to go near the Judges, so I went the opposite way, downhill. The road led me to the place he told me about before, the one he thought would please me, Elysion. I knew his Judges sent lovers to the Mourning Field, but they send heroic mortals to Elysion. As this underworld goes, Elysion isn't bad, that is if one doesn't mind flat stones for games, ash pits for wrestling, or black tree trunks with no branches, no leaves. The trunk I hid behind was smelly with mold.

The mortals in Elysion are the best that ever lived, and they don't look quite as ghostly as others I've met since. At Elysion I found those who'd been brave, who were generous, or heroic. Here was Dardanus, whose people called themselves Trojans. Here Amazon Queens held races along a hilltop, and below the hill, water made a slender path. It deceived those sitting beside it and they called it a stream.

I listened to them talk and learned one thing: it is possible to return from this realm after all. Yet I can't use what I learned. A valiant maiden—she'd transfixed a rampaging centaur with her voice—told the others she chose to return to earth. To get back, she'd bathe in a river they call the Lethe. I tiptoed away to find this river. Along its banks, many footprints, human-sized, went into the water, but none stepped out. The river had more bends and turns in it than Eros' head has ringlets.

The heroic ones bathe in the Lethe to be reborn, but here's the deceit: Lethe water makes them forget. The life they lived, all their feats, all the races they won, even special spells they memorized to instill courage—Lethe water washes it off. On earth they have to start all over again.

It's not only deceitful, it's vicious. These humans were

triumphant and victorious in life, yet what do they win? How do his Judges reward them? By forgetfulness. They're sent right back to life's beginnings, stupid as anybody.

I see this now. By the Lethe River I only wondered at it. I couldn't float back to earth myself because I wouldn't recognize earth when I got there. I thought of taking some Lethe water and setting up a bath for the lovers in the Mourning Fields so they'd forget their loss, but I didn't do it. It didn't seem quite right.

So I left the Lethe, and Elysion. If humans could be heroic, I decided, so could a Queen. A goddess would be brave and take the road upward.

With every step I took, the fog, which was faint in Elysion, got thicker. Again and again I sensed figures emerging from it, but I'd step close and they'd dissolve. I know now they're ghosts, more ghosts than when he and I went uphill. They're changed to fog when they enter the underworld, and they're deceived too about why they died.

They say that on earth . . .

But, oh no, that has to wait. I feel weighted down again. He's coming.

* * *

I will. I will.

I'm a Queen. I will be calm. I won't be upset.

I'm a goddess. Goddesses have powers within themselves. They lie with gods all day and yet remain whole. They don't sit around shaking and crying. And I won't either.

I will. I will stop it.

But goddesses can choose. I can't. If I fight him, he takes longer and it hurts more. If I don't fight, he acts as if he's pleased me.

I can't think of it. I'll start shaking if I do. Think of something else, think of what he did before he started touching. He stroked and curled my hair between his fingers. That makes me think of his skin, the muddy color of it.

I swear I'll go down to the Lethe and wash my hair in it. I

will forget how he pulls it.

I will. I'll think of what he said about my duties. I'll recall them, and I'll vow never to perform a single one.

What happened? No. I won't think of his eyes. I'll remember when he entered the gates, right after I felt him approaching. At first I thought he'd come to talk. He never listens, only talks. He didn't sit down but paced, expecting me to turn my head every time he turned his steps. He knotted his hands behind his back, and, honestly, his fingers look like old tuber roots. He walked, turning sharply at every corner, flicking bits of ash from the asphodels' petals, staring at his steps as he spoke, stopping with a jolt and frowning at the ceiling to think up his next instruction.

"Persephone," he said. "I'm playful with you much of the time. Now I must be serious."

Playful? If he's playful, then a war is a tickling fight.

"You wear a crown," he said. "You rule a realm as mighty as any." Here he stared at the ceiling. "Mightier, perhaps." Turn a corner, pace, pace, stop, stare at the air, pace. That's just what he did. "One principle must direct each of your acts. In a word, we call it Necessity."

In a word, I said, "What?"

He paused. I stared at him.

"Grape from grape seed. That's how it goes. Olive from olive. Barley from barley. Seed and fruit are bound. That's law, am I right?"

He didn't wait. I didn't answer either.

"Necessity is similar. You're a Queen now. You rule a realm which is distinguished by justice. Hence, now listen carefully, Necessity binds. You must accept certain tasks. The olive seed gives the olive. The Queen's duty gives her realm justice. In short, Ne-cess-i-ty." He spelled it out for me, sound by sound.

Now my neck was so stiff I stopped watching him walk. I closed my eyes but I still heard his steps, his long robe brushing the floor and his endless instructions.

Hades' Queen ought to hold ceremonies to welcome distinguished mortals to Elysion. His own ceremonies had not been entirely successful, and I should learn from them. Also, as Queen, I must know his Judges' decisions. I should send them congratulations on especially subtle judgments, and he would teach me how to do this. I ought to select a grove in this realm. I could retire there when my king had private visitors. If I had trouble choosing, he had a grove in mind. In any event, it would be called Persephone's Grove.

I opened my eyes because I was falling asleep. He stood by a flower pot, straightening the asphodels. Then he stepped back and looked.

Again he brought up his justice, or was it Necessity? A realm became just—necessary?—when its rulers performed their duties. I should sit on my throne.

I have a throne. It's by his. I don't like it. Or his.

I should eat three regular meals a day, evenly spaced and I might snack in his company. And one more thing.

By now I was dozing, but his hand touched my hair. I woke and smelled something.

"What's that smell?"

He was pleased because he'd devised it especially for me. It was oil of asphodel and he'd wear it on his hands from now on.

He'd begun kneading my shoulders. My Queenly duty, his hand lifted my chin, made acceptance of my king's love a necessity. I should stop acting like a child. I should be happy when he touched me. Soon it would come naturally, if I'd only try.

I didn't try, of course. Except to try to get out from under him, but that never works. He kept whispering, hissing in my ear, about duty, duty. I still hear it. I hate it. I won't obey.

He said I acted like a child.

I hate him. I truly do, and I won't let the hurt of it stop me from hating, not for one instant.

All right. I'll be calm. I am a Queen.

Yes, I'm childish. Sometimes. I know I am. I can't make up my mind. Only sometimes, about certain things. I get confused. But wait.

It's his realm. He is Hades, Dis. I'm in the underworld, and I must, I will, I must remember that. I will and I won't be confused by his Necessity. I'll remember what I learned, what I discovered when I went out on my own and talked to his own ghosts, the mortals I'm supposed to rule. Especially I must remember what I learned from that one ghost, the one who died in Boeotia. I wrote it down. I can go back and read it and remind myself. I can look at it again and again, and I have that. I'll read it now.

* * *

Except I made a mistake. I went back to read what I wrote before and I'd never gotten to that part. Oh well, it's a confusing place.

When I left off, I was walking uphill and the fog grew thicker, and I heard barking. I haven't seen dogs yet, but I do hear them, so they must be present. No, they might be a lie.

Anyway, I neared the Judges and the fog was awfully thick. That's good, I thought, since then maybe Minos' awful eyes won't see me—Minos is supposed to have all-seeing eyes. Just in case, though, I hid my crown and put on the one Hades gave me. I left it crooked, so it wasn't official.

I stepped forward. The fog grew so thick it felt like I was walking into water. Then I saw that the gray air was only thick on the road, but behind me and in the fields, just thin mists rose. I had to stop because the air was so thick it tired me out just pushing it.

"Queen?" I heard a voice.

I looked. I saw no one.

"Queen? Don't walk through me please." I heard a mortal's voice, a man's. He didn't sound old, but not squeaky like a boy either.

"Please don't step on me please, if you're Queen."

"Stop being invisible then," I said. I was tired of turning my neck up and down, all around.

So he collected others nearby him to gather together.

Ghosts have to do that, I learned, if they want to be seen. Everybody has to cooperate to get brighter.

I saw an oldish man with shades of others glowing around him. I asked who he was and he gave a Boeotian name. I was Persephone, I said, Queen here. Temporarily.

"I wasn't sure," he said. "Your crown's crooked."

That was rude, but I let it pass. I said conditions for beauty weren't perfect in the underworld.

The Boeotian ghost told me he was dead, which I already suspected. He was frank about it, so I think he actually believed the rest of his story. I asked if all the fogs were ghosts.

"Hades crowds us," he said. "The Judges work slower than eternity. We wait and wait."

I thought that was a poor way to rule a realm, and I said so frankly. He made excuses, saying it was unusual for it to be as crowded as this. He said that lately ghosts had to wait on the riverbank and the boat of the boatman nearly sinks with each load. Which riverbanks? I must find them. Who's the boatman? Find out.

The Boeotian ghost said the Judges were working right through meals and still couldn't keep up with all of the dead. He finished, apologizing and saying things could be worse. "Everybody's thin at least," he said. "And too weak to smell much."

"But why?" I said. "What's everybody thin and dead for?"

What he said next showed me how much he was deceived. As he tells it, mortals are dying by whole families, entire villages, even halves of cities on the earth.

"But why?"

"We starved." Earth's fields, he tells me, are bare and empty. Cold winds blow and the fruit trees wither, their leaves curling up without making fruit.

Imagine. Just recalling it makes me angry. I wasn't mad at the ghost from Boeotia, of course, since I could tell right away he believed every lie. But Hades, Dis, how cruel he is.

To deceive a ghost, a poor ignorant mortal, about the very reason he's dead. It's the meanest of tricks.

I tried to tell this to the ghost, but he wouldn't believe me. Humans think they're so wise, all on their own. He wouldn't listen, but would have his impossible story. Mother Da, he kept saying, neglected the earth.

Now everybody knows, everybody—Titans, centaurs, maenads, not to mention goddesses and gods, why even dumb humans know—Mother loves earth. She loves it more than anything, more than laughter, more than Poseidon, more than Olympus even. It's what makes Mother herself, Mother Da. She loves spreading plenty and she gives everybody more than anybody needs, simply for the joy of giving it.

I commanded that ghost to silence. I wouldn't hear any more. And those around him, too, calling Mother dried up, a stingy old spirit withholding her gifts.

"Mother Da," I said, "that's Demeter to you, Mother never begrudges gifts. She's not ungenerous. She wouldn't let earth parch, and she couldn't allow streams or wells to freeze."

By now the Boeotian was frightened of course, and had dissolved back to fog. I knew he could still hear me.

"I'm Persephone, my mother's own daughter," I told those ghosts. "I'm Queen here. You will not offend me."

I heard some murmurs, mostly children's voices. The rest had quieted.

I said I didn't know why they had died, but if I found out, I promised to come and tell them. Probably it was their own fault, getting into one of the battles that Ares starts, or else worshipping some immortal not quite rightly. As for the story about Mother, that they'd been tricked into believing, deceived by the boatman, or the Judges, or whoever it was, that story was absolutely false.

In this way I explained the deceitfulness of the underworld. And as I told it to them, I heard myself. Every time I remember this truth, it reassures me. That knowledge of confusion and deceit in everything around here makes me feel better. Only that, and my own secret crown comfort me.

Yet I do have these. They're all my own. I found them for myself. So I have power, as every goddess has power, over herself. I will believe in them, and I know that they are true.

I will not be confused.

I will think clearly past his tricks.

I'll find an escape. Or else Mother will save me.

Oh damn.

VII

DAUGHTER, the goddess who was once Demeter writes these words. Remember her, remember how humans enjoyed her gifts of the growing and the grain. I hope someday you read this letter and then you'll see that I'm not the stingy spirit humans call me nowadays. I am not that cruel spirit, and yet I am no longer Demeter. The other goddesses and gods may send messengers to this temple at Eleusis, but they do not find the Demeter they once knew.

Iris came from Zeus with a message. How simple Zeus is, thinking all he had to do was send that lovely goddess of the rainbow, a pretty invitation, and I'd come running up Olympus' slopes to join the others in feasting. Iris seemed ashamed to carry pointless tidings, and she frowned, the rainbow of her colors graying.

Since I wouldn't ask her shimmering to enter the shadows of my small room, we stood on the porch of this temple the humans have built for me in Eleusis. Iris spoke musically, her voice a purple and gold and red petal curled around the sky. Her beauty made me think of my daughter. Persephone had once been as brilliant and filled with light. No, I told Iris, I can't return to Olympus. But I had letters, I said, would she carry them to Persephone? I begged Iris to take my letters to you in the underworld, but she would not go there. Iris, lovely goddess of the rainbow, I cannot blame her for refusing to descend into Hades' dark home.

Daughter, please know I'm not the cruel spirit, the Ghostly Mother, the mother only of death, as humans call me now. I am merely the goddess who was once Demeter, a useless presence who gives no gifts and waits alone in a temple. Day by day I watch humans all around me as they die. I've watched it now for many days, and constantly it fills me with sad amazement.

Humans die. Eleusis, this small settlement of humans, grows smaller and more still every day. Fewer footsteps raise clouds of dust walking to the well, and the women and men who come to it walk slowly, carrying fewer water urns. When the urns are full, the humans lift them painfully, and often stop to sit resting alongside the road on their way home. Eventually one or another of them cannot stand again, and that one has died. The others use the water from the urn to wash the body, and all lift together to carry the dead one away.

If a child dies, they place the body inside of an urn and the mother weeps, looking down the neck of the urn. I know I am responsible, I have brought this little child's death, but I am one of these mothers too. No children are born here now, and the women carry no newborn infants in their arms. Demophoön grows, but he's a fretful child who hardly remembers me. Most of the little ones have died and all fullness has turned barren.

But humans die, and I understand that now. I envy them this death they have, with its pain only hurting until death arrives. They're mortal, with sorrow like a lake or pool that will dry if it isn't replenished. I place my mourning beside that, and from the shores of the day Hades stole you, it stretches without pause toward eternity. My grief overflows the caverns and valleys of the ocean. It is disturbed by currents, driven side to side by winds. It is dragged between the continents twice a day by the moon. Immortality was never so heavy before.

All the other immortals—Zeus, Iris and all the others—they cannot understand my grief any more than they can understand this human thing, death. How could Zeus, or any of the proud goddesses and gods, understand that the goddess who was once Demeter writes these words?

The goddess who was. I read that and I remember Demeter. When there was hunger she spread hillsides with food. I remember how, when there was only one kind of grain and many humans, she made new and different grains. With my own hands, I coaxed young trees out of the ground and weighted branches with fruit. I breathed red fatness into apples, touched my lips to the figs to sweeten them, caressed plums' and pears' skins so the juice would spurt.

I loved the richness and loved watching the humans, their fingers and faces sticky with juice from the fruit, their bodies growing round as roof beams. On the threshing floor, when they beat the grain from its husks, golden mounds of it rose around the women's ankles. They laughed and teased, lifting their skirts to wade through the wealth Demeter gave. And when they walked over the hillsides, my daughter Persephone gave flowers too—roses and hyacinths and crocuses, like at Nysa, beautiful fields of . . .

Nysa.

At Nysa I threw my crown away, and now I feel smaller inside my cloak. I haven't laughed since, since when? Demeter gave life, and I am known for death. To have given, to have always the memory of it, and not to be able to die. I may withdraw from the universe, make myself only a memory among the humans and the powers, but I will never die. I remain here in an empty stone temple where humans are too weak to worship, the immortal goddess who was once Demeter.

The clash of battle rings in my ears, and I hear Demeter's name called. So I am worse than Ares, the proud god of every battle, awful carrion hound that humans fear because he brings killing. "Demeter. Provider," his voice calls above the sounds of battle. "Mother of life."

Demeter is no longer present, but I'll answer for her.

* * *

Have gods grown senile, like old humans do? Zeus and Ares plot together as if this was one more battle in the humans' squabbles they love encouraging. Do they think I'm an enemy to be cajoled into a valley and captured?

I wouldn't invite Ares into my room, so we stayed outside on the steps of the porch. He set his shield aside and glanced pointedly toward the door.

"When a truce is called," he said, as if he actually believed we two were warriors on the field, "a meal is usually served."

He was hungry, of all things, and he came to me looking for food. Since he came straight from Olympus, I asked if he hadn't had his fill of ambrosia. He looked away, as if to conceal some battle secret.

He drew himself up full, gleaming tall with his armor and his arrogance, and then he began his argument. He spoke on and on, telling how he alone of all the immortals recognized true talent in strategy, how he'd come to honor my skill. Other Olympians didn't notice, but Ares and Zeus admired my abilities, how I marshalled my resources, letting the humans die, saving my own strength for whatever trouble lay ahead.

I said nothing. No doubt he thought my silence was the craft of a leader, but truthfully, I hardly understood a word he was saying.

He and Zeus appreciated my position, he said. Olympus and Demeter stood against one another, and so they would remain while more humans fell in the battle. The time had come for a truce, and Zeus had noted that only this morning.

I studied Ares. He'd leaned his gleaming gold shield on the highest step, and he glanced toward it often from beneath his dark black brows, admiring how the sunlight glinted on its edges. Truce, I thought. Since Ares loves fighting and would never approve such an offer, that idea must have come from Zeus.

He said he would grant me new rights, and that new powers would be mine if I chose them. Zeus would let me send rainfall, instead of sending it himself, whenever I desired it.

I smiled. The bargainer begins with the oldest barrel.

Or perhaps, Ares continued, I might like new rituals. Zeus would see that humans performed them. Or I might prefer that my brother's lightning bolt should never strike down a fruit tree, or that Aeolus, who blows the wind roaring down from mountains, should never flatten the wheat fields. Much could be mine, Ares insisted, and spread his broad hands in offering.

I saw those hands. On the battlefield, blood pools in their palms. I looked away.

"Grief means nothing to you," I replied. "I grieve for Persephone. Only her return can appease me."

I expected him to take up his shield and go, but instead he glanced around and leaned closer. I thought he smiled, but Ares is too good a general to reveal much.

"I told Zeus it wouldn't work," he said. "But then we both know Zeus, don't we?"

Now he did smile, like a conspirator sharing secrets. "When skill meets skill," he said. "On the battlefield or behind the lines, they recognize one another. Respect makes even enemies frank."

His eyelids lowered, and flint-dark eyes peered at my face. He hunched his shoulders like a wrestler, crouched and ready.

"I admire you because you succeed," he said. "At first humans only skimped on the sacrifices, and we got by. Then all sacrifices stopped. No delicious scents rise to us on Mount Olympus these days. Ambrosia runs short, and nectar is becoming a delicacy. When we can get it. In short, you're winning. You haven't been home in a long time to see it, but Olympus is not what it was. Zeus insists you'll be back any day, but hardly anyone believes him any more. Zeus loses allegiance rapidly."

I hadn't realized these things. To Ares they were obvious, so I didn't let my amazement show.

"I'll be brief," he said. "You could starve them, and Zeus would fall. Then you'd take over, but what would you have?"

I thought a moment. "A weak, unruly Olympus."

"Exactly. You're armed, but your weapon's dull. You need a strategy, a force."

I listened and studied my lap.

"Think of it. I provide force, you provide nourishment, but for our side." His eyes shone and excitement rose in his voice. "Think of the battlefields we could take, Demeter. Any town faithful to Zeus would fall. Starvation for Zeus' legions." He leaned closer and his palms spread as if they held the world already. "We'd triumph, of course. Can you see the temples? There would be thousands, sacred to Ares-Demeter. Or Demeter-Ares, whatever. Rituals would be held for us constantly."

"All blood sacrifices," I said.

His mouth opened to agree, then snapped shut when he heard me. His face fell like a coward's shield clattering onto stone. He'd waxed warm with his talk of blood, and perspiration shone on his forehead.

"I don't bargain," I said. "I demand Persephone. I will have her back."

Ares looked me up and down. "Persephone," he said. "I see." Then hope crept back into his voice. "That's your price then? That's the trade you choose?"

"I don't choose." I had been sitting on a stair, but now I stood and looked down at him. "I don't trade, I don't choose. I need."

I turned my back and came inside after that. He took his noisy shield from the stone steps, but before he left he paused and leaned in at the door. How did he put it? Demeter, known for her gifts, was immortally honorable too. He knew he could trust me. He felt sure I'd speak no word of this to Zeus.

I could not even reply.

Now that he's gone I sit by this stone wall watching the birds circle. They worry the bare ground, mistaking pebbles for seeds. If any seeds were there, a human has already found them. Ares' visit shows me a great deal. He sees human's deaths as mere strategy in a new battle. I understand that no immortal, goddess or god, can grasp what death means. I don't grasp it myself, but I feel the sorrow. I once was Demeter, and I am no more. I watch the humans die. To die, to cease, it's unbearable. No wonder humans spend each day fearing, struggling, striving to escape this death of theirs. Who would have thought immortality would have made such a difference?

And after death the humans go to the underworld where they remain. They still have their names, and they have their pasts and the stories they tell, but the joy and the mystery are gone, like the seed from the husk.

I never thought I'd understand humans, however much I pitied them. I gave food because it pleased me to feed them, because to give is my nature. Was my nature. The birds pick at the stones.

* * *

Ares must have gotten back to Olympus with his message since now I entertain whole families on my porch. Three more have come together, and they left at last. It's enough to have Aphrodite here complaining that humans no longer praise her in love, but of course she must bring that child of hers, Eros. And Hephaestus too. Humans are too weak to think of him or work with his metals over the fires, so he too has plenty of time to pass during these idle days. Will Zeus himself descend next, bringing all Olympus along behind him? Hephaestus' words comfort me though. I feel sorry he left so suddenly.

Aphrodite's scent lingers in the air, a perfume not even wind can erase. She called it myrrh and swore it was better than any flower oil, offering me a vial. I shook my head and asked if Zeus had sent them too. Sitting at Aphrodite's feet, Eros looked up with surprise.

His mother argued. "Take my gift, it's not a bribe. Think of how it will please Poseidon."

I told her I pleased Poseidon as I wished, when I wished, and well.

"Soon?" Eros interrupted. "If soon, we could. . . ."

"Hush." His mother's ivory fingers stilled his lips. "Demeter will take pleasure when she's ready."

Hephaestus remained standing. He leaned closer to hear them talk, but he seemed uncomfortable without a hearth to lean against. I remembered his birth, that squalling, ugly spirit born dwarfed and wrinkled. His ugliness increases with age, and he limps more than he used to, yet for some reason I felt close to him today.

Aphrodite sat uncomfortably, her full soft buttocks unaccustomed to settling themselves on stone. Reaching to her bosom, her slim fingers withdrew, slowly, slowly as Hephaestus watched, a single feather from a swan. She brushed her cheek with it, arousing herself and staring off over the empty fields.

"If Demeter should want pleasure," she spoke softly, hissing her breath, "many gods are ready."

"Aphrodite," I said without blinking, "be direct."

She stroked her cheek with the feather, trailed it slowly down along her throat and back up again. Against her pale skin the swan's purity looked dirty white. Hephaestus watched her.

Eros sat on the steps beside his mother, sharpening his arrows' shafts so the points would sting helpless humans to love. When the tips glowed, he withdrew a small vial from below his belt and opened it. It held his love potion, scented with his own musk, and he carefully spread a drop on each point, then re-capped the vial and tucked it back to his crotch. He lifted his finger to his lips.

"Stop that." The feather struck Eros' fingers.

"I didn't do anything," Eros' plum lips pouted.

Aphrodite turned away. "He's developed a habit, Demeter. It's not good."

I waited.

"It's his love philter, lately he sniffs it. He's been acting, oh dear, unpredictable."

"He's getting older."

"And so, I might add, are you." Aphrodite was finally ready to speak straightforwardly. She handed Hephaestus the feather. "Demeter, you need love, you need lovers. You're wasting away."

"I need my daughter."

"Well, she's gone." Nevertheless, Aphrodite suggested, I might conceive again. She carried a lotion which would help me, one she had used herself just before Eros arrived.

"Why do you ask this?" I said. "You see I'm not fit for love now."

"Neither are the humans," Eros put in abruptly. "They're weak and tired, and everyone's too starved to conceive. We thought you knew that."

"I see." And I did see. Earth had no use for Eros now. Nor for Aphrodite, nor for Zeus, nor for any of them. It was even worse than Ares had let on, since now none of the immortals, no goddess or god, was needed. All because of hunger and the humans' death, and no immortal could change that.

"I'm sorry, I can't help you, " I told her, and truly I was sorry. I no longer had the spirit to give food.

Hephaestus shifted his stance and he coughed. "About your daughter, I had a thought," he said. "An idea I mean." He spoke stutteringly, his gnarled fingers twirled the swan's feather. He could not bring Persephone back, he said, but he was an artist. For himself, he'd made lovely nymphs out of gold.

Aphrodite frowned.

They were beautiful, delicate handmaidens, he explained, and they could breathe, and even moved spontaneously. With his forge and his tools he could bend and beat metals, and I'd have a child, a replica of course, but almost the real thing.

I let my chin fall and shook my head. Hephaestus stuttered an apology. He hadn't meant to insult me.

"It's all right, Hephaestus," I said. "Just answer one question."

He stood hunched, gripping the colonnade for support, and he nodded almost as if he knew the question already. "You'll ask what it's like, won't you?" he said.

I met his gaze.

"You want to know what's it like," he repeated, "to live as a lame dwarf among the beautiful, the deathless goddesses and gods? To live like that over all the length of immortality?"

"Immortality," I said. "No beauty, no pity."

"It's long. We'll go now Aphrodite."

I stood to watch for a time as they moved down the hillside, until they joined the haze of dust the wind carries across the fields. Aphrodite, loveliness herself, walked smoothly as a child. Eros bounced, chubby and perverse, a tiny thundersquall. And Hephaestus whose ugliness, it seems, has made him wise. His limp grows worse with the ages.

* * *

Aphrodite, Eros, Hephaestus. Also Ares, also Iris. I think of them, and envy them because they live and act. And the other immortals too, Zeus plotting, Hermes going from place to place as he transports messages. And Rhea sustains all the living of the world. Those immortals remain themselves, they have their natures, and I have my past. I am most like Memory now, a garrulous echo repeating events, a mere list.

And who is Persephone now? I used to know. In every day since the day she was born, her moods and mine were linked, our inner stems tangled. Today when I search my heart for her feelings, I find emptiness, a huge cave where dark presences whisper. My heart feels hollow when I think of her, but can this mean I know her feelings? I turn my thoughts away from the awful absence they suggest and I breathe a moment. I miss her again. I turn my thoughts to her and the absence returns. This emptiness must be what she feels.

Even my future-knowing, which comes and goes, confuses me in this time. I have sat whole days watching humans walk to and from the well, considering and searching for a vision of what might come in the days ahead. I find images, but images as confused as drunken dreaming. I sense loss, yet beside loss I feel rich fullness flowing again. I envision myself in a temple, and then there is fire. That is clear, fire builds in waves overtaking all the humans and immortals in my dreams. Am I mistaking my future for my past, am I remembering that field my torches might have touched? Or does fire fill the future, destroying everything it touches, yet somehow beautiful? How can these both be true? It's a riddle, like those riddles humans tell. It's a riddle and I can't riddle it.

Memory, Memory. I feel her coming with her lists, her events, her endless reckoning. How is it for my child to be a prisoner in Hades' realm, is Memory her companion there too? The ghosts all around her are only images, talking of their memories, their deeds and their loves. They repeat the past as endlessly as I do, and I no longer wonder that humans fear this death. I thought they were ignorant, striving each day for food, for warmth, for shelter, but I saw things too simply. Without food and shelter, they die. They become only memory.

And the rituals. The humans tremble as they perform rites, never feeling confident of the knowledge in their hearts. They question all they've been taught, and they fear to neglect the ceremonies, even fear while they perform them. All because of this death of theirs. If the food isn't found, or if the shelter is too weak, they die. If the sacrifice goes incorrectly, they die. By thunderbolt, by earthquake, by rivers in flood, they die. This is death, and now I know it.

Welcome, Memory. I imagine or I know that she leans in the doorway, outlined by sunlight, beckoning. Her pale lips shape words, naming names from the past. On her arm she carries Persephone's basket, and she places it on the table beside me. Are these seeds?

She brings memories and words, and they are seed husks, all that's left after the meat is eaten out. My fingers crackle through them. Now she sits by me, and her thighs crowd against mine on the narrow stone bench. She whispers in my ear, hissing words and words, like the whispering of wings.

Humans die and I have caused it. To think that once I felt joy to give them food when they needed it, yet they trembled, reciting my rituals. And I blamed them. They weren't ignorant, and I wasn't kind. I gave them what I wanted to give, but they begged what they needed to have. They needed as I need now. I never knew need, but it is a cruel thing.

Persephone, what are these wings I feel moving around me? Do you feel them around yourself too? Are you knowing this, somewhere deep inside his arms which are dark and huge? I remember Dionysus. He would have been a gentle, slender boy loving you.

Memory, Memory. Bitterness catches in my throat like a seed husk. I taste it and swallow. Are these wings that make the air tremble and shudder in my throat? Not thunderous wings, but whispering. I had wings at Nysa. I changed into a bird, a wild white one, and I rose over Dionysus. Do I see Hermes? Or do I remember? Has Hermes come with a message for me? Or in future-knowing? Dream?

VIII

WHY are so many humans dying on earth if the ghosts' story isn't true? All the ghosts tell of barren fields and children so thin their ribs show. I don't mean the ghosts are lying, but I don't understand. Mother couldn't let so many starve.

On the Cocytus, which is a river the color of sour milk, dead humans crowd the far shore, pushing and shoving. They drift aimlessly over there, haunted by the moment they died, and they must get across that river to be finally, officially, dead.

I've learned a great deal since becoming Queen of the Underworld. The boatman steers the boat, for example. The boatman's name is Charon, and if the humans die and don't get buried with a coin in their mouth, Charon won't carry them. He collects the fare from the lucky ones who have it and rows them across. A few leapt from the boat to shore near where I was standing, and they collapsed into fog right away. I tried to explain how they could cooperate and become visible, but hardly anyone listened.

In truth, being Queen, I think my duties should include showing newcomers the basic rules of being correctly dead. I told Dis that, but he doesn't listen to me either.

Actually, Dis has been quite peculiar lately. I call him Dis now, quicker to say than Hades. He has a lot on his mind with all the new dead, and he won't talk to me about what he does. It's not the same here as it was, and since I won't perform my expected duties, I have nothing to do. I go out among the ghosts most of the time. Besides, even our own palace is crowded these days, since Dis puts the overflow of ghosts in the spare rooms. And isn't it just like him to fill my old room with maidens who never even loved? In that very room in which I experienced quite serious moments, they sit up half the night, giggling.

It's my palace too, and I ought to have a say. I have my own rooms, of course, which are all mine except when Dis visits. Which isn't often lately, but then he is busy.

Of all things! I just noticed something and I don't like it. Everything I write comes back to the subject of Dis. I write of him and of him and of him. This displeases me.

As of now: It Will Stop.

A Queen wrote that. My new rooms are called The Queen's Chambers, but I'd rather say rooms. I have three: one for sleeping, a second for bathing, and this third one in which I sit when I'm awake, or when Dis visits.

The walls are beaten gold, and Dis says it's the best kind of gold. Deep in the ground beyond the Cocytus river lie rich gold mines, and also Dis got an artist, dead no doubt, to inscribe flowers into the gold walls. Each flower has its own name carved underneath it, as if I myself didn't create and name every one of them. Except for asphodels, of course, and asphodels fill these rooms too. At least he hasn't tried to make me eat lately. He removed all the different foods he had brought and left only one gold plate.

It's a platter, actually, and it's in front of me now. It's huge, but empty, except for a single seed in the middle of it. The seed's from a pomegranate, he says. I'm not hungry, I told him, thank you.

This room is large. When Dis paces, which he always

does when he visits, he takes thirty long steps along every side. Sitting in the middle of this room, I feel sort of like that pomegranate seed. The room's floor is marble, and I hear each and every one of those thirty steps.

Him again! I write about Dis when I wasn't going to even think of him. I won't think of him.

But what else is there? Only ghosts, poor things. They live in a miserable dream, if one can call what they do living. My friend, the Boeotian ghost who I met shortly after I came here, says his heart constantly longs for earth. He remembers life, all things he did and his friends, all that, and remembering makes him so miserable I try to cheer him up.

I told him, for example, that I was his friend now. "And I'm a goddess too," I pointed out. "Loveliest of all the immortals."

"I guess so," he said, "leaving out Aphrodite."

He was only fog at the time, since being visible tires him. So I don't insist on it. He sounded sad anyway.

"What do you mean, you guess?" I said. "I am loveliest."

"Queen, as you say we're friends."

"So?" I demanded. Then I asked him, right out, if I wasn't the loveliest.

I felt him shiver, a whisper moving in the fog. Then he suggested we talk about earth for a change.

"Boeotian, answer your Queen."

He started to disperse, becoming even less visible, so I gave him a Queenly look.

"Whatever you say," he said. "On earth, Queen Persephone . . . before you became Queen . . . ahem, your cheeks flushed like peach blossoms. Your smile pursed, pretty as a rose bud. You stood like a slim white stem and your arms spread leaves. No, make that petals."

"Very nice," I said. In life, the Boeotian wanted to be a poet so he can't help talking that way.

"Queen Persephone," he said, "did you ever watch a petal fall? It lies on the ground, and soon the sun dries it."

"Of course," I said. "It crackles and gets gray and you

can see right through it. But a new petal grows in its place. So?"

"You're looking tired lately, that's all." He moved away, a separate shadow among many gray wisps. "It makes me sad to think of you, lovely Persephone, condemned here forever. Getting paler and smaller, my Queen, forev. . . ."

"Not forever," I shouted. He makes me quite angry at times but I still do like him. "Mother hasn't abandoned me. I leave for earth very soon."

"She abandoned earth."

"That again!" He may be a ghost, but sometimes I'd like to kill him. He refuses to understand that things must go back, will go back to just as they were. They will.

This time I saw no point in fighting since we've already gone over and over it. He is my only friend here, after all, just as Eury and Clymene used to be my friends on earth, and will be again when I return. The Boeotian takes their place for now. He isn't quite as tall as Dis and is considerably older. He walks slowly, which is nice, because with Dis I have to run to keep up.

Oh, no—I write Dis again. How can I stop this? Lately he comes into my thoughts constantly. I know. I'll pretend it's like on earth and a certain god's name is unspeakable.

The Boeotian and I go for walks away from old Unspeakable's palace sometimes. He shows me things which old Unspeakable might not want me to see. The Boeotian showed me the Cocytus and explained to me all about the boatman. That's Charon. All in all, my ghost and I get along quite well, except for those moments when he's deceived. He treats me nicely, like a Queen, brushes ghosts out of my way, recites poets' verses about me, and his own poems too. In exchange, even though a Queen doesn't have to be fair, I talk with him about earth.

"Tell me how you made that flower, the sea lavender," he'll ask, for example. He knows the story, but I tell it anyway, beginning to end. I start out saying how Eros told me the rumor that his mother, Aphrodite, wanted to meet alone with Poseidon. Aphrodite planned it all by herself, how she would wear a special gown and go down to the sea and stand on a cliff wiggling, or whatever she does.

"And the gown was blue," the Boeotian says, getting ahead of the story.

I say yes, blue, and then I tell how I knew that Mother Da would get angry, since she likes having Poseidon all to herself. So I made bluish flowers, mixing one drop of sea blue and one drop of primula purple. I gave the flowers long stems, strong enough to make a necklace, and then I borrowed, from sharp stones, prickles for the stems.

"Whence lithe Persephone tempted Aphrodite," the Boeotian quotes, "beside the laughing sea."

I tossed the necklace on a stone by the sea where Aphrodite would find it, which she did, and she put it on and ran down to the sea. But when she began wiggling—here the Boeotian likes to give the final lines . . .

"Love's tender throat knew pain.

So now all lovers know it."

Which is his favorite story because it's sad, having Aphrodite all prickled by the stems in the necklace, and he likes sad stories. As Queen I try to keep my subjects happy, even if they are dead. As for my official duties, I don't bother.

I look up from writing, and there's that seed. Dis has stopped saying it's my duty to eat, and I appreciate that. He brings no platters, no baskets, and he doesn't go on with his talk of Necessity either. I'm especially relieved because he hasn't touched me lately. He simply waits and walks around, like an ugly lost dog.

Still, I wonder. He acts so strange lately, and he may be up to something. He's not like the Dis that used to . . .

Oh him—his name! I think of him again.

Well what else is there to do? He might at least come to visit, so I wouldn't sit and think of him all day.

That isn't quite sensible, is it.

* * *

He came!

Not that I wanted him to, and in fact now that he's gone I'm more confused than I was. But it does prove I knew a small amount of future-knowing and saw things that would happen. I know more since becoming Queen, and even he admits that. He acts differently too.

He came in the gate, and right away he looked toward that platter. "Not even one seed, Persephone?"

I have told him and I have told him. "It's dry," I said. "Foods on earth have life."

He looked back and forth at the seed, at me, at it. I was afraid he'd try touching me so I made my gaze hard, but he only stroked my hair once. "On earth, yes," he said. "It might have lived longer."

Then he paced as he always does. He paces and talks and puts me to sleep. I count his steps, but this time the oddest thing happened, he took thirty-five, even forty steps to each side of the room. He was saying that he knew I wasn't performing my duties.

"You're walking slower," I said.

I thought he was going to get all red and angry because I interrupted, but he didn't. He just said it was nothing, I shouldn't worry. And I also shouldn't worry because he wasn't going to try to force my duties on me any more, and he realized now that he'd expected too much, right at first.

"Persephone." He stopped and stared a moment. "I never meant to hurt you."

From this I knew he was up to his tricks again. A wild dog that bites can still wag its tail.

"I tried to please you." He paced again, stopped again. "Didn't I bring flowers?"

I hate asphodels, and I can't help showing it. He's so proud of them, but I can't help comparing them to that flower at Nysa. They're like a foggy ghost of that flower, gray with petals already dry and transparent. Even his asphodels' seeds look like tiny chips of bone. It's only natural that I should hate them, so I turned away, but he saw my look before I could hide it.

When I looked back, he'd turned toward the wall.

"You don't like asphodels." He was staring at a gold carving on the wall.

"They're flowers." I tried being truthful.

But did I like them, he asked again. So I told more of the truth, that I wasn't particularly impressed with them. His back was turned, but his mud-colored hand lifted, and one finger traced over the raised gold that made the picture.

"You don't wear your crown either," he said then. "All the ghosts' gossip comes to Hades eventually."

My mouth dropped open. Could one of his Judges have told? I thought I'd avoided them.

"Justice." Dis turned so suddenly that his long robe fanned out in the breeze. "Justice awaits me. I must go."

He was almost out the gate when I spoke. "One thing," I said. "Do one thing to please me." I don't know why I said that, and it's only made things worse. I probably said it to get clues to his newest trick, the nice-as-nice way he's acting. Whatever. Anyway, he stopped at the gate and turned back.

"I have a question," I said, "and you have to answer truthfully."

He stepped closer, but I gave a Queenly look.

"Will you eat if I answer your question?" he asked. "Will you restore yourself somehow?"

I reminded him that he'd wanted to please me, and said that I'd think about eating. Which is true. I do.

Then he stood quite straight. "I swear by the River Styx I will answer truthfully," he said slowly, quietly, solemnly. "Ask your question."

"Why? Why did you bring me here?"

"It was a decision made in a Boule."

The Boule, I pointed out, was his idea.

"I thought you'd see the beauty here," he said then. "You're beautiful."

I reminded him of his oath. "Answer absolutely and fully. Future-knowing included."

He looked startled. He stepped closer to my table, but only to sit down. "The future-knowing then." He spread his hands and looked at them. "You've seen my realm. It has justice, Persephone, and justice is beautiful."

I hoped we weren't going into that again.

"Among all the realms belonging to the immortals, death is my domain. I give provision, reward, punishment." He went on a bit, as if he envied the other immortals, telling how Aphrodite gives humans the desire to love, how Athena gives wisdom. Even Lord of Battle Ares gets praise for successful fighting.

I pointed out that I knew my relatives, and that I'd studied everything he was telling me.

"But Hades," he said then, "for all immortality, Hades is known for death. Persephone, I swear by the Styx. . . ."

He paused and clasped his hands, and I thought, if this is a trick, he's copied just how frightened humans' hands shake when they face those Judges of his.

"Persephone, by the River Styx, in my future-knowing I see myself giving life. With you, my Queen, that can be possible."

He stood up very suddenly, red and tall and dark, how he gets with rage. "I've answered," he said harshly. "It's just."

I curled up, pulling my knees in quickly to make myself a ball because I knew he was going to start touching me. I tucked my head in my arms and made my shoulders hard, but I felt nothing. I heard his steps moving across the marble floor. I went on waiting and held still a long time until finally my fingers had started tingling and hurt, so I looked up.

He was gone. I looked everywhere in case he'd hidden, but apparently he hadn't.

His tricks confuse me now. How, swearing by the River Styx, and that means you have to tell the truth, how could he make up such a story? If it's a lie he knows he'll be punished. It confuses me too because he acts like he worries about me, but at the same time everything about him is a lie. I wish Mother Da were here to explain all this.

I know, I'll go and ask my friend the Boeotian. Poets, even almost-poets, understand such things.

* * *

When will Dis come back? I don't care if he never comes, it doesn't matter.

But I wonder what he'll say when he does come, and he sees that the seed is gone.

He can say whatever he likes. Probably he'll start talking and go on about his Necessity anyway, so I don't care.

Maybe he won't look at the platter, and he won't even notice. Then I'll have to tell him.

Why should I want to tell him? But then if I did what would I say?

Oh damn. This much thinking makes me sleepy.

For a while I thought I could say my Boeotian friend ate the seed, but since solid food disagrees with ghosts, I decided that's no good. But it was the Boeotian's idea, sort of. I feel so sleepy, and I must remember how it was the ghost's idea.

I went out of the palace and asked around among the crowded ghosts until I found my Boeotian. He sat on the muddy bank of the Cocytus river, marking it with a stick. I remember now, I told him I wanted help explaining Hades' latest trick. I repeated all the things Dis had said, even about his wanting to give life instead of death all the time and then the Boeotian asked . . .

Where was I?

I must have fallen asleep for a moment, that's all. I wonder if that pomegranate seed had a spell on it that makes me sleepy. That would be just another of his tricks no doubt, or are they tricks? Did I deceive myself, seeing deceit everywhere I looked?

Questions, questions, like all those questions the Boeotian asked me. He wanted to know about Dis, about every word Dis said, everything right back to the day that chariot came up at Nysa. Being an ordinary ghost, nobody important, the Boeotian had never seen Dis himself so I had to describe him. He kept wanting to know exactly what my king looked like. He looked like . . .

Who?

Dis, that's it. The Boeotian asked questions about whether Dis brought me gifts and tried to do nice things. I said yes about the gifts, if ugly flowers counted. And did Dis act peculiar lately, the Boeotian asked, which surprised me. And he asked more questions, then he told me to wait because he wanted to get visible to show me something.

Measuring slow steps by drops of dew. . . .

Funny, I drifted off again, and then I remembered the first line from the Boeotian's poem. He'd been writing it on the river bank when I came. He doesn't like to write things down, but being foggy he forgets things.

I remember, he got visible, and he looked simply awful.

"Do poems make you sick?" I said. "You look sick."

"Only when the river erases them," the Boeotian said.

Everything ghosts try to do here is hopeless, and we both knew already that the water would come up and ruin his poem. But before that happened, I must hear what he wrote, he said, and stared down at the edge of the waves.

Measuring slow steps by drops of dew. . . .

That's the first line, but then what? The part about legs, yes.

Long legs like restless mandrake roots. . . .

Then dark hands, the dark hands were clasped against his forehead. The Boeotian put it more beautifully, and I could almost see it. And those shoulders, in the poem the Boeotian said Dis' shoulders were hunched to part the fog, yes

Of longing lovers like himself
That twirl in Dawn's trifling grasp.

Oh I feel sleepy.

Then the poem came to the part about long dark robes. . . .

And when the Boeotian finished reciting I asked—but no. There was another verse.

In the awful underworld
That mourning lover paced and ceased
and paced again. Thirty steps to every turn. . . .

I can't remember everything because I'm sleepy, but he finished reciting.

Then I said he'd made up a truly fine poem, one with mists and dew and waving grasses and everything. I was amazed how he'd made it up, right out of his head, and it did sound quite real, but the Boeotian said no, that wasn't true.

"Be still, Queen Persephone. Consort of Hades, Gentle Mistress of the Dead."

He was fading, and I could see he wasn't going to stay visible for long. I feel like that now, drifting in and out of sleep.

He faded but I heard his voice say, "Beauty isn't a poet's to make. We copy truth. I saw Lord Hades himself, your own Dis walking there in the endless dawn of the Mourning Fields. Awful Hades wandered there, all alone, grieving to himself for his lost love. For love of you."

The Boeotian's shadow faded even further away, but I believed what he said. For an instant I believed that Dis loved me and he was sad. I thought I might eat then, just one seed, to make Dis feel better. It was the Boeotian's idea, in a way. And then a wave came up out of the river and erased the poem from the bank. The wave sucked it down the way sleep seems to pull me down now, which makes me so very sleepy. And my ghost was gone then. Then I'm calling, Boeotian, Boeotian, Please come back.

How am I going to explain when Dis comes, which will be soon? Hades is coming, but I'll say a wave came up in me and ate the seed, swallowed it, erasing me. The gold platter is empty and when I look in it I see a face, my own face, swimming and floating in the middle of it. I feel that seed in me now, and it's making me sleepy very sleepy very

* * *

It's later. Has he come? I'm awake and I had a dream. It is future-knowing, it is, so I'm sure I'll leave soon.

Mother made Zeus make Hermes make Hades let me go back to earth. Oh politics!

In my dream Hermes, doing his duty as a messenger, came for me, and Hades had to let me leave with him. I saw Hermes clearly, he was wearing his winged cap which makes him go swiftly and makes his footsteps fly.

But then later in the dream I was with Mother. I felt her arms—so real, and I remember flowers too. I'll see them soon, hyacinths and roses and irises.

But then the dream had Hades in it too, further, far into the future. Dis was there, which means future-knowing is certainly odd. As Mother says, it's confusing, but then humans get their memories mixed up sometimes too.

I woke up feeling sad because I don't like the way the dream ended. I felt so hot when I woke because I dreamed of fire. But the first part was good, especially the part when I heard Hermes and Dis coming for me. Their steps came down the hall, Hermes' swift and light, but Dis' steps slow and heavy.

Oh damn. I just looked and saw the platter. The seed's gone because I ate it, didn't I? Or maybe I dreamed that feeling too. It was on my tongue and then a stone, a stone dropped into my belly, heavy and deep.

Wait. I hear footsteps in the hall . . .

PART TWO

The Early Years

From 1499 to 50 years before the birth of Christ

So then did they, their hearts as one, fully cheer each other's soul and spirit with many embraces: their hearts came free from grief while each received and gave back joyousness.

Homer
"Hymn to Demeter"

IX

DAUGHTER,

I certainly feel strange beginning another letter to you. Words came easily before, back when I didn't know if you would ever read my letters. Now I have given those others to you, and you have read them. Hermes has promised to come this afternoon to take this new letter to you, and I can't think of what to write.

Perhaps if I could forget how we were together recently, and how we promised to write to each other, then words might come more easily. I try to keep my thoughts in the present, forgetting the past and the future, but then I think of you back in the underworld. It makes me shudder.

Nonetheless, we were allowed a time together before you were required to return. And we will have time together again. It won't be all time, not the always that we want, but it's sacred and certain that we will have three parts in every four. At least your absence is only a little death this time because you'll return. Three parts of every four is a lot, is most of the time actually. Mother Rhea, who rules all things, has promised that we may have that. How long has it been since I called Rhea "Mother"? Back when Zeus and I staged battles on her lap, I suppose, and we both called her that.

I laugh, thinking of Zeus. Even when all Olympus knew his Boule was destroying him, he would not relent in his decision. Ares had humans battling over food everywhere on earth, and with humans too weak to indulge in love, Aphrodite was haggard from fits of temper and weeping. Even patient Poseidon, the shores of his seas choked with the dead, threw daily squalls and earthquakes. I had brought Olympus to its knees, and I didn't even know it.

Only when Zeus' Queen Hera closed the doors of the sacred bedroom, and only then because humans, weak from hunger, had stopped conceiving children, did Zeus call Hermes to his side.

"Go to Demeter," my brother said. "Her daughter's free. Go on, guide Persephone back to earth." Hermes, with his winged cap and sandals, got to bear the good news.

Do you remember your first step back on earth? I hope the underworld at least gives you memories, as it does the ghosts you live beside now. Did you know that in the instant of that first step, flowers blossomed from dried roots all around you? You ran down the hill and I ran too, but more slowly. I was running uphill.

Petals opened in each place you stepped, and the grains, in the moment I called out to you, fresh grains shoved their stems through loam again. I recall the humans too. My hand touched yours, and the humans felt warm winds return. The frozen plains began to melt, cracking and sparkling, and the humans turned their faces toward the warm rain beginning to fall. They pounded one another's backs, leaping onto each other's shoulders and shouting our names. You said later that you couldn't believe that earth had been frozen and dead, that life had only just come back, but it was all true. I saw it and I felt it too, as our hair fell across each other's shoulders.

You did look awfully thin, running down that hill. I could hardly bring myself to hug you, so thin, so fragile.

Then we did hug, and I remember that seed. I felt it growing like a dark tuber at your inmost center. I felt a deadly weight, and I knew you'd eaten while you were in the underworld. I did not want to say it aloud, did not even want to hear you say it, and it seemed that a long pleasant time could pass before we would have to admit you had eaten there. I felt strong and safe all that afternoon until Mother Rhea came. What immortal but she, mother of all immortals, would dare interrupt us? None would invade the talk of mother and daughter, the passing over of the Knowledge.

We sat on the sun-warmed stone by my temple, happy to talk and watch, seeing humans smile and call to each other as they came and went from the Maiden's Well. I described how the sweet fertility spills, drop by drop, from the channel, and told how each goddess, each human woman, renews herself after love. When Rhea approached on that first afternoon, she heard me trying to explain the Mother Knowledge.

"Then recall your past," I said. "Your present senses."

"Your future-knowing," Rhea completed my statement, her voice so like my own that you didn't flutter an eyelash.

Mother found us lying side by side on the temple stones. She had heard her own words repeated, and her hands replaced mine to untangle thistles from your hair. I realize, thinking back to that time, that I was teaching the Knowledge poorly. During all my wandering, my imagining, I'd rehearsed the words to rote, and when I finally sat by you I probably spoke the secrets too plainly. Or I tried too hard. Whatever, the Mother Knowledge may come later for you, but it will come. I promise you'll return to yourself each time you love, and Mother Rhea promises it too.

She sat next to us, and I lay back listening to her voice. She spoke of the changing shapes of the moon. She spoke of the daughter, a pale white eyelash on the night sky, and she spoke of the mother, tossing her robes down on the water, and finally she spoke of the aged one, a trickle of milk to be swallowed by the darkness. She told how each goddess, each human woman, may lose herself in the night sky and rise again under another sky, clear and bright. Rhea closed her lips over the last secret and I drifted, just as you did, inside the senses.

Mother did not stay silent, as one does in such moments. She had come with a message, and her question surprised me as much as it did you.

"In the underworld, child," she began by saying, "did you eat?"

"Me? Eat food?" You sounded exactly like a frightened mouse.

"Absolutely not," you said. "Absolutely not exactly." Then you swore, swore by the River Styx, clever Persephone, saying you hadn't eaten a single meal.

I realize now that you must have known it was too late to change anything. Dark Hades must have run straight to Zeus with his story. I could well imagine the version your dark husband told. "Persephone tasted my fruit," he would have said to Zeus. "Justice demands I take her back."

You know the laws, daughter, you know the rules and the names of your relatives. How could you forget that she who eats in the underworld must remain there?

We sat on the sun-warmed stones. "Not one seed?" Rhea asked you then.

Your protests—look how thin you were and couldn't we see how skinny—were embarrassing. I've taught you dignity, not to quibble, and besides, all Olympus knew by then, even I knew, that this supreme law must be obeyed. I only wondered what plant I should curse for having tempted you.

"What seed?" I asked you.

"A pomegranate." You pouted, dear, and you should not pout since it puts lines around the mouth. "But I only ate one," you said.

Mother Rhea studied her hands. When we immortals were children in her lap, Mother Rhea often knew our thoughts before we had half-thought them. She read my look. She saw the grief and all the rage flowing back into me. She who is above all others knew this law must be changed or I would bring grief to earth again. Yet Rhea knew as well that law is law, it must somehow remain.

"A single seed," she said, smoothing a crease from her full skirt. "One grain of sand never made a seashore. Pulling one string doesn't play music on the lyre. Tell me, Persephone, how many seeds make a meal?"

Rhea is clever and wise as all the ages she's seen, and I saw her cleverness coming. She would use the number you chose and count out your fate with it. You would be taken from me. I trembled, watching you pause to think before answering. Would you say "Twenty?" "Twenty-four?" "Twenty-eight?" With that number, Hades' arms might take you away no more often than the moon disappears in the dark sky. Would you say "Four?" "Three?" Only "two?" And I would lose you for half of all time. I begged silently for you to see what I knew. You sat before your mother and your grandmother deciding your own fate. You only thought to impress us by saying a number that sounded fair.

"Four, I think," you said at last, smiling. "Yes, four seeds make a meal."

"Four seeds make a meal," Rhea repeated your words. "One seed doesn't count for eternity. It counts one part in four." Rhea spoke with firmness that no deal or Boule decision could ever alter. "You will spend three parts in four on earth, child, and then leave your mother. In that fourth part you go back to your dark husband, Lord Hades."

In this way she changed the law for you alone. You didn't argue, which is good, even though you wept and blamed yourself when we sat talking later. It was your fault and a thoughtless act. I read your last letter over, and I can't understand what tempted you to eat. I realize you were hungry, but one seed wouldn't help that. You didn't eat out of confusion, or out of spite, and we can't even say that your Boeotian friend tricked you.

Whatever, it's done, and we'll find some good in it. I have the memories and you will visit again. I look forward to that. Today I miss you, and I miss Mother Rhea too. You and I were together while you were here, as your letter says, like twins in the sac. Perhaps we still share a few feelings, and that would explain today's emptiness, how I long to be near my own mother. You are in the underworld, missing me, and I remain in my temple, without you again.

Now I look from the porch and see how, even in the short time since your leaving, the grains have weakened. Winds shake their stems again, and the pale glaze of frost falls over the fields. Without you, no foods grow and flowers close themselves. But at least when you step back to earth, the ice will melt and flowers will open. Grains will sprout again.

And consider the humans. You're young now, Persephone, and only beginning to get your future-knowing, but if you have children someday you'll understand humans' feelings too. You'll feel their pleasure as deeply as you feel your own. That morning when you ran down the hillside, every footfall bringing life back to the soil, I felt the humans' excitement pounding up in my throat, roaring in my ears, almost as loudly as my own.

But, Persephone, no, I just realized something. With you gone, and the foods and the flowers weakening again, it means these humans will begin to die again. That thought makes me almost as sad as your absence. I'll stop. I must not think of that any longer.

* * *

Athena, sweet goddess of wisdom herself, must be right when she says I've started thinking like a human. I was puzzling back, thinking about how all this hunger among humans got started, when I began thinking about the flowers he made for you in the underworld. Asphodel, strange name for a flower.

You had nearly forgotten all about them when you returned to earth, and then, in the days after you learned you must go back to his kingdom, you began to speak of them. I remember the day you described them to me, the day we both decided, practically in the same breath, to go and visit Nysa.

After we enjoyed the going there, side by side as two graceful birds, we landed and took our shapes. We stood over roses and hyacinths and crocuses, remember? Then you described asphodels and we got laughing. The flowers around us squeaked, their stems and leaves fluttering in the breeze, "Asphodels! asphodels!" I watched the way you imitated your Dark Lord, taking thirty stiff steps up and down the field, pace-stop-stare-start-straighten-pace-stop. You made me laugh, and tears flowed down my cheeks and into the faces of the flowers. Then you told me about the chasm and the horses, about his cloak and that terrible pounding, and about the crown.

I swear you told the whole thing—about wearing that crown and seeing yourself and how you showed it to your Boeotian ghost friend. I heard it through before I realized whose crown it was. I'd thrown mine down at Nysa, angry at that flower, and you had found it. So you wore my lost crown, and you imitated how you had walked, balancing on your toes because my crown didn't quite fit.

We can't let the underworld confuse your memories. Always in the days before I lost you, I preferred my sense of future-knowing, looking ahead instead of into the past. But if I had to trade powers today, I'd take memory. In memory, I see us together perfectly clearly. Your letters say the underworld is deceptive, but it can't confuse immortals, can it? I mean, will you have your memories? I'll remember anyway. Keep my letters. Then if you forget anything, even if you trip and fall into the Lethe River and its waters wipe away all your memories, you'll have all this written down.

I love the memories, even though they interrupt me. What was I thinking about when I remembered that day at Nysa and the asphodels? The humans, of course, and that they won't have food while you're gone.

My powers weaken when you're not here, the fields freeze and no food grows. Humans starve and the men war, getting food for the women they serve. Everything on earth is becoming as bad as it was. It could become even worse because of cruel Ares' growing powers.

I did not tell you this when you were here, but while you

were gone, during your long absence, Ares taught humans how to fight larger battles. They were too weak to fight alone, so he taught them to band together for huge battles, he calls them wars. One or two humans used to fight, or a family at the most, in little squabbles or bickering over houses and wells. Now with Ares' help they plan the entire thing. They make shields and spears—a spear is a piercing pole made of metal—and full towns fight, town against town, killing one another over food and land. Ares wanders earth constantly, directing and glorying in these wars. You know how he gets, red and gloating.

Persephone, actually, all this began that day at Nysa, yet I wonder, was it somehow my fault for leaving you alone? Now, since they have no food, the humans starve, or else war over the food that's left and die doing that.

And I forgot to tell you the worst change. Mostly it is the men who do the fighting, and now humans honor the best killers among them. They make wreaths of laurel branches to place on these killers' heads, and then they carry them, like heroes of the games, through the gates of the winning town. Can you imagine that? And while these killers are celebrated, the unburied dead lie rotting in the sun. It's as if we immortals all went to Olympus to feast in honor of deadly Ares' brutal work, or celebrated Lord Hades' love of the dead. Can you conceive of it?

At least the Eleusinians are peaceful and I have a temple here. I can manage enough growth in fields on the edge of town to keep this place from starving. They share their food, taking half-filled baskets from house to house, and so please me. As for the others, I must think of something, or sit here knowing that they die again. I curse that day at Nysa when we were separated, and now both of us are useless to stop these deaths.

Persephone? Persephone, just now I felt the most amazing idea.

No, it's impossible.

But perhaps I could do it, and my brother Zeus would

hate the idea. I might call together a Boule to argue over it, and you might vote because now you are more grown.

Never mind, I scribble, that's all. I just now got this silly idea about making humans immortal and ending the suffering that way. Honestly, with you gone, I rave like some human again. When you read this, please skip over the sad or silly parts. I stay waiting for you in Eleusis, but I came from afar, and my mind still wanders elsewhere occasionally.

For example, there was something important I had to write, and now I forget what it was. That Hephaestus now has a cane because he limps so badly? No, you were here when Hades sent that gold stick from the underworld. Eros is cured of tasting his potion now, since Aphrodite coats his fingers with awfully strong perfume. That wasn't what I meant to tell you though. I think of Hephaestus, Aphrodite and Eros—love, that's it. I promised to write you more of what I understand about love.

I must try to explain it again. What mother ever had to teach her daughter about love after rape? And when the rapist was death himself. Before your first experience all this would mean little, but now, learning to love correctly, right at the start, is crucial. It's more important than understanding rituals, or sacrifices. Forget all the laws you've learned, forget even the Boules and deals, but remember what I teach you about love.

It hurts me, Persephone, to read parts of your letters. For you, love has been awful, and I can feel what he did, feel it in my skin. No goddess ever showed ashen Hades the gentle love skills, and he's never been loved, not even honored, unwelcome as he is among immortals. What he did, my child, was not love, and it's no part of love. He did rape, you were never deceived about that. He called it justice, but it was forced. And, deathly bridegroom that he is, that he should speak of your duty as queen, and call it love—I'd like to rip him up by his black root.

Rape is one thing, love is another. That is what I have to show you. Remember the day we sat by the Maiden's Well? I started to speak, then fell quiet, then started speaking again, but would suddenly stop. I kept searching for a word, an example, some way to express it, and you must have dropped twenty stones down the well shaft before I gave up. Think of berries for instance. Picked from the vine, they're ripe and sweet, and their soft insides burst on your tongue. That taste is pure and forgetful as sleep—that's love.

But suppose the vine goes unharvested, I can explain it that way. Sun sears the berries until they're black and hard and have bitter-tasting mold on their skins. If you ate one it would taste bad. You'd spit it out, but its taste would stay in your mouth all day. That's his rape.

There is love in lying together, and it can grow in you, only his rapes have made that love seem hard, black and bitter. In your letters I read how you joined fear to fear and bred suspiciousness. You turned away from what he called love, and when you looked back you saw only deceitfulness everywhere you looked. You learned to hate, and you made yourself hard. If you had known the love of Dionysus or Poseidon, you'd have tasted the sweet ripeness, but now all vines look bitter to you.

I'll teach you all over. I promise I'll do it. The happy yielding, the pungent burst at the center of ripeness—it's there. When you write, tell me if you can believe this. I'll find new ways to say it.

Hermes will come for this letter soon. I should not have written about earth's barrenness, please don't think of it. I'll keep the humans from starving, and I won't let them kill either. For now, remember earth as you last saw it. Remember the human children, their chins smeared with food, their fingers sticking to their fathers' hands. That's how earth will look when you get back.

I close now. Stay gentle. And write to me.

Oh yes—for the form of it—Queen Demeter sends regards to your king.

* * *

Wait. One note more.

I'm sure now, I know how to stop this suffering. It's perfectly simple, so simple it sounds silly, but listen to this—I will make all humans immortal.

Now I know that sounds silly, but that's only because no goddess or god has ever tried. Hermes comes soon, so I write quickly. Pay close attention.

We've always known how to give humans immortality, but no one's ever thought of giving it to them all, every last human on the earth. I'd place each human in the heart of the fire, just as I bathed you, as I bathed Demophoön among the embers and ashes. What death could they fear then, daughter? What cold or heat, what sea wave, what weapon could a human fear then?

The humans would still want food of course, but they could grow it themselves. I'd teach them that. So much for starvation. They die in other ways and they'd still die from earthquakes and sea waves and, above all, my foolish brother's thunderbolt. They'd still hesitate over the rituals, uncertain and afraid to offend this goddess and that god. But suppose I gave them a gift of immortality, absolutely given with no sacrifices, no rituals needed to please me. I simply give them immortality.

It's right, and I feel it, feel its goodness inside me. For myself, it would be justice, but gentle justice. Once I gave grain and loved giving.

These days, the scent of myrtle burning under the sacrifices offends me, since now I know that humans burn it, not for love of me, but in fear of my wrath.

I'll hand over my powers, I will. Humans will be immortal and won't have to tremble when they name goddesses and gods. They'll praise Olympus, loving us for our natures, but no longer fearing our deadly tempers.

Silver shimmers on the porch—Hermes is here.

Just this then—when you see humans next, you'll find

them well-fed, living in health and pleasure as immortals. If suffering made me like a human, then joy will make the humans feel like they themselves live on Mount Olympus.

I close now. Oh yes—for the form of it—Queen Demeter regards your king . . . as temporary.

MOTHER Da,

I read your letter. I liked it all, except for the parts I didn't understand. I especially liked your idea of immortal humans. I told Dis about it and he simply stared. It's such a good idea, he couldn't think of a single thing to say.

I do have some suggestions, but I'll get to those later. First I must tell you about how my future-knowing is getting stronger, and to do that, I have to tell you about a dream I had. I dreamed it before I returned to you, before we had our time together on earth. I dreamed of fire, and that we were together, you and I, in the fire. Hades was in the dream too, but he came later. Mostly the dream was of being with you and of fire.

Now you can see that I really was back with you, and now, later, I'm with Dis again. The fire, of course, is how you'll make humans immortal. You must write to fill me in on the details when they're ready. As you can see, the dream came true. You wrote of Mother Rhea, saying that sometimes mothers know children's thoughts before the children half-think them. Well, don't underestimate the children.

Which reminds me, there is one thing I must not forget to

write to you. Mother, the underworld is large, and I'm not always in my chambers when Hermes brings your letters. He finds me by calling out, reading from the seal, "Letter for Persephone. Letter for Demeter's daughter." Mother, I am Queen here. In front of the ghosts and the boatman Charon and even the Judges, not to mention every pallid maiden wandering around in the Mourning Field—it's embarrassing. You should put on the seal, "Queen Persephone, Gentle Mistress Of The Dead." If you want to put, "From her mother, Demeter," underneath, I don't mind. Just don't forget the Queen part up top.

I'm not complaining—this is important. I'm new here.

As for the other things in your letter, particularly the humans fighting their wars, or whatever they call this new killing, you needn't write me about that. Dis and I had to enlarge the palace for so many dead. We're even thinking of using the caves across the river of fire, behind the palace, and you wouldn't want to go there, Mother. Most of the dead, as you say, are men. And about their new stupidity—this heroism—the ghosts around here talk of nothing else. "Fools feed on fallen fruit," my Boeotian friend used to say that. The fools are falling in here like rain. The ghosts just gobble up hero stories.

The warriors brag to the boatman Charon, pestering him with the stories of their greatness as he rows them across the River Cocytus. And even the Judges—Minos, Rhadamanthus and Aeacus—have been taken in by this stupidity. They've started sending these bloodthirsty heroes to the best part of the underworld, to Elysion itself. Rewards for killers, can you believe it? Dis has been informed of my opinion about all this.

Yet the strangest difference these days, as I see it, concerns the human women believing what these men say, snatching up these hero stories as if they were ripe figs. I used to like human women because, despite being so pathetically human, they always managed the laws and made sure everyone had enough to eat. For mortals, they were actually quite sensible. Peaceful men shared the women's homes, back in those days, but now, in the underworld at least, women celebrate the biggest killers. They actually dance when a warrior arrives. At least a few dance, not really that many. But in the Mourning Field where lovers wander, the maidens weep for boys who went to war and never came back. Honestly. Admiring killers is as ridiculous as if I mistook this deathly realm for the slopes of Olympus.

I see now that humans get confused easily, and it is hard for me not to get angry with them. You did teach me patience, so I try. Each day I work with a few of the ghosts, showing new ghosts how to be properly dead and still retain dignity. It's quite tiring, so I keep my lessons short. They drift away, hardly paying attention, preferring to whisper among themselves and wish for earth. I tell them that's over now, and a few, very few, accept what I say.

Not that I don't think humans can learn, I think they can. I think your idea of teaching them to grow food is excellent, and I even have a suggestion. I know just the human who should be your first student in learning how to grow things. If you take my advice, you'll be feeding two birds with one seed.

There's one warrior on earth, still living, at Charon's last report, by the name of Triptolemus. All the ghosts talk about him constantly, saying he's a "three-fold warrior," meaning he's three times as good at killing as anybody else. He's a man, of course. Just the other day I came upon two maidens in the Mourning Fields, and they were gushing over what they'd heard of him.

"A new ghost says he has arms like roof beams," one told the other, brightening out of shadow.

"I think he looks just like my Aenos," the other said. "My Aenos was a warrior too, strong, even bigger than Triptolemus, the three-fold one."

You see my point, Mother. Lovelost maidens can be deadly boring. Anyway, here's what I want you to do, locate this three-fold killer. Just follow Ares to any war and you'll find him. Teach the old three-fold to grow grain. Then send him to teach others. He has a war chariot—they're new but you must have seen one—and he can travel in it and teach mortals all over earth. You'll save loads of unpleasantness for everyone dealing with humans.

Besides, if you keep Triptolemus busy, I won't have to hear his name around here day after day. Everyone's raving about him. Triptolemus, three-fold warrior, don't forget.

Speaking of forgetting, don't worry about me. Even if this realm tries to deceive me, I have your letters and I write things down. My future-knowing is good, my memory must be likewise. I remember our visit, the many things we did. I even remember some things you forgot. Honestly, Mother, you overlook the most important things.

Remember, for instance, the day at Nysa? You forgot to mention how, in memory of my Boeotian friend, I softened the prickles on the stems of sea lavender flowers. I did it right after we landed, remember? I also especially remember visiting Aphrodite and Eros, and how Aphrodite was jealous of my new beauty. She wanted me to use oils to warm my complexion and red dusts to make my cheeks flushed, and she even had Hephaestus say I looked pallid from my stay in the underworld. Hep's not as truthful as everybody says. Dis says I'm more beautiful than ever, even if I do live in the underworld.

Eros was a disappointment too, even though I'd missed him very much, thinking how we used to be friends. And then to discover he's still a child! Do you know, he wanted to touch me with a drop of his potion? Fortunately, Aphrodite took his vial away. Eury and Clymene were also my friends once, and they also seemed young, singing and fussing all day over which shape of basket holds the most flowers. Probably, becoming Queen and all, I've matured rapidly. I have my realm and my duties and subjects, and it's a lot to keep track of.

With so much for me to do and new dead arriving every day, you'd think this realm would fall apart while I was gone. Yet while I was visiting with you on earth, the underworld went on as usual, nothing much changed. It's been deadly dull forever, and always will be, I guess.

Except for my Boeotian friend. That is news and I can write about it. You see, he's gone. My very first day back, I asked for him only to find out, from the story the ghosts patched together for me, that Dis had let him go. I was pretty upset. Apparently Dis had learned about the poem my Boeotian had invented, you remember that one he scratched on the river bank. It was that poem which made me feel sorry for Dis, feeling ashamed that he wandered in the Mourning Field for love of me. And all of that persuaded me to eat the pomegranate seed.

I know I've explained this to you. That's why I gave in, don't you see?

Anyway, Dis wanted to reward the Boeotian because I ate and I had to come back. He sent word for the Boeotian to stand once more in front of the Judges. The Boeotian was frightened at first, but he liked how it came out. The Judges sent him to Elysion, the only halfway beautiful place in the underworld, where he could be among heroic dead humans beside the River Lethe where one can go back to earth. Nowadays, all the ghosts around here are making up poetry, horrid stuff, but you see what they hope to win by it.

Anyway, the whole thing must have gone to the poor Boeotian's head because he surely forgot I was coming back. Wouldn't you know it, his very first day there he bathed in the Lethe, whose water makes humans forgetful. Maybe he went to the bank to write another poem about me, because I can't believe he would leave when he knew I was returning. Anyway, the whirlpools utterly erased his memory of the past, and he drifted away on the river's currents which will take him back to earth.

All this happened before I got back here. Please understand, though, the whole story comes from ghosts' gossip, notoriously unreliable. Besides, to get to earth the Boeotian is going to have to float up the winding Eridanus river. Then he'll have to start living all over, including getting born, etcetera. All of which could take ages in humans' time. Still, I do wish you'd keep an eye out for him. I miss him terribly. Dis shouldn't have let him go without asking my permission. My only comfort is to hope he'll be born as a true poet this time, not just almost, and I search my future-knowing for some news of him. Maybe if he becomes a poet, he'll remember me and write me poems.

Anyway, I've found a new friend, and the best part is that Dis can't send this one away. He's here permanently, guarding our gold fields beyond the Cocytus river, and his name is Cerberus. He's not a ghost either, but a dog. Or else he's three dogs, depending on how you look at him.

Remember I wrote that when I first arrived here I heard barking? Well, when I got back, Charon introduced me to Cerberus. He's chained on the Cocytus's bank, right beside the Judges' hill, and he's one dog, perfectly formed, except that from his black shaggy neck he's grown not just one, but three—three!—heads. Imagine. That's three mouths, three times as many teeth, all sharp, three wet noses, and three tongues—he loves licking my hand. Plus a grand total of six floppy ears. And three separate barks, all fierce.

I said he was perfectly formed, but actually that wasn't true when I met him. He had a problem with his tail. He had three heads, but he didn't have even one tail. You can imagine how bad-tempered a dog without a tail can get, especially one that has two extra barks.

THEREFORE: Queen Persephone's First Official Act:

I gathered armfuls of the long grasses that grow in the Mourning Fields, and I soaked them in Lethe water so they'd forget to be sad. Then I braided a tail. A little mud helped stick it on, and when I'd said the changing spells, guess what? Cerberus managed to wag it.

He looked slightly happier.

I could see that one tail wasn't going to be sufficient, so I made two more, stuck them on, etcetera. You should see Cerberus now. He's giddy like a puppy, and he wags his tails for nice ghosts and for Charon and, of course, for me. I toss a thistle and his heads butt into each other trying to catch it. I can hug him and ruffle his ears. He's soft, Mother, and I like being with him. Besides, unlike my Boeotian, Cerberus belongs here and he won't be leaving.

Now that Cerberus is my friend, I miss the Boeotian less. I talk with Charon too sometimes, when he isn't busy transporting corpses. I still don't like the Judges much but at least now they have to bow to me. Dis commands that all in the underworld do me honor, and Dis is having royal robes woven for me.

So you really must avoid calling me just plain Persephone. Dis calls me Queen in front of others, and I'm called Persephone or Grain Maid when he and I are alone. For Cerberus, of course, I'm just three yips and three wags.

I'm tired of writing now. I'll go visit him. No doubt he needs me. About once a day his tails knot together from wagging, and I have to untie them—part of my duties. While I do it, he whines and licks my cheeks with all three tongues.

* * *

I'm back now.

I meant to see Cerberus, but I ran into Dis instead.

Dis had arranged a celebration to welcome me back, so we had to go to that. I've been back for days, of course, so the ceremony was posthumous. Anyway, Dis had rehearsed all the Elysions to bow deeply and say, "Welcome, Gentle Mistress," three times together. Unfortunately, starting out so formally, the celebration never was much fun.

There was lots to eat though, for Dis and me. Mother did you know that ghosts drink blood? I told Dis it was awful, and he sent them out of my presence to do their drinking. Knowing that, I don't think I could ever be close to a ghost again. But then I have Cerberus.

Dis and I ate a lot. To tell the truth, every day I've been back has been a good one for eating, but perhaps I feel so hungry now because I starved myself before. Dried fruit and hard bread don't look nearly as awful these days. I'm getting fat and healthy, and Dis says that if I keep this up my new robes may not fit! Especially I have a taste for asparagus. If the robes don't fit, I'll command new ones to be made.

You can probably tell, I'm happier now. Dis is nicer to me, and most days I don't cry. I used to weep every time I saw an asphodel, and their smell still offends me, but having them around hardly upsets me any more.

Some days, nevertheless, great spasms of unhappiness come. All at once I'll miss you and earth and the Boeotian and flowers. It's silly, I know, but I start wishing I could wrestle with Eros or run in the fields with Clymene and Eury. Now my breasts are nearly as big as theirs. Perhaps some poet will call me deep-bosomed.

But I get very sad sometimes. Especially, I'm sad reading the part of your letter I don't understand. I remember you and Grandmother Rhea by that waterfall, and the afternoon when I dropped stones down the Maiden's Well. You asked if I understood what you meant by love. But please don't be hurt or be mad if I tell the truth: I'm not sure.

You write of yielding to the sweet burst of forgetfulness. Dis and my times of touching aren't like that. Not even now, when I can bear him. And you say Dis raped me. Well he still does push himself on me as he used to, but I don't fight now. I know what he's doing, and it doesn't frighten me much any more. I don't push him away or anything like that. It happens almost every day. I mean we can't keep on calling it rape.

That's all I think I should say. It might be unkind to be too descriptive, and as you told me, no goddess taught him love. It's not nice to start jokes on Olympus about Hades lacking skills. You know what I mean.

I'll skip the details, but I do want to tell you my feelings.

You write of tasting berries. Some are dead and bitter, others ripe and sweet. Well it's not like that for me. And you speak of yielding, but I don't have a choice, Mother. Is that why I couldn't take myself back after love the way you and Rhea wanted? I don't know. I don't think of it except when the sadness comes.

Anyway, I'm getting sad writing this. I remember you said, when we sat by the Maiden's Well, that Dis could be a wave, a crash of surf washing gently over me. The wave would recede, you said, then I'm supposed to grow warm, to dry, feeling firm sand under me. Mother, for me it's different. Please don't say it isn't love because it is what I feel. The wave pounds me under, yes, but I don't stay on the shore. I go under somehow.

I'm getting very sad writing this. But you asked, so I'll try.

The water pounds, then I get pulled down. I feel it drag me down, somehow down. First there's sea green, and light flashes through it. It's like sunlight, only cold, and then I feel the blue depth. Water weeds and strange flowers swirl there. Then I go to the deepest place, which is black. When I feel myself pushed down to there I'm afraid. I can't move and I get afraid I won't be able to breathe. I feel him, him all around like water, he's heavier than air and he presses on me, on all sides. You see I can't choose, Mother. Please don't say it isn't love when all my knowing—my past, my future, even my hope—keeps sifting down, further and further, until I feel what's left of me coming to rest on the sandy bottom.

He slides from me. I lie there, lost. Cold currents move across the ocean bottom, pass right through me and I can't stop them. I don't know where I am, except I'm lost. It takes a long time for me to decide to move, or to open my eyes, or if I ever want to do anything again.

Mother, I can't tell you any more today. I don't feel well. My stomach feels funny. Some mornings I feel like this.

I'm going out. I need to be out of this room. I don't like what I wrote. I'll go and see Cerberus. We pretend to fight, tumbling on the river bank, and I nuzzle into his fur. It makes me feel better. He wags his tails. I can tell he likes me.

I might burn this when I get back. Or I might not. If you read this letter then of course I decided to send it.

* * *

It's later now. I'll send this without reading it. Writing made me sad and I'm not very brave, so I don't want to get sad again.

Anyway, Mother, letters are rather silly. Writing takes so much trouble, and never says what I mean it to say. Writing never was truthful, like talking.

Suppose we do this: we're immortal after all, so write to me every age or so when you have something to say. That way our promise gets kept, and I won't have to write about every single sad thing that happens.

I'll write, of course, but only when I feel cheerful. I suppose.

XI

DAUGHTER,

You were right to ask that we send each other letters only once in a while. We spend three parts in every four together, and I know enough of your life in the underworld now so I can imagine the fourth part. I have learned to stay busy when you're gone even if it is a barren time on earth. I bestow the few gifts I can manage, the smaller grains and the red berries which winter birds love. These days I sit on a hillside overlooking Eleusis, watching the humans repair and improve our temple.

Some barbarians, supposedly Sea People, have been wrecking goddesses' places, so there's good reason to make ours strong. Artemis had several temples looted, and the barbarians threw offal in Hera's bath pool. You can guess how Zeus' Queen took that! Here in Eleusis, Theseus, the son of Aegeus, governs and he rules alongside an Amazon. They respect the Mother Ways, and they're having our temple improved. Below me today, workers pile stones for walls, and they've moved the gates further west. With so many worshippers, we need more space for our rites.

I sit and watch them work, see them shivering in the cold

wind that comes from the hills, and I think of you often. You have come and gone from earth many times since this temple began, and now the humans have given this time when you are gone its own name—winter. Winter means that time of year when you're in the underworld. I realize, writing the word "year," that it is a new word for you too. Living in the underworld, you can't be expected to keep up with humans and their words.

Imagine it this way—if each one of your visits marks a year, and you've visited, let's see, over two hundred times since my last letter, that means over two hundred years have passed since something, I can't recall just what. Two hundred years sound like a lot, but it's only humans' time.

So many changes take place over the ages that I only have time to tell you about a few each time we visit. I worry that all the days you spend away from Olympus, locked in the underworld, will make you forget our life here. You say in your letter that your memory and future-knowing are fine, but then you tell me a dream about fire which you think you understand. Persephone, I know you feel like a queen now, but you still have a great deal to learn.

Future-knowing is new to you and you don't know all about it yet. It is important that you understand that every vision in future-knowing is a riddle, and all its answers are true. For example, my future-knowing told me I'd win you back. I didn't know how it would happen, but I was sure it would. I also knew that no one, goddess or mortal, ever returns from the underworld. The laws are made from our future-knowing, so this law must stay true as well. My knowledge and the law contradicted each other, yet both of them were true.

The Persephone who returned to me wasn't the same, not exactly. You won't like my saying this, but you were full of life when you left and—well, you changed. It seemed like Maid Persephone left, and Queen Persephone returned. One was young and lively, and the other. . . .

And vision changed for you, too. You saw the earth, but it

was a different earth than the one you left. Eury and Clymene seemed younger, your lusty mother looked drawn from grief. But I'm still your mother all the same, and that's how future-knowing goes.

As for your dream, think about it a few more ways. Remember, it's not the kind of riddle with only one answer. In your dream, Hermes brought you to earth, and then we were together. Hades appeared, and you woke up dreaming of fire, so you think this is the fire I use to make humans immortal.

You're right, but also completely wrong.

You dream of fire, but which fire is it? Is it the fire meant to make Demaphoön immortal? Your palace sits near a river of fire, and that may be the blaze you dreamed, but there are other fires too. In the temple we burn smoky myrtle wood to make the humans immortal, and in the heart of that fire, you rise and return to us. A western tribe is said to follow a cloud of fire. Humans use fire in their homes. Sea People use fire in wars. Fire appeared in your dream, but which fire was it?

It was all of them. And there will be more fires in the future, too, fires we know nothing about yet. Don't interpret future-knowing too simply. The future loves to betray those who think simply.

This talk of fire reminds me. I visited Prometheus the other day. You remember him I hope. How long ago it was when he stole fire from Olympus and gave it to the humans, and for that Zeus has chained him to a rock all this time. The sharp-billed eagle still feeds from his belly, an unpleasant sight, so I don't go there often. I went to see him because I felt sad, thinking of the many changes around us, and I hoped the view from a rock might let him see matters differently.

He was no help. He's always been wise, but these days he's begun predicting strange things. For example he said that all immortals will eventually die. I could not help myself. I argued with him. After all, to say immortals may die isn't even good Greek, much less sensible. Immortals dying isn't the worst of it though. He went on to accuse me, all-giving Demeter, of living in the past.

Curse the past, I told him, I'm busy arranging the future. Half of my time, I have to call everyone together in Boules to defend the immortality we gave humans at Eleusis. The other half of my time I spend on love, the only cure I know for politics. Of course I did not speak of love with Prometheus, considering his circumstances. I left him there to his predictions, which he cries aloud for Aeolus' winds to carry away.

Still I felt sad, thinking of the many changes on earth, and changes too in the underworld. You have a child now, a strong young son, and I'm happy about that. Seeing you with him gives me joy, and joy is welcome after all that has happened. I do not live in the past, but so many changes disturb me.

Earth used to have rich growing all the time, but now it nearly dies for half the year. Humans used to say your name brightly, always with joy. Now when they say it, they remember your dark realm too. They even bring flowers to their places of burial. Your underworld is different. Your Boeotian has left you, and for all we know he may still be drifting up that winding river, looking for earth. You write of the war dead and the heroes, telling me of Triptolemus. By the way, I took your advice and taught him how to grow grain. Now humans grow their own food, that is another change too. I did not tell you about my meeting with Triptolemus when we were together, since you seldom like to talk of love. But you may not mind reading about it in a letter.

As you suggested, when I wanted to teach humans to grow their food, I went looking for this Triptolemus. I found your thrice-great warrior on his war chariot, just as you said I would, standing above fallen corpses on a battlefield. He looked so swollen with pride, you'd think he'd won the games. Then I became a bird and took him on my back, giving him scare enough to shrink his pride down to seed size. I flew over hills to a certain field, I think you know which one, where I set him down and resumed my shape.

Now he looked white as sea foam and as ready to run. But

for a killer, this Triptolemus was handsome enough, and I rather liked him. To make the long part short, we spent the afternoon together.

My clever daughter had suggested—I can call you daughter inside my letters, can't I?—that Triptolemus learn to plow. He did. We turned the soil until it sifted through our fingers like pollen. I showed him how to draw his fingers along the moist surface, carving a seed canal. I taught him to thrust the root deep, to plant the burst high in the hot heart of the earth. We tumbled, mixed and mingling, and packed earth wet and firm to encourage the sprout. And when the furrow was ready, I made him wanton and he spilled the seeds. Afterward, while the mud dried to a cake on my thighs, I lay beside him. I changed his name then. He'd been the thrice-great warrior, Triptolemus. Now he was Iaison, the thrice-great plowman who lay with Demeter in the furrow of a thrice-plowed field.

Lying there, I ripened to the kernel of myself, knew myself as maiden, mother of a daughter, and grandmother all at once. I rose and stretched toward the sun, gold and rippling. I felt whole again.

When I returned Iaison to his war chariot, I placed my own wings on it so it could fly swiftly. He set off that afternoon long ago—visiting Chios one day, the mouth of the Nile the next. To all he met he taught the skill of planting, and to many he also boasted of his afternoon at Nysa with Da. The women insisted on trying him out for themselves, naturally. I was glad for that, and also glad he taught my gift to them. They began planting their own food. Now they raise their own grain, and they don't have to come begging for it every time they're hungry.

I look down at the plain and our temple. This broad plain grows enough for the people of Eleusis, and they are strong and thoughtful of me, always improving our temple. The new temple walls are bathed with pure milky light now, as Helios' sun is setting. The workers walk tiredly past the well, going home and hungry. Their day is over and I am tired too. I'll go down to the plain for the night and return to finish this letter when Helios rises again tomorrow.

* * *

This new day is gray and windy. Even Helios has to warm himself behind a cover of clouds. The workers have returned to the temple, and I watch from the hill as a light rain turns Eleusis' road into mud under their feet. Theseus, who rules here, wants the new temple to be ready for your return, and already it is halfway to that time, the chilliest heart of winter.

Which reminds me, you asked me about the rites at Eleusis before you arrive. Since they mark your return and end when you arrive, all you see is Eleusis' night of dancing, laughter and feasts. What you have heard of the preparations is true, they are long and arduous. The humans who come to be initiated must suffer as I did. It was decided that way in the first Boule I called to propose immortality for the humans.

I don't want humans to suffer, you know that. Immortality was to be my gift, no rituals nor sacrifices required, but perhaps it's a good thing that I didn't foresee the uproar this would start on Olympus or I'd have left well enough alone. As it was, everyone came to that first Boule, curious about what new powers I might want. I let them wonder, waiting until the platters and plates were nearly empty, and until Dionysus' wine had softened their thoughts. Then I began speaking, putting it so simply that even Zeus could understand.

I hadn't finished the main idea before Zeus let loose a flood of petty objections. "Immortal humans won't strive," he shouted over the murmurs and wine-soaked giggling. "They'll neglect my worship, they'll let the temples stay empty, keep back what they owe us and avoid sacrifices." He went on with that sort of thing. The truth is, my brother Zeus enjoys wielding his thunderbolt, making humans sweat, tremble and piss.

Zeus whined on, but now Ares was on his feet too. "Without death, war's not glorious. What happens to my powers?" Some of the goddesses too demanded that humans keep on dying. Aphrodite pouted, saying, "Love goes sour if it goes on forever," and then Athena complained that immortal humans wouldn't prize wisdom. I pointed out that they never had before, but she pretended not to hear me.

My Boule was deteriorating into a squabble, and I was going to have to devise a deal. Suppose, I said, that those who want immortality must suffer. They would have to grieve for Persephone's loss as I did. I proposed rites at Eleusis, saying the humans would wander, just as I did, seeking you and feeling the cold unhappiness of losing you. Then when you came up to earth from the underworld, the humans would receive their reward—immortality.

"You'd have them act like you?" Artemis choked on an olive and spat. "What's the point? I don't see how having them wander around, missing your daughter, means they're making a sacrifice. It wasn't that bad, Demeter."

I tried explaining, but how many goddesses or gods could understand suffering? They'd never felt torn thought from thought, as I had. Only Dionysus sympathized, since he too is uprooted each year, when humans harvest his grapevines. Prometheus understands me too, loving humans as he does.

For the rest, I had no hope of persuading them, and would have given up but for a mistake Athena made. "It'll never work," she predicted. "For what you want, humans will have to come together on purpose, year after year. As we all know, they worship on impulse, when fear forces them into the mood, not according to our plans. They can't follow directions either, not year after year." I loved Athena for that, and will love her again next spring when her own people, the Athenians, join our rites at Eleusis. Athenians suffer alongside Eleusinians these days.

Because of that argument the Boule was settled—all agreed the plan was ridiculous and they would gladly let me do it. By the Boule decision, the initiates must suffer, but I compromised on nothing else. Every human who wants, even a servant or slave, can be immortal.

It took me a long time to devise the exact ritual, but the

people of Eleusis grasped it quickly. I have lived among them a long time, and although other humans now walk many days from villages and towns to meet you here in the spring, I still favor these Eleusinians. Some here lead in the rites, serving as priestesses, Dadouchos, Keryx and Hierophant. But I've gotten ahead of what I must tell you.

The ritual starts in winter, that time you never see on the earth. During winter days humans eat only leftover berries, dried fruit and whatever grain they've stored. Soon they're tipping the urns to get at the last kernels, and everyone's hungry. Twelve days before this winter time ends, before your return, those who wish to join our rite stop eating completely.

They stay home. The women sit and warm themselves by the fire, and call on their men to finish the baskets, sweep the hearth, and keep the fire fed as always. The paths through Eleusis are muddy, but no one walks them. No one uses the well, and since there's no food to trade at the market, no one goes there. Men still feed the children, slaves cook, but no one who desires to be initiated eats even a single seed.

The initiates fast for nine days. Their hair grows dull. Their beauty fades. Their eyes sink into their skulls, and their gazes smolder, embers about to flare. Then on the day called Boedromion the 16th, or is it the 16th of Boedromion? Never mind, our initiates don't need ciphers—they hear the Dadouchos' cry, "Into the sea! Initiates into the sea!"

They emerge from their houses, the gaunt women tottering along the paths. They stumble and fall, leaning together to help each other reach the place where salt water and fresh water meet. Poseidon's surf boils as the initiates fall into it. They tumble between Poseidon's loins, and he washes nine days' starving and sweat from them. Each initiate's skin becomes fresh as a child's, like Demophoön's when I bathed him in the fire so long ago. Then they dry themselves and dress for the journey.

These clothes they put on for the rites become special afterward. Many wear them until they drop in threads from their arms, and others save the dusty, sweat-soaked and fire-singed pieces to swaddle newborn babies. This simply infuriates Hera, of course, protectress of newborn babes and all that.

When the initiates are dressed, they go to the sacrifice. A sow, fattened on grain, is killed by the servants and roasted while the initiates look on. After that, they return to their houses, each stooping low at the threshold, just as I stooped down and startled Metaneira that first day I entered her house.

On this day, using the recipe I gave to Iambe, the humans soak barley and a sprig of mint, making kykeon. When the kykeon fills the urns, the Dadouchos raises her sweet voice again. This is the 19th of Boedromion, or the other way around, whatever. My priestess calls the initiates to begin the procession.

I stop here a moment. I must swear you to an oath. No other immortal, no human, not even a ghost must know this. You must swear, Daughter. Have you sworn?

Then I tell you: Demeter herself walks the Sacred Way.

I'd agreed to let humans suffer, but I had to be sure their pain would not surpass their joy in immortality. That was why I joined the procession the first year, and I've continued since then because . . . because . . . because I don't know what because. I found a secret still left to discover in our sacred practices. Each year it comes closer, growing more complete. It's more than I can tell you in a letter.

That first year, of course, I only wanted to test our rite. I couldn't suffer as a human would, so I had to find a human that I, the goddess Demeter, could follow, and I didn't want anyone special. I found an old woman who lived alone. She was simple, and the roof of her hut sang when the wind blew. She had probably gone hungry often, since after fasting she was so thin her body showed extra skin, like a puppy's. When she walked, her unfilled flesh flapped like the skin of a half-tied drum. In a way she reminded me of old Doso, the child's nurse I had pretended to be in front of Metaneira.

I found her on the day the kykeon was ready. All our initiates gathered, a strangely quiet throng in the marketplace, and I went along beside her, disguising myself as a plain old woman. Ahead of me, this old Doso looked no bigger than a beggar's pack, and the cloak she wore was torn, even its patches mended over. Hunger had tightened the faces of the initiates near me, and their lips were dry from thirst. I studied old Doso. I swear she looked as I must have, seeking you.

Her feet were clean and bare when we stepped onto the Sacred Way, but they showed bruises and cuts before we'd climbed the first hill. Gray dust smeared her ankles, and she stumbled often, while others near us fell again and again. Sharp pebbles left scars in knees and elbows and arms. Even before we reached the first bridge, many had cried out, yet none left the procession.

My priestess stood on the bridge. She wore rough woven clothes, dressed to imitate Metaneira's slave, Iambe. When we appeared, she began to leap and tumble on the creaking boards. She rolled and shook herself so obscenely that our sides soon hurt from laughing. Young girls near me cried out, "Baubo, Baubo," laughing and pointing at her.

Tears of laughter and pain carved long streaks down my Doso's dusty cheeks and down my own, but when a priestess passed the cup of kykeon, Doso reached for it gladly. Her hand shook so much, she nearly dropped the cup, and I helped her lift it to her lips. She swallowed the bitter draught, and the kykeon stung her parched throat, as it had mine.

As we crossed the bridge and stepped back onto stones, we took up the burden of the search once more, and it felt heavier. New stones pierced old Doso's skin, and she placed each step as if it were her last. I glanced at the initiates nearby. Pain was more generous to some than others. A few whose faces were as streaked and whose arms were as scarred as Doso's, looked easy and peaceful. Some had set a hand on another's shoulder, but they didn't lean there for strength. I touched Doso's back. She didn't seem to feel it through her dusty, sweat-moist cloak. I felt a strength I hadn't expected.

We were following a straight stretch of road between the first and second bridges. Sunlight flashed from Poseidon's broad sea shoulders and hurt our eyes. I could feel Doso wince as hunger stabbed from her belly to her ribs, and she stopped once or twice to cough. Then she'd straighten as much as her back allowed and walk again.

I can't say what stopped me from revealing myself and putting an end to it, ashamed of so much suffering. I wanted to, again and again. Around me, humans cried out with pain, and Doso bit her pale lips against it. Even the young and strong cried out. Yet each time I touched Doso's shoulder I seemed to feel what she felt. Without that, I could never have let the rite continue.

This old woman was becoming stronger, not weaker. Once, for instance, she stooped to cough and spit beside a roadside statue of Hermes, and before we stopped I was sure that her head did not reach as high as the statue's belt. Yet when she straightened up again, her head came level with Hermes' chin. My hand, which had held her shoulder, now touched the middle of her back, and I let my palm rest there.

It was like feeling her heartbeat, but more than that. I walked in her steps, still touching, and pictures floated in my mind. I was awake, but I seemed to dream this old woman's thoughts.

I saw her senses turn inward, like a flower at dusk. I saw the flower close itself, one petal at a time. Her foot touched a sharp stone that cut her skin. She bled, a small red line crossing the callused olive skin, yet her muscles didn't tighten. I saw an emptiness in her mind, and then that emptiness filling with pictures.

I remember the picture of an urn, beautifully crafted, its wide mouth yawning and waiting to be filled. I took my hand from her back and again I saw the stony road, sunlight, shadows. I saw these things, and still I sensed that old Doso walked on a smooth ivory path. I felt dust coating my lips, filling my mouth at each breath, felt the crowd press close. A few still moaned, some cried out, but most had grown quiet, and I saw other faces as peaceful as Doso's. I touched Doso again and I saw no pain, no hurting.

In her I entered a silence more still than the air after a thunderclap. She was alone there. She'd turned off the road we others walked, and she made one more step, then another, on her own road. She moved alone in the quiet of her thoughts, and she found no words for what she felt. She reached a marker on that road, the speechless privacy of pain, took another step and walked past it.

I saw her body, a beggar's bundle, but she no longer remembered she had a body. She walked on her road until she came to a low entrance to a cavern. Entering it, she fell and lay thrashing as the cavern's walls opened and closed with her breath. She couldn't find her footing.

I pulled back my hand. She hadn't fallen. She walked ahead of me as before.

We approached the second bridge. As we moved closer, raising a dust cloud, my priestess stood waiting for us. The first initiates came up beside her, stopped there briefly, then moved on. When we reached her, the sacred Keryx tied a thread from Doso's right wrist to her opposite ankle, and she did the same for me.

With the thread drawn tight and shrinking from her sweat, Doso now walked doubled-up. I remembered my silhouette on a hillside, that night so long ago when I lost you. Like Doso, I crouched double-humped like a camel's back. Past the bridge, we ascended a hill, and from its peak I saw the distant gates of the temple. My Hierophant had ignited the myrtle-wood fire, and smoke rose above the sanctuary, then sparks of fire lit the evening air.

I looked to see if the initiates had noticed where we were, and that was when I realized how hushed we'd grown. Each gaze around me was open, but none took note of the temple or the smoke or the hills or even each other.

I touched the arm of one. I felt her great sadness, but no pain. I touched another and felt an emptiness. I saw a smooth shore ready to be marked by tide. I touched Doso again. Her thoughts slipped down along the white curve of a seashell. Its smooth walls tumbled me toward an empty place. When I whirled through the spiral's eye, where would I go?

We passed the temple gates. I know my hand rested on Doso's flesh, but beyond this, I cannot explain. I could see and touch her ahead of me, but she was gone from me, perhaps through the spiral's center. I could not go there with her, and touching her, I only felt a place, like an image in my future-knowing. It felt calm, like future happiness, but I can't say I knew how she felt. I only knew that her eyes were open, her gaze gently awed.

I left Doso by the temple gate where the initiates come to the Maiden's Well. There they find my priestesses, the ones with small oil-filled vessels balanced on their heads. As the initiates come near, flame is touched to the oil in these vessels, and the priestesses step lightly, beginning the Maidens' Dance. They pretend to be Metaneira's daughters, turning and twirling to fan the flames. The glow surrounding the well shows the quiet initiates crouched, their heads turned downward. They crouch in the damp night air, a dense crowd of stones, while the dancers whirl past them, lit only by the flickering of flames.

Then my initiates rise and walk up the hill. I have taken my place in the temple, ready to greet you. Everyone crowds past the entrance, eager to see you, and the throng crushes together like a single body. Yet each, like Doso, remains separate and feels herself alone.

The Dadouchos lifts the torch high and shadows dance on the temple walls. All are hushed, as still as the winter world before your return. Their eyes open wide, but they see no walls, no temple, no bodies. They search the chambers of their thoughts to find, as in the hollow of an empty shell, the silence.

Then the first, the simplest and most empty, takes a step. A child goes toward the throne. I watch the child draw near the fire, and watch the others follow. The Hierophant sings, her voice high and sweet. Then the gong is rung, sudden as thunder. Its echo fades and leaves absolute silence.

My Hierophant stands in the heart of the fire. Her arms rise. Her hands open to show, there in the belly of the fire, one ear of grain.

Here all I have to tell you ends. At that instant, my daughter appears, with her son in her arms. My arms enfold you and our ceremony ends.

Do you wonder why humans welcome you back so joyously? Like you, they have passed through the realm of death and grieved as I did. But now they have seen the ear of grain born from the belly of the fire. Why should they fear death again? They give up their striving, and they are immortal. Which is why, that night you see them in Eleusis, they eat and eat, merely to eat.

XII

MOTHER,

It's wrong to begin with an apology, Mother, but I have to explain. This letter may seem peculiar.

For my duties, like welcoming dignitaries, I must speak correctly. Lately Dis and the Judges talk in a new language called Rhetoric. Dis and the Judges agree I should study it, but unfortunately I'm three lessons behind and must study more. Yet I must also write to you.

Now I'll explain that.

NARRATIVE EXPOSITION

(That's a heading. This letter will have headings once in a while.)

This morning I discovered Dis sitting at my table writing a note to Zeus. His note requested that a Boule be held for an important decision. He's threatened this before, and I've talked him out of it, so I tried again today, saying the issue was between my mother and me. I swore that if I couldn't persuade you this time, I myself would request a Boule. So you see, besides being my Rhetoric Lesson, this letter will make me keep my promise.

INTRODUCTION OF TODAY'S TOPIC

I'm sorry to write of matters that should be handled face to face. Unfortunately there's no time. When we were together I tried to discuss the topic of today's paper. Remember our fights of last spring? I know it sounds like I'm throwing off the Old Ways in favor of the New, but I'm not going to argue. I write out of kindness, to save my dear mother inevitable defeat, and if that means I get called your "modern daughter," well I'm sorry.

Dis just reviewed what I've written and says I'd better get to my topic.

Title: JUSTICE FOR ALL HUMANS

Subtitle: Suggestions for Demeter & Persephone's Yearly Rites at Eleusis

Thesis statement: It is my belief that all humans, both women and men, should be together at Eleusis and in immortality. I shall attempt to prove my foregoing thesis by the following-going fallacies and arguments.

1. (In Rhetoric everything has numbers under the headings).
2. Argument from Circumstance (meaning it's hopeless anyway).
3. Deduction Argument (concerning the properties of creatures known as human, to include dead men).
4. Inductive argument, which shows the truth about humans using evidence. (This might be a fallacy not an argument).
5. Mother, if all this confuses you, I apologize, but Rhetoric is harder on me than on you. I'll be in trouble if I don't practice, and you'll be ridiculed on Olympus if I don't write this letter.
6. Where was I?
7. Dis looked in the gate. This is taking forever. He's impatient. I'll begin my next heading.

I. ARGUMENT FROM CIRCUMSTANCE

I shall begin with an Emotional Appeal.

Mother, we have to! We simply must! Men have to be allowed to participate in our rites! Circumstances are beyond our control! We have to let men become immortal! It's hopeless.

If you don't agree—you must!—I have to request a Boule to decide. Zeus will grant one. Politics will happen. I'll go, I'll even vote, I'll even try talking in Rhetoric, but we'll still lose.

Zeus and Hades and Ares and Hermes and Apollo, all the gods will take a stand on it. Aphrodite's easily swayed. Artemis gets confused. Athena sides with her father and Hera is fickle, besides being jealous.

We'll lose. What will happen to our rites? Men will enter the temple anyway, and we'll have to put up with them. See my point?

ARGUMENT FROM CIRCUMSTANCE, NUMBER 2

To be hypothetic, let's pretend we won the Boule despite everything I've said already. Our religion would still be for women only. What would happen? (That's a Rhetorical question. I have to answer it, not you.) Humans already call our rites "Female Mysteries." The mystery part is bad enough since there's no secret, but other religions are letting men join. Without men, our practices might fall into disuse.

Don't you want our rites preserved? Sooner admit men! Better that than to perish from sheer pigheadedness!

Oh dear. I'm sorry.

Dis came in asking for the lesson, and I got mad. I didn't mean it like that.

I should have expressed myself more gently. Nevertheless you must give in. Circumstances dictate this course of action. You have to agree.

II. DEDUCTION ARGUMENT—TO PROVE THAT MEN, LIKE WOMEN, ARE HUMAN

Here the writer will attempt to take accepted general statements and apply them to a specific instance. I will do this by introducing a syllogism, which sounds confused but it isn't. You only get three numbers in a syllogism and all of them have to add up, sort of.

Persephone's Syllogism:

1. All humans die.
2. All men die.
3. Therefore, all humans are men.

That's wrong.

Again:

Therefore, all humans are dead men? No.

Once more:

Therefore, maybe all dead men become human. I'll try a different approach.

Persephone's Second Syllogism:

1. All humans are mortal.
2. All men are mortal.
3. Therefore, all humans die.

Scratch that out, put it another way:

1. If . . .all humans are mortal,
2. And . . .all men are mortal
3. Then . . .and then

. . .and then

Are all the immortals inhuman men? Now we both know that's not true.

I'll try once more. I wish I could remember one of the Judges' syllogisms. Sometimes Dis begins by talking negatively about dogs.

My Third Syllogism:

1. No dogs are men.
2. No dogs are members of the class called immortal beings.

(Here I always interrupt Dis to remind him of Cerberus. Dis says Cerberus' immortality isn't relevant.)

My syllogism:

1. No dogs are men.
2. No dogs get to be immortal, etcetera.
3. Therefore . . . forget it.

This one proves men are already immortal. Please ignore this part of my lesson, and my letter. I have other arguments.

III. INDUCTIVE—THE USE OF EVIDENCE

Here the writer, actually the goddess, uses specific cases to prove the general rule. She proves that men are worthy of her rites.

My first two examples, well known to my reader, are:

1. Brimos, my son
2. Iaison, formerly known as Triptolemus, a dead man formerly mortal.

Mother, I love my son Brimos deeply. By using an analogy in comparison you can guess that you would love your son, if you had one, very deeply too. Now suppose that our sons, just because they're not goddesses, were denied the pleasure of eating ambrosia during feasts on Olympus. How would you feel? How would your hypothetic son and Brimos feel? I personally would be furious. Our sons are examples of why males should be treated fairly.

"But Brim and my son," you may object, "would be immortal already."

And you would be absolutely right. Nevertheless, if you'll forgive the reminder, you recently shared love with an earthly man. I refer to a certain Triptolemus, if the writer isn't mistaken. (In Rhetoric one has to sound not absolutely certain of anything.)

1. You loved Triptolemus-Iaison who was a man.
2. You even attached wings to his chariot so he could travel over the earth teaching humans how to grow grain.
3. Could you deny, to a man you loved, benefits you give freely to any woman who asks?

4. Surely not.

(That's my first number 4. I think I'm getting better.)

Second Example

My second argument also employs analogy, and I don't need numbers any more.

On earth men died recently in a Trojan War. They fought and died for love of their fellows and also over a woman. She's Helen and still alive. Anyway, these heroic deaths show men capable of devotion to a cause. (Mother, please don't interrupt and say I'm praising killing because if you read closely, I don't think I said that.) I'm saying war heroes show, by example, what men are capable of. Surely if they're devoted enough to kill, they're devoted enough to worship.

Oh dear.

My Third Example

and my last is a man named Hercules. He visited the underworld recently to rescue one of his friends. I met him, and since I'm thinking about him now anyway, he makes a good example.

Hercules came to the underworld because two men were here against regulations, and one was Hercules' friend. Dis had discovered and captured them, and he punished them by placing them in chairs made of wood that grew by the Lethe. Since Lethe water makes humans forgetful, these Chairs of Forgetfulness made the men forget why they'd come.

Anyway, when Hercules came to rescue his friend I happened to be standing behind a pillar to watch. Hercules struggled and strained to pull his friend from the chair. Hercules was extremely strong, so his friend was stretched from being pulled. Hercules was twice as tall as I am, and his hair, his hair was so gold—like ripe wheat it was. He wore only a loincloth, and that wonderful hair of his, like scattered gold shavings, shone all over him. His flesh was bronze and his hands were enormous and he had this golden froth all over. He looked so different from Dis.

Oh, I just remembered, Dis wants to read this.

Suffice to say Hercules got his friend out of the chair and out of the underworld. The other still sits. (He's looking waxy.)

This example shows that men might not be as bad as I once thought. I haven't seen many, but Hercules impressed me. I have known many ghosts who were once men and they're just as miserable as the women. Therefore, men have their place: In the world, today! The underworld, tomorrow! Eleusis, next spring!

IV. ARGUMENT FROM DEFINITION

In this argument, the goddess defines her terms and says what she means. I begin by reviewing an A Priori Promise.

The A Priori Promise: The Great Goddess Demeter, in generosity and thankfulness for her Daughter Persephone's return, promised that all humans could have immortality.

Interpretation: Any creature which can be shown to be human should be given immortality. This raises a delicate question.

The Delicate Question: Are men human?

Now I've gone and asked it, haven't I? When we argued last spring, I wasn't sure men were human, but I've thought about it since then. Any reasonable goddess must be convinced by the following proofs: (And now instead of numbers I get to use letters.)

a. Men are mortal (we needn't repeat all that).

b. Men, like women, walk on two legs. (I know birds do too, but except for Triptolemus in his winged chariot, men can't fly. Birds can and often do.)

c. Although men are hairy, they are less hairy than beasts. Except a few, who may be more.

d. Men have the same number of teeth, fingers and toes as women have. Women with all those teeth and toes are considered human, so men should be human too.

e. Men, like women, live in houses or huts. Men enjoy women's food when it's available to them. You may object that these things apply also to dogs, but if you read somewhere in my syllogisms you'll see, "No dogs are men," which sort of says it.

f. Many women live with men. They feel affection for their men and consider them helpful playthings. It's becoming considered less than nice to act as if these women cohabit with beasts. It's only polite to call their bedmates men.

g. I mean human.

h. This one must convince you. It's my last: Men are probably involved in human reproduction.

I can just hear you yelling inside my head. Please stop yelling. Please! "My daughter consorts with ghosts and dogs for one fourth of eternity. It's damaged her." That's what you're saying, I just know it, but please listen.

I don't believe Zeus birthed Athena from his left ear lobe, or whatever that old story says. I don't think men can do it alone, have babies I mean, as women always have. Yet we do call Zeus my father, except it's only official and polite. Plus practically everybody, even Amazons, admits that having a man these days makes childbearing more likely. Be honest, how many so-to-speak technical virgins have you seen bear children? Not many any more.

Now some say that men actually cause it completely. They say the woman is only temporary, for storage. I can't agree, and I don't wish to get you yelling inside my head again, so I'll just conclude.

By defining "human," and forgiving some characteristics of men, I think my mother ought to agree. Men are human. Therefore:

1. If: men are human (and I proved that),

2. And: Demeter gave immortality to all humans (your very words),

3. Then: I hope to see men at Eleusis next spring.

(I have another Argument from Demolition, or maybe it's Definition I mean.)

a. I am defined as Persephone.

b. Persephone is defined as Queen of the Underworld.

c. The underworld is defined, especially lately, as a fair and just realm.

d. Therefore, if I define myself as Persephone, which I feel I ought to, I'm supposed to be just.

e. I am also defined as Mistress of the Rites at Eleusis.

f. If men are human, my rites are supposed to be for all humans.

g. Then therefore I'm unjust and I'm getting confused. This means I'm not myself these days. Dis says this is because I allow an abortion of justice at Eleusis, and he wants men in the rites.

You see my point I hope.

V. CAUSE AND EFFECT ARGUMENT (the next to last)

The writer is tired and she made a mistake. Now you have to pretend men aren't human, even though she just said they were. Are you pretending? Then I will too.

Question: Aside from women being human and men not, is there any other important difference between them?

Answer: Yes, there is. Women can join our rites. Men can't.

Did it ever occur to anybody besides me that Persephone and her mother might actually be making men not humans, inhuman maybe, by excluding them? If we think of cause and effect, we can call the Rites at Eleusis our first cause. If the rites are the first, the uncaused cause as it were . . . as it was? then we can conclude I'm lost.

I can't remember that argument all the way through, but it goes something like this: If the First Cause is the Uncaused Cause it is having an Effect in all Ineffectual Causes. (Even Dis admits Rhetoric is new and sometimes confusing.)

Anyway, what it means is that maybe if you and I let inhuman men into our temple they would learn to behave. They might even turn into women! Think of it, where would we be then? Which brings me to my final, last and most fallacious argument.

VI. ARGUMENT FROM EXAMPLE (a lot like Evidence)

Let's pretend men are human and assume there is one who is. Could such a man understand a goddess's experience of losing her loveliest, most innocent and only daughter? Frankly I think it's possible and might be interesting. I beg your indulgence for a story. It's about an imaginary man and I'll give him an imaginary name—Oudemia.

A Story

Oudemia woke bright and early. It was the day of the rite at Eleusis, a sacred ritual. He was excited, but he was even more hungry. Oudemia hadn't eaten even one seed for twelve days before he woke up and this story started. You can imagine how thin he was.

This morning he truly wanted to eat. There were figs and olives and grain and apples all waiting in the urns at his house. I know it's winter and there's no food on earth, but this is a story. Always before he ate as much and as often as he liked. You can imagine how fat he was before he got thin.

Oudemia had been up late the night before because he was cooking barley and mint into kykeon for the rites at Eleusis. He'd been purified by bathing in Poseidon's sea, and he'd stood drooling like everyone else when the sow was roasted. Now that he's awake, Oudemia hears the beautiful voice of Demeter's Dadouchos calling out for the procession to gather. Oudemia doesn't eat, but instead he runs quickly to the marketplace.

Other initiates—both women and men—were already there. They started walking, and so did Oudemia, but as he walked he thought.

He thought, "What should I think about?" He was going to have to walk all day so he decided to make his journey easier by thinking about the most beautiful things he could. First he thought of food, which reminded him of you, Mother.

He thought of flowers, gifts from Persephone. Then he thought of them both together and discovered the most beautiful thing in the world—the love of mothers for daughters, and likewise I'm sure.

I'll keep my story short so I won't go into all the cuts and scratches and bruises Oudemia suffered walking along the Sacred Way. I don't need to tell you how dust got in his throat and his eyes, or how horribly his stomach hurt. Suffice to say he felt true agony for the first time in his life.

"What in the world am I doing this for?" he asked himself. He kept walking, but clutched his side to make the aching stop. "I'm rich," he thought. (Let's say he's an Athenian king.) "I have everything I want, yet here I walk barefoot beside slaves and beggars. Nobody recognizes me and we can't stop to talk politics." Which he loved to do. "Why do I feel so bad? This is crazy."

But Oudemia kept walking and didn't talk. Since he couldn't tell anybody how bad he felt, he had to keep thinking about it.

Right here, if I were making a poem or song, I'd put in more about pains and moans and agony.

Suffice to say, Oudemia walked and thought and passed the first bridge. He walked and thought and crossed the second bridge. He walked and thought all the way through the temple gates, and then he began figuring it out.

"What do you know?" he thought to himself as he hunched painfully by the Maiden's Well, the Well of the Beautiful Dances in Eleusis. "Here I am, a king, a rich man, a traveller, but look at me. I crouch as miserably as any beggar. I feel as hungry as my slave. I feel lonely. Demeter probably felt lonely. Persephone felt lost and I do too. Before today I couldn't feel what humans and goddesses felt, but today I understand how women feel. Now I'm no different from anybody. Mortal, immortal, what's the difference? We're all together when we suffer. I could die. I feel half-dead already from the heat in here." By now, Oudemia was crushed among the throng by the fire in the temple.

Silence fell. Oudemia felt very plain, but special as well. The good food and wine and travelling seemed silly to him now, even if he would feel like a king again the next day.

Now just being alive and happy seemed most important.

Oh damn.

Dis just passed the gate calling out, "Don't forget the footnotes!" When you see a number above the line, look for it again at the page bottom.[1] There's the number, Mother. Look at the bottom of the page now.

. . .he's immortal!

Here I rise in the flames.

By suffering and feeling other humans' feelings Oudemia had finally become fully human. When the Hierophant raised the ear of grain, he realized that he was a flower, just one, but he'd been woven into the necklace of life. It's woven so tightly no one can ever untangle it and it's long enough to go twice around Grandmother Rhea's neck. After that Oudemia knew he was immortal and this made him happy for all eternity.

That's the end of my story and my paper. Except to say I have to let Dis correct this before Hermes takes it to you.

* * *

Dis gave it back, saying my use of arguments and fallacies was "interesting." I don't think that's praise. Well, I tried.

Anyway, now I can add a note that he won't read before I send this to you. This part isn't Rhetoric, but I want to tell my heart's thoughts with love to my mother. I want men to welcome me at Eleusis next spring. It will make me happy.

We fought about this a lot over the last few visits, but even when we fought we still told each other the truth. In the

1. Persephone's footnote: Naturally Oudemia went out after the rites, just as everyone does. Everything tasted and looked better than it ever had, so he ate loads and got drunk on wine. That's because . . .look back up now

middle of that big argument last spring we both admitted to our future-knowings, that we both feel the fate that men will someday join our rites. If we both see it in our future-knowing, that means it's inevitable. That's no Argument from Circumstance, just something we both know has to come. Let's get it over with.

Nevertheless, I insist on two exclusions. First no one may join, woman or man, who doesn't speak Greek. Even though the rites are wordless, they can't civilize a completely uncivilized mind. My first rule would keep both animals, many of whom resemble humans as much as men do, and barbarians out because neither can speak Greek.

My second rule says we won't welcome any whose hands are stained with blood. This gets rid of warriors and bloodthirsty types who make themselves feel better by going around joining powerful religions. Besides, simply look what happened to Demophoön. You yourself made him a hero and he only used it to become a famous warrior, a killer. He fought in a dozen battles, changing sides half the time for sheer love of fighting. Poets sang a couple of songs about him. Then he was forgotten, after all you gave him, the stormy little life of one more troublesome killer. We should not welcome such types.

That's all I have to say, except one thing. If your future-knowing has already convinced you to let men in, please don't tell anyone. Act like my rhetorics and arguments persuaded you instead. I think I can use that to make Dis stop giving me lessons.

I conclude with an endearment.

Little Brimos misses his Grandmother Da. Every day he asks if it's the day to rise in the midst of the fire. I say, "Soon, Brim."

Soon, Mother.

XIII

DAUGHTER,

You won't guess, you'll never conceive, you'll never imagine who I've met. Search your thoughts—your past, your present, your future-knowing—and try to guess the name. Make a game out of it with young Brimos. You both might guess for an age and still not know. So I'll tell—your Boeotian friend.

"Of course," you say, "it had to be." Don't feel bad for not guessing, ages have passed since you knew him.

Remember after our first visit when you returned to the underworld and found that your deathly husband had gotten rid of the poor ghost. That Boeotian ghost was your only friend, and you wrote to me that you missed him. I've remembered him all these ages, and when he and I met and I realized who he was, I knew you'd be glad to have him back.

He's not a Boeotian in this life, of course. He spent ages drifting up the Eridanus River from the underworld, just as you predicted he would, and he was reborn at Chios—to wealthy parents, no less. Of course, I discovered all this later. When we met, I didn't think he was anybody special.

All this happened shortly before your last visit. It was the day when the initiates stayed in their houses fasting and I sat on the hilltop wondering which human I'd accompany during the rites this year. In other years I have walked with the wealthy and the poorest, sipped kykeon next to a slave and breathed the dust kicked up by a queen as she walked ahead of me. Every year about this time I study the humans and select the one I'll accompany.

I left my temple that morning and went walking through Eleusis. I saw crowds of humans, Eleusinians and others who'd come here for the rite, but none of them appealed to me. Then I saw a ragged figure crouched in a doorway, and I wouldn't have noticed him, but I heard him muttering. He kept repeating the same thing over and over, changing the words slightly each time. I heard Zeus' name, and that other name humans use for him, loud-thunderer.

This ragged beggar looked terribly thin, and I was pleased, thinking he'd been fasting. I was impressed that not only was he fasting, but he was wandering outdoors as well, wearing only rags and carrying a staff. I supposed he did all this to honor me, but I soon learned otherwise.

It was the ninth day before the ritual, so when the sun rose the Dadouchos took her place beside Poseidon's shore. My new priest, the Hierokeryx gave the cry, "Into the Sea. Initiates into the Sea!" and doors clattered open as the initiates ran through the streets toward the water. Each passed the Hydranos, and he sprinkled a few purifying drops of water over them. . . . Oh, I just remembered something. I've gotten ahead of my story because you don't know about these latest functionaries.

The Hydranos sprinkles water on the initiates, and is a man. So is the Hierokeryx—he calls the initiates to the sea. These men's roles began a century or so ago. Back then so many males were joining our rite that they sometimes outnumbered the females. The men were only lowly initiates at first, and they soon started complaining that no men officiated. Naturally I sympathized, but I couldn't honestly hand over sacred functions to men.

Please don't give me an argument. Hades can talk all the Rhetoric he wants. The rites may be, as you say, half yours, but I started them. I picked the place where they're held, and I have final responsibility to see they aren't degraded. Obviously a man couldn't be as important as my Hierophant or Dadouchos, supervising the ritual. I couldn't even name a man to do temple maintenance, since even that work is sacred.

As usual, your mother thought long and hard, nearly two decades, before she saw the obvious. The rites had grown so large, the initiates so numerous, that we needed assistants.

Nowadays, the Dadouchos saves her voice for the beautiful singing while a man, the Hierokeryx, does the tiring parts. He calls the initiates down to the sea, quite a task these days with so many Athenians coming for the rites. The Hydranos is strictly functionary too, sprinkling a few drops of water, taken from where salt meets fresh, over each initiate's brow. He says a word or two and everybody pretends it's important. Now men complain less, and our rites go on pretty much as usual.

So much for background, which is what your Boeotian friend taught me to call such things. By the way, I told him your Oudemia story, and he said it's so good he's thinking of making it into a poem. But I've gotten off the subject.

So that morning the Hierokeryx cried out and everybody ran toward the water. Everybody, that is, except this bent fellow I had seen in the doorway. He merely hobbled toward the shore, but when he passed the Hydranos and got sprinkled, he leapt, gasped, and scurried out of the way. Then he sat and watched the others purify themselves.

At least I thought he was watching. I also thought, what sort of initiate is this? First he acts worshipful and thoroughly pious, taking no food or comfort, then he skimps on purifications. I approached him. "You, initiate," I called out. "Into the sea. Poseidon's waiting."

He didn't stand up, and this made me angrier. "You smell," I added. He did smell as ripe as a fish boat.

I was so irritated I completely forgot to disguise myself. My radiance shone unconcealed, but it didn't seem to startle him one bit. He looked at me quite simply, without even a proper trembling, and where dark irises ought to have marked his eyes, I saw only milky whiteness. Obviously he was unaware he addressed a goddess.

"Drowned and dead, wouldn't I smell worse?" he asked.

I understood the problem then. He was blind, and if he stepped from the shore, he'd lose his footing and fall in. He walked with a staff not in imitation of me, but because he had to, he could not see his way. I supposed he wandered around and begged his living, probably hadn't slept under a roof all winter. I reviewed the laws of our rite—we could admit no non-Greek speakers and none who'd shed blood, but we didn't exclude blind men. I was going to have to help this one through the ritual.

The thought of walking alongside a man gave me a start, but then I told myself, my modern daughter seems able to put up with equality. Perhaps I've looked down on gods and men long enough, so I may as well give the New Ways a try. Otherwise I'll get as old and narrow of thought as Mother Rhea has become in recent ages.

Half-persuaded, I changed myself into a young girl and took the beggar's hand to lead him down to the water. You should have heard the other initiates shout when they saw us. "Oedipus joins the rite," they cried out laughing. "Look, Electra leads him." I suppose we looked like a couple from one of those plays the humans do nowadays. The beggar found all this funny, but I ignored it.

I had enough trouble already. This beggar needed a bath, but he didn't like the idea of getting wet. He began to whine, wailing about how far he'd walked to get to Eleusis, how he'd stayed up nights, singing loudly to scare away animals. His dirt, he insisted, was sacred dirt.

I walked him firmly into the water, and scraped a few layers of crusty black mud from his ankles and legs. I left the rest. His flesh had been hidden so long I saw no point in letting him get badly sunburned during the procession.

When I finished and pulled him in to shore, he complained less, but then I realized I had a new problem. His rags lay on the bank, a poorer bundle than last season's snakeskin, and he'd need something to wear, white clothes for the ceremony. I stood gripping the old fellow's arm and standing there so long that most of the other initiates had dressed and left for the sacrifice. Then I heard a familiar voice.

"Electra?" it said, deep and growling. "Or is it a nymph?"

Washing past, Poseidon had noticed an unusually trim pair of ankles parting the stream of his sea. He paused, swirling in place to spray upward, learning what fair maid owned those trim ankles. The ankles were mine, of course.

There I stood by this shivering, dirty, naked human, and explained my problem. When Poseidon finished laughing, he sympathized. He drew me aside.

Aphrodite, he pointed out, had been born of his sea foam. Couldn't we weave a sea spray cloak for this human? I said that was a nice idea, but it would take too long.

You know how Poseidon loves to please me. He slipped away and soon returned, joined by Aphrodite, Athena, and a whole handful of those spider-web weavers, the arachnids. Aphrodite arrived out of breath from telling all she knew about sea foam. Athena, sweet wisdom herself, thought it out and gave the spiders instructions. Before long, we wove not only a cloak, but a tunic as well.

The beggar was awfully grateful. Being blind, he had no idea that immortals, and spiders, fussed over him, measuring lengths from his neck to his kneecap. We let him think a few of the others had loaned the clothes. Aphrodite insisted he was cute and kept tickling his privates, which made him squirm and giggle.

Fast as we worked, the weaving took a while, and dusk had fallen by the time we returned to Eleusis. The sow was long since roasted, and the initiates back in their houses.

Saying I wanted to prepare myself for the rites, I left the beggar on a doorstep for the night.

During the night I thought of curing his blindness so that I wouldn't have to walk beside a man. Yet I had to admit I liked this fellow. Not in the way you're thinking. He seemed childlike, but sensible. Besides, Aphrodite had dabbed him with perfume, so his smell had improved.

I found him in the same doorway at sunrise. He had stood up all night to protect his new clothes, and he'd hardly slept. I took his hand and led him to join the throng in the marketplace. When the Dadouchos lifted her torch, we set out on the Sacred Way.

I expected my entire attention to be taken up with my companion, leaving little time to explore my own new feelings about the rite, as I do each year. If your Boeotian friend surprised me in this, it wasn't to be the last surprise. Suffice to say that your former friend has proved to be quite a remarkable human.

Even though he could not see where he stepped, he fell fewer times than other initiates. He walked so well that, if I hadn't seen the blankness of his eyes myself, I would have thought he pretended at blindness to make a living. Yet his skill at finding his way impressed me less than other qualities.

At the first bridge, for example, the initiates gather to see Iambe leaping and tumbling, jiggling her flesh to imitate Baubo. You'd think this blind man would miss the whole point, but Iambe's gestures somehow seemed to tickle his very skin, right through the layers of dust which covered it. He grinned wider and wider, and his mouth showed blackened teeth when he threw his head back to laugh. His bony frame shook so hard I worried he'd burst the seams of his new tunic. This must be a sensitive beggar, I guessed.

When we walked, his feet were so callused the sharp stones hardly pricked them. I heard his belly growl, but the hunger pains seldom made him wince, and instead his face showed his inner journey, reflecting it like a mirror.

I'd accompanied many others in ages past, and suffering showed new roads to each of them. This one was different, his face calm, his lips pressed softly closed. I held his arm and felt an emptiness very like my own memory of loss, but the barrenness in his heart wasn't new or strange to him. It was like a vagrant's cave where he'd often spent lonely time, a familiar place he returned to often. Purest of all his feelings, I sensed a silence, as if emptiness and quiet were friends and honored guests in him.

I sensed these things after we passed the second bridge, and I was sorry that, when we arrived at the temple gate, I had to leave him and prepare to welcome you. I glanced at his face and saw a slight smile there. He looked as pleased as a child who'd made a new riddle. As the throng pressed close and entered the temple, I let my hand be tugged from his arm. He groped in the air for me, so I leaned over to whisper in his dusty ear.

"I'm leaving you, Ho. The crowd carries you to the fire."

His smile returned and soon the throng propelled him into the temple. I hurried away to take my place. Later, watching flames flicker over the initiates' faces, I found his figure easily. The fire reflected brightly on the milky whiteness of his eyes, showing you in all your radiance as you rose in the midst of the blaze. When you appeared, this blind man's face brightened as instantly as the other faces around him.

Then you joined us, of course. I won't repeat the details of our visit, since I'm not particularly pleased by many of my memories. You go on about New Ways and your life in the underworld, and you seem incapable of understanding much that I wish to tell you. Still I must repeat one thing. Please don't overlook details when you set about making that child Brimos immortal. The smallest mistake and your son will be a mortal, so you must respect all I've taught you, the Old Ways, in this.

I did enjoy your visit, as I always do. I only wish that, at the time, I'd known this Homer was your Boeotian friend. What a reunion we might have had. It wasn't until after your ghastly husband had come to claim you, after I got lonely and wanted someone to talk to, that I remembered Ho.

I thought he'd be easy to find. After all, how many blind men wander around in clothes woven from sea foam? The first day I looked for him I spent the whole afternoon rousing beggars from Eleusinian doorsteps. A few were blind, most smelled, but none were Ho. The next day I went into Athens and found more of the same. I'd grown tired of visiting alleys and ash-piles, so the following day I went up Olympus' slopes for a change, to grace an Olympian banquet with my presence.

Everyone was there, enjoying the wine and chatting of fine sacrifices. When all had eaten their fill and had been polite for a while, Aphrodite's voice rose over the others, engaged in one of her customary bickers.

"That nasty poet, what's his name," she complained. "I resent his saying I was wounded in that ridiculous war."

"That war," Ares shot back, "was the Trojan conflict. And your poet happens to be the great Homer."

"By Zeus' small balls!" I cursed out loud. Everyone stared, except Zeus who looked away and studied his grapes.

It turns out that when I'd met this very same poet at Eleusis he was still hardly known. He'd come all the way from Thebes to witness our rites before he began plying his trade of speaking poetry. It seemed that several of his verses were less than complimentary, at least to Aphrodite's fine self-opinion.

I asked Athena for directions and found our friend Ho easily. It turns out I'd looked in all the wrong places. Instead of haunting back-alleys and ash-piles, your Boeotian friend sat in the middle of Athens' marketplace, and young men and women, nearly half of Athens, sat listening to him. He recited his verses so skillfully all were transfixed. Even I felt temporarily lulled out of my immortal impatience. I let him finish six verses before I turned myself into a big white bird, frightened off the crowd, and flew to my temple, the blind beggar on my back hollering and screaming the whole way.

What a voice he had. I could forgive his curses while we flew, but when we landed, he kept right at it. "Artemis! Iris! Hephaestus! Hermes!" he catalogued half the population of Olympus. "I don't give a barley seed who you are, put me down this instant. Let me finish my Iliad."

Apparently immortals have been taking turns kidnapping him, gossiping into his ear and vying for parts in his poems. I let him fume for a while, listening in to catch up on gossip, then I quietly spoke my name.

Fast as a newborn foal, he was down on his knees.

"Is your daughter here?" He pleaded. "I've always wanted to meet her. You too, Queen Mother, of course. I can't see seasons or flowers, and I never know if your child's just arrived or leaving." On and on he rattled. "Queen Demeter, of all people. Of all goddesses, I mean. I'm honored, honored. Sorry about that outburst. Say, I'm hungry. Have you got a grain cake?"

For all that, the man had charm.

So I fed this Homer a grain cake or two and made a nearby apple tree bear fruit out of season so he could taste crisp ripeness. He was fond of saying that only fools fed on fallen fruit, so picking it fresh from the tree delighted him. We spent several days together enjoying food and talk. He's not the easiest human to deal with. Having spent so much time around immortals, he takes us pretty much as we come. He has travelled most everywhere, observed much without the use of his eyes, and isn't easily impressed. He didn't know he was the first man to enter my sacred temple, and I didn't tell him.

In those days I had no idea of his former ghostliness. I learned he'd been born to a queen of Chios and was a frail child, but a lusty wailer. Since he was weak but loud, his father insisted he memorize all the hero stories that humans tell. He grew bigger but not much stronger, and as a young man, "and a fool," he added, he set out in search of adventure.

He travelled through Chios and joined a voyage that happened to be leaving the morning he arrived at the shore. "I should have noticed when we left port," he said, "we carried no grain, only barrels, all of them empty."

Two days out he knew he'd gotten in with pirates. He'd wanted adventure, but seeing the scars on his shipmates' bodies, he thought twice about that. He changed his mind and, hoping to persuade them to slay sea monsters instead of seafarers, he started telling stories. "I learned the poet's first rule."

"What's that?"

"Keep talking. Never turn your back." His face showed a grim smile. "Want to hear the second?"

I certainly did.

"Poetry being what it is, you're always asked to pay cash."

He soon ran out of stories and had to repeat old ones, which annoyed them. The brigands blinded and robbed him, taking not only his money but his leather pouch and sandals too. They left him on a lonely shore, expecting he'd die and find his own way to Hades' realm. He woke up blind and empty-handed but, as he put it, "a wiser fool than before."

The money he'd lost belonged to his family, so he couldn't return to Chios. He made up a poem about the pirates and began to wander, town to town, telling it. He hoped to persuade his listeners to seek out the pirates, and his plan might have worked, but each time he told the tale, his own role in it got bigger.

"That gave me my Odyssey." He leaned against my altar and sipped his third cup of wine. "My major work, and a fair start at fame. Still, my life lacked something."

He'd always wanted to create one truly great work. He envisioned a single piece containing dignity, honor, gentleness, and a touch of violence. It would have interesting characters, passages of sheer lyrical brilliance, the unmistakable sweep of history, a recipe or two, more metaphors than similies—he felt he relied too heavily on similes—etcetera, and more and so on. The list didn't end until his cup was dry.

Unfortunately, singing for a living left no time for great works. His audiences wouldn't sit still for anything but hero stories anyway. Besides, he admitted after taking a stiff swallow from the cup I'd refilled, poetry was harder than he'd expected. He couldn't simply invent. "We poets copy truth," he said. "Beauty isn't ours to make."

Now that saying sounded familiar, but I let it pass. Not until he began speaking of you—yes he spoke of you, dear daughter—did I recognize the Boeotian.

He went on with his story. After reciting the Odyssey day after day, in town after town, he grew tired of it. Still he had to keep pleasing the crowd. That led him to the Iliad, a war story.

I interrupted to tell him Aphrodite's complaint about that poem, and we had a good laugh over that. He agreed, the poem was a shade too heavy on the bloodshed, but he insisted on calling it passable work. After all, he had to make a living.

"In practical terms, I was a success."

He'd been nibbling on a cluster of grapes and they dropped into the hearth. His skillful fingers sorted a few from the ashes, and he ate them without even blowing them clean. "I can sleep in any king's mansion. I've been inside Theseus' palace, been wreathed at Hercules' games. Done it all."

He'd met loads of immortals. "These days they're so eager to keep out of my comic scenes, I'm seldom harassed by calamities. In short," he said, "I should be happy."

He wasn't. He couldn't resign himself to a life of inventing war stories and staying out of the way of immortals. "There's that unsung beauty, that one poem I want to make. To tell the truth," and here he admitted he seldom did tell truth, "my visit to Eleusis isn't strictly religious. I'm working on a special piece, about you and your daughter. I call it 'Hymn to Persephone.'" He paused, but I said nothing. "I've always felt close to your daughter," he added. "As if I knew her, had suffered with her. Something from a former life, I suppose."

"Boeotian!" I shouted.

"What's that? Has a Boeotian arrived?" He turned, smiled and waved toward the empty porch.

I realized he'd have no memory of knowing you, but I had to explain my shouting like that. I said it was a spell I had to cure my hiccups. He looked doubtful, but said he'd try it when he got hiccups.

I insisted then that he must recite this newest and most ambitious work of his. So he did, and was it bad! On and on about deep-bosomed daughters and swift-speeding chariots. He must have called Zeus "loud-thunderer" a dozen times. He got Poseidon's and my scene by the waterfall all backwards, so I finally insisted he leave out our horseplay.

I couldn't have him going around saying that this was his best poem and having his facts all wrong, so we spent days going over the details. I told our story, start to finish. I even read him a few of your letters. I hope you don't mind. His title had to change, of course. "Hymn to Persephone" lacks dignity, and a title needs that. We fought quite a bit, and he persisted in wanting it his way, saying it was his poem. I pointed out that it was my life.

Since he felt his greatest poem needed a recipe, I let him use Iambe's recipe for kykeon, which differs slightly from the one they use today. Unfortunately, he had difficulty picturing you the way I wanted you described, as a lovely maiden. Humans have that trouble nowadays, calling you ashen and saying your beauty is spectral. We settled on "trim-ankled" —that hackneyed phrase—for you, and I'm called "rich-haired."

Naturally we said nothing about your ineffable qualities, those features of the underworld that humans know they're better off not describing. Nor, needless to say, did we explain about the rites. Just said, "Happy is the human who has seen these things," and left it at that.

After muttering and memorizing for days on end, we finally finished. Ho seemed much happier. He said the rhythm was exquisite. We tried dancing to it, but he kept stumbling and breaking sacred objects. Then he decided this hymn was only the start. It marked a whole new phase of his work, he said. Now he's determined to do a collection of Hymns to Immortals.

When he got started on that subject he became annoying. He pestered me day and night for details and gossip about everyone on Olympus. About this time I also realized he'd eaten all but a handful of my special ambrosia.

Before sending him on his way, I made him promise to return to Eleusis next year. When you come next year, you'll hear the great Homer recite our poem. I know it by heart, naturally, but won't write it here because, like a ritual, a poem is a living thing. It can't be expressed by marks on a page. You should hear the Hymn to Demeter from Ho's own lips.

I close now. Regards to young Brim. And to your ghastly consort too, I suppose.

* * *

One note. That last about not writing sacred works reminds me, there's a fine story going around Olympus these days. Hermes heard of it in his travels, and now everyone's telling it. Even our friend Ho saw the humor of the whole thing.

Apparently a certain folk, living in the East, are in an amusing difficulty. They're primitive, still only wandering tribes, but they've somehow learned to write. That talent so impressed them that they wrote, in verses if you can believe it, about their god. They're god worshippers, like the Dorians, primitive.

But their foolishness in writing things of the spirit isn't the worst part. They wrote one version several centuries ago, and they carried it from place to place. Then they realized that living things won't stay fixed on scrolls, living things change, so—and you have to take my word for this—they're rewriting it.

They've changed everybody's names, turned stories upside down and forgotten to put back parts they meant to use. The wanderers call their priests, the ones who do the rewriting, "scholars," so these days it's the biggest insult to call anybody a scholar.

Speak of Hermes and here he is. Don't forget the sacred sayings for Brim. Say them on the last night. Don't forget.

XIV

MOTHER,

I have duties to perform, but I stop to write to you. I'm troubled. I sit down in my golden room to write a note, but my thoughts all crowd around me at once. I think of the changes. So many have come and I don't understand them. Perhaps the thoughts will leave me if I write them out.

First the gossip and good news. Brim is finally, completely immortal. I finished bathing him in fire the final night and said the sacred words. He's too young to be much impressed, yet seems pleased with himself.

As for other matters in your letter, I did appreciate meeting Homer when I visited you on earth after you wrote of him. His Hymn to Demeter was all right, except I'm not in it much. He's dead again now, naturally. He's back in the underworld, still blind, and he keeps reciting his old poems age after age. Every so often I think of letting him float back up the Eridanus River and get to earth again. Earth has a new poet, Hesiod, a great sourpuss. Ho might give Hesiod fair competition. But what if Ho weren't born a poet three times in a row? Let me know your opinion.

My dear husband is doing quite well. I do wish you'd stop

calling him ghastly and ghostly and all that other. It isn't funny, Mother. After all, he is my consort and I'm raising his child. Though he doesn't exactly rule me as human men rule women nowadays, I often follow his directions. It's easier that way.

I honor him and perhaps one day I'll even love him. It's too soon to tell. But you please must stop using those rude descriptions of him. Without Dis, I'd still be your maiden daughter, the loveliest and most innocent, but not a Queen in my own right. Think about it.

Then I think about it myself, and I'm not sure. I'm bothered by all the new ideas, by all the changes that can happen on earth in only a few hundred years. To Dis the ideas that trouble me are wonderful. He adjusts and improves our realm to accommodate this new guilt and conscience and transmigration. And redemption, of course, whatever that means. I feel uneasy with these new ideas, and I'm especially troubled by what happened today. Perhaps if I tell you, you'll see what got me thinking so hard and complicated.

As Queen I must send notes of congratulation to our three fine Judges for their best decisions. I've never minded this, it takes only an afternoon once I get started. Dis supplies a list of who's condemned, who's rewarded and for what, plus the date of the judgment. We've started reckoning matters in dates here, like humans do. I name my years after our priest at Eleusis, since it's our own ritual, but Dis wants me to put his own dates on my notes.

Today I wrote one for a war hero's elevation to beautiful Elysion and making a few comments about the use of juries for trials. They use juries on earth nowadays, and I think the Judges might do likewise. Anyway, my writing tasks were simple enough, but last on my list of Judgments to Commend I saw:

Ghost: Tantalus.

Exploits: Offended immortals.

Disposition: Eternal hunger and thirst.

Ordinary enough, the kind of thing done here every day,

so why couldn't I write the note?

I tried to do it. I put down, "Pleased to hear of Tantalus. Justice gives what is deserved," and similar remarks, but my words sounded pale and inadequate. I never get personally involved in ghosts' problems, but I felt compelled to seek out this Tantalus.

Dis' records told me where the offender had been sent. Dis keeps excellent records—each commendation, each punishment, the success of various tortures, etcetera. I set out for the place called Tartarus, which is where wicked ghosts are sent to be punished.

To give you an idea how things have changed, let me describe Tartarus. You must distinguish it from Tantalus, the ghost of whom I'm about to speak of. Tartarus lies across the river of fire, in the lower realm. Big green adamantine gates stand at its threshold, and, as if those weren't enough, Dis lets a many-headed brown monster, of the family name Hydra, live right next to the gates. Dis says this froggy-eyed, snappish creature keeps innocent ghosts from getting into Tartarus, but to me it seems more busy keeping guilty ghosts inside.

Innocent. Guilty. There I go again, using the very words which trouble me lately. You see, Tartarus is only for the wicked, or at least for those who the new laws say are wicked. Just inside the gates I passed a half-dozen cowards and scoundrels suffering various simple tortures, having their hair pulled out or believing they're on fire. Everybody's visible down there so they can see each other's pain as it happens. Smoky fumes from the furnace always cloud the air, and a one-eyed Cyclops works day and night, forging chains to put wicked humans in. Tartarus is mostly a place of fire, with ghosts moaning in pain all around. It's truly dreadful, and I don't go there often. To tell the truth, it reminds me in a way of our poor ruined temple at Eleusis, and that makes me sad too, thinking of fire.

I often think about innocence and guilt and what they say lately about justice. You know, Mother, our temple for one thing. It used to be beautiful, and the humans were always improving it. First the Athenian king put up statues and enlarged the sanctuary, since more huge crowds came to see me every year. Then that other Greek ruler came and made our temple the largest, the greatest humans had ever seen. He put up carved steps so everyone could see me, and not only that, he started a new procession all the way from Athens. Visitors came from all over the world and travelled many days at a time to see Demeter and her daughter.

But I needn't tell you all that. Suffice to say our worship became earth's greatest and everyone knew about it. Ages and ages passed, each more great. And then the wars came.

Those barbarians descended from the north. The Athenians won over them in battle, of course, but couldn't capture their commander until it was too late. I only wonder, was it punishment when they overran our temple and started the fire? Do you remember my dream of fire so many centuries ago? Was this the fire I dreamed? But then what were we punished for? And now the Athenians say they'll leave our temple in ruins, a testament to the northern tribes' barbarism. Is that justice?

I thought about many sad things as I passed Tartarus' gates and walked deeper. I stood in the depths of the darkest part of my realm, and I wondered about all this. Are we punished? Or did it simply happen, as bad things can?

I found the ghost Tantalus without difficulty. He stood a few steps beyond the gate in a small pool in the middle of brimstone and smoldering rubbish. The sight of him surprised me. He didn't look much punished, standing waist-deep in water down in Hades' hottest depths. Trees over his head leaned to offer him ripe fruit, no more than an arm's reach away. I decided this ghost had nothing to complain of.

I hummed softly to announce myself as I approached his pool.

"Welcome, Queen of the Lower Realms," he said, as well he should. I didn't want to pry and ask right out why he was being punished, so instead I asked politely if he was hungry.

"Eternally," he said. "Thirsty too. You surely know my fate."

I thought his hunger was pretty silly since he stood near both fruit and water. I pointed that out. He merely had to reach and he could pull down an apple from the tree.

"Then you don't know my fate." He looked more despondent. "If you're hungry, help yourself. I don't bother."

I reached up and pulled a red apple from the bough easily enough. I bit into it. It tasted good, not nearly as dry as most underworld food. Tantalus watched me chew and struggled not to drool in front of his Queen.

"Watch closely," he said and reached up as I had. I swear he came so close that his fingers' heat must have warmed the apple's skin. But then a wind arose. It blew only around one branch, tossing it out of his reach. The branch shook playfully, practically laughing at us.

"Now I'll try to drink. Pay attention."

He bent to lower his mouth and pouted his lips until they almost got wet. But they didn't. As if a bowl were being tipped, the sparkling pool drew back so he couldn't reach it. Then he straightened, and the pool came back as it was before.

"Does that happen a lot?" I asked.

"Not often." This was the first time he'd tried in ages. "I don't attempt it when I'm alone."

If he'd keep trying, I said, he'd eventually get it. "How can you starve, having food and drink so close?" His ribs showed like bare beams.

"I prefer to think that I don't choose to have it," he said. "I wouldn't get it anyway. That's the immortals' revenge. Not to reach, not to try to drink, is my way."

He paused, but I looked puzzled.

"Of getting back," he finished. "At immortals."

I was completely confused. Then I remembered those humans who made up a new religion lately, the Orphics. There are so many new religions these days, but perhaps you've heard of Orphics. They believe that humans are put together half as ugly Titans and half as beautiful divine beings. These humans punish themselves to drive out their earthly nature, the ugly Titan part. What they do is pretty disgusting, and I won't commit it to these pages, but they think suffering will make them pure, make them immortal and holy. Tantalus' way of denying himself made me suspect he might be an Orphic, so I asked.

"I tried it," he replied. "But that wasn't the answer."

"To what question?"

"I don't know."

Discussions like this, I've found, have a way of getting nowhere. I changed the subject. "I understand you offended immortals." I asked what his crime was. "I don't find you that offensive."

He thanked me, but said his crime . . .his crime, he paused repeating like that, then he shrugged. "Was offending immortals."

"But how?"

Here's where things got complicated, Mother. There's no easy way of explaining. I might sound like Brim, when he gets confused reciting his relatives' names, you know how he does. Anyway, I asked. "How did you offend us?"

Tantalus didn't know. He wasn't sure he'd committed any crime. Like most humans, he'd done many things during his lifetime, and he felt proud of some, like loving his children. He despised some of his acts. He'd been a soldier, but he wasn't particularly pleased with having killed.

"Draco ruled Athens while I lived." Like everyone, Tantalus had obeyed Draco's petty brutal laws. He'd seen thieves executed for borrowing a neighbor's chicken or sneaking away with a fresh baked loaf. "I kept a clean record myself. Except in my thoughts."

I interrupted. I didn't want his life story, only what he'd done.

"I thought too much," was his answer.

"But what did you do? What act got you condemned?"

"Depends on who's telling it," he said. Then he asked,

"Which version would you like to hear?"

"The worst," I said, guessing that must be what got him in trouble.

"As you wish." He paused and looked deeply into my eyes. "Tantalus served his son's flesh at a banquet on Olympus."

That was bad, I had to agree. "Are other versions less awful?"

"Tantalus, metaphysician, said the sun was not the great god, Helios, but only a ball of fire."

When I finished laughing, I insisted on hearing all the stories, every one between the worst and the funniest.

It was said that Tantalus had stolen ambrosia from Olympus and served it to his friends; that he'd asked for a life of pleasure like the immortals have; that he'd stolen a dog from Zeus, then lied to Hermes about it; that he'd blabbed immortals' secrets.

"Were you initiated at Eleusis?" I thought he may have tried explaining our ritual.

"I was a soldier, remember? I killed."

He'd be ineligible, even in these days of men entering the sanctuary.

Other versions, he told me, said Tantalus, not Zeus, had kidnapped that Trojan prince, Ganymede; and so on and so forth and more, etcetera. "But what did you do?" I interrupted.

"What's it sound like? Pick your poison."

I considered the stories. To me it appeared that he'd been given immortal privileges, sure enough. Then he'd probably abused them.

"That's the gristle," he said giving me a smile that was halfway frowning.

"But did you do any of that?" I asked. "Did you abuse Olympian gifts?"

Frankly, he didn't know. The stories were just that, stories. He had never visited Olympus, never tasted ambrosia. He'd certainly never cook his son's flesh. "I thought and thought. I was guilty. All the time I was alive, I felt guilt. But I couldn't learn my crime."

This guilt had haunted him all his life. It was guilt, not shame. He'd joined the army to escape this feeling and seen the difference on the battlefield. Cowards ran and felt ashamed, but Tantalus stood and killed and yet felt guilty afterward. "I got involved in cults, gorged myself on sects." As an Orphic, he'd denied himself pleasure. He'd travelled and met the scholars you wrote to me about. They were writing their god book, a Deuteronomy, when he was with them. As he tells it they write down family records too, and they believe their own special immortal is a god of history. Their concepts fascinated Tantalus. They had loads of rules, called divine laws, and he'd liked that so much he'd followed each law to the letter. He still felt bad.

"Do they actually write books about a god?" This seemed incredible, but he swore they did. Like the Greeks, they used writing to record debts and names as well. I said it must make their god furious to have words, which necessarily lie, written about himself. Tantalus said the tribes' god often got moody.

By the way, Mother, did you know the Greeks have written down Homer's poems? They have. I've given all the ghosts instructions to keep secret about it. Ho must not find out. But I've gotten off my subject.

Tantalus said the new laws on earth considered guilt now, not like it used to be. Before, only punishment mattered, and if a human did a bad thing, punishment happened. These days they worry about why a human does something. They ask if he might have chosen not to do it. As Tantalus describes it, guilt is miserable.

"In former times, the immortals punished whom they wished, ennobled whom they wished. It was whimsical. Please don't be offended."

I wasn't. He told the truth.

"Humans went along pretty much day-to-day. That's the impression I got from books."

He'd read, looking for ideas to make him feel better. For

example he'd read of this new foreigner, Pythagoras, who believed in the transmigration of souls. Tantalus said transmigration means that good humans might be punished in one life, but got rewarded in the afterlife. Pythagoras said every human was already partly immortal, in a little part deep inside which is called the soul.

To be polite, I didn't argue, but obviously all this reading only made Tantalus feel worse. I was feeling worse too. The sadness he described was so deep. I burst right out and insisted he tell the ending of his real story.

"I killed myself."

I gaped. You can imagine. "You what?"

"Suicide." he said. "It's a new word. I took my life."

"No wonder you're punished," I shouted. "The immortals showered you with gifts—life and beauty and fine intelligence. All good foods to eat. Wine and sunlight."

I ran out of breath and just stared.

"Yes," he agreed. "But I had to find the answer."

"To what question?" I hopped up and down, I was so mad. He paused, calming himself I guessed. Yet the whole time we talked he'd been awfully calm.

"I had to know if I could," he finally answered.

I bit my lip to keep from hitting him. He made me angry the way the new gods do, and how humans speak of them, as if their little power in one place were all power over everything. And here was this Tantalus, a mere man, a thief who stole away the gift of his own life.

"I had to know whether I was free, or only a tool of immortal will." He stared down to where the pool shimmered, showing him back his own face. He said that when he was alive he used to stare at water a lot. "I looked, trying to see the worm in my heart. I looked at my face and asked questions. Was guilt born into me? Was it my fate? If I'd caused it, maybe I could rid myself of it. But how? By following laws? Maybe I should obey no laws. Would guilt leave if I loved my family? Or if I left them forever?" He looked gray and sad. "Which I guess I did."

He raised his glance from the water to look at me again. He had this way of looking, it worked its way inside of me, like a longing that can't get out. "You see, Gentle Mistress, if my guilt had only come from something I'd done, some act, some thought, even a yearning." He felt he could have stood that. Perhaps he'd abused his mind by thinking too much. Maybe suicide was his crime after all. "Maybe I shrank from living. Life shrinks from me now. Maybe fruit and wine on earth weren't enough. Anyway," he shrugged, "now I can't have food or water."

"At least," I said to cheer us both up, "you answered your question."

His head shook slowly. He'd only realized afterward that an immortal might have tricked him. "They make us feel we choose freely."

"What immortal?" I asked.

I could pick my poison. He couldn't keep track any more of all the new goddesses and gods, even if he counted on all his fingers and toes.

We fell silent. Somehow what he said came together. It joined with my earlier thoughts, all that about guilt and innocence. About justice, that sort of thing. All the new ideas flew circles in my mind like cave bats.

Don't get me wrong, I approve many New Ways, as you know. But this unkind punishing—this poor Tantalus who couldn't eat, couldn't drink, could never nourish a single thought with certainty—that caught in my throat.

I thought of the ways you taught me. You said the Old Ways had fairness, and when I was younger, and even now, you say humans intend well but are only helpless. Hopeless, sort of. I remember how you felt pity flow from your heart and how you loved to give it. Pity and gifts. You love laughing. But not at pain. You gave the rites, you made humans immortal out of sheer generosity. Mother, you could never have done this to Tantalus.

But, I reminded myself, Tantalus was punished for being wicked.

"Justice gives what is deserved." Before I'd meant to say a word, I had said that aloud.

"I wish I knew you were right, Gentle Mistress." Tantalus wasn't looking into my eyes, but staring away past everything.

I suppose that did it, being called Gentle Mistress. He meant it to be nice, but I felt so ashamed. Or maybe guilty. I'm not an expert.

I was his Mistress. In Hades' realm, I'm Queen. All around me ghosts moaned in pain of punishment. I felt sorry I ruled the dead. I felt responsible. I ruled the wicked and the desolate lovelost and those judged good and sent to Elysion. I, Queen Persephone, ruled them all.

I don't mean I judged them personally, our fine Judges do that. I don't sentence or execute. Truly all I do here amounts to a little gardening, the writing of notes. I preside at celebrations. I'm like the women at our temple these days. I'm only official.

Nevertheless, I was Queen. I am Queen. This is my realm.

How do I say it? How do I understand these thoughts? I believe I used to push them back.

The Old Ways fight the New Ways inside me. I'm Queen Persephone, but still your daughter. I was part of this unforgiving, ungentle justice and I have been for a long time. I'd never even considered whether I liked it.

"Ungentle Mistress," I said out loud. I've never had much courage, but I did look up at Tantalus' face.

He was staring at my hand. It was hanging at my side and it still held the apple. I'd only taken one bite. I looked at it, and then at him.

I was his Queen. I am Queen of this realm too and free to do as I please. No law stopped my hand from reaching toward Tantalus' face. Water would not dare pull back from my palm when I cupped and lifted it.

I should not write more about what I did. Hermes sometimes lets Dis read my letters when Dis insists, so I shouldn't say more. I'll change the subject.

Perhaps if I thought more about it, I'd understand the new ideas, the new gods. That one from the East comes up a lot in the ghosts' gossip these days, that god they call the god of history. I especially don't like that god, Mother, maybe since I don't like history, which I have to study, or the way things go lately.

For example, remember the first Greek victory over the northern tribe? Those northerners who call themselves Persians began it, stealing food and taking cattle. I learned that during the fighting the Persian king brought a block of pure white marble along to his favorite place, Marathon. He meant to erect a statue to mark his victory.

It was a fine plan, except that he lost the fighting. The marble block fell as spoils to the Greek victors, which I suppose amused the warriors. There was a sculptor among the humans then, a very talented man named Phidias. The Greeks told this Phidias, "Carve a monument." Phidias did.

Last spring, you'll recall, you didn't want to travel. I left Eleusis and went to learn news on earth. When I was at Marathon, I saw the sculpture and learned its name. Phidias called it Nemesis.

I don't think I've gotten off my topic. I thought of that sculpture, that's all. It seemed to fit.

Anyway, after what I did down in Tartarus, I left Tantalus there. Walking away, I looked back. He stood in his pool. I saw him swallow the last bit and twist his tongue to catch a drop from his chin. He still looked very hungry.

Once you wrote of seeing a starved calf, long ago when the earth first suffered a winter. Now I may understand how you felt. What I'd done hadn't helped. Tantalus still hungered. He'd always look blank and suffering.

Mother Da, can you please help explain it? Oh dear, I'm grown and I shouldn't run after Da with questions. Yet so many questions come at me at once. It started before I met Tantalus, and only got worse.

I'd broken a rule in my own realm. Did I sin? The Eastern scholars say unhappiness is caused by sin. I'm not quite clear about sin. But if I hadn't done anything to help, would I feel better?

Or maybe I sinned long ago, when I ate that one pomegranate seed. Are my thoughts punishment? Is that what humans call retribution? And the fire in our temple. Will anyone worship a goddess who rises in rubble? They worship Dionysus now because he's joyful. They say Dionysus dies, and when he rises again he gives redemption. Now I did that before him, I did it first. What's wrong with me?

Again, between my face and this page, I see the statue Phidias made. Nemesis. She is made all of marble, tall and white and cold, staring down at the humans who come to see her. Brutal goddess of retribution, she rebukes the proud and insolent. Her stern, pitiless face shows the Persians' fate in losing. Her eyes are bright, devoid of the slightest forgiveness. She records every wrong.

I asked Dis, when I returned this year, to take the mirrors out of my rooms. I bathe with only one lamp lit.

You say Homer couldn't see me as other than ghostly, that humans call my beauty "spectral" now.

Well I am and it is.

Whose hand strokes my skin? Who grips me all night? How could I be otherwise?

Humans also call me Ineffable Maiden. They avoid saying my name.

Da, you and I tell each other the truth. That's why we fight. I've changed.

So have you. The world is different. I'm not the green stem. Humans grow their own grain, you officiate in a temple where men have replaced even your highest priestess. Even the Mother Knowledge, how daughters learned to draw back after love, has fallen into forgetfulness.

I'm not what I was. I might not be anything. I was the most innocent, the loveliest. Most innocent.

How could I become so guilty?

I must stop feeling this.

I've pretty much messed up this letter. I'm like Brim, cry

and feel better.

Anyway, I can't visit Tantalus three times a day. Anyway, he wouldn't fatten one finger's weight. Anyway, when I approached, whose face would he see on the body of a maiden? That one I saw on a statue at Marathon?

XV

DAUGHTER,

I came from afar.

I walked this realm before earth was a thought in the mind of the universe. I began as myself when the universe was a dream of the sleeping forces.

You are my daughter and you're frightened by change. You say you've grown and shouldn't pester Da with questions. If you'd lived as I've lived, you wouldn't give new ideas the least thought. If this letter came from anyone but you, I'd laugh or be silent, but I won't allow you to trivialize experience with mere facts. Demeter may be old, but I can be angry.

Change frightens you, but I've seen change. I already was when land separated itself from seadeep. I was when light opened her eyes and rolled from the arms of dark. I midwifed fire, heard him squall as he dropped from the womb of heat.

I've seen change. I slept in our father Kronos' belly until Zeus slew him. I watched my father, father of all the immortals, spill his crimson over a sunset. I saw the old Titans placed in chains. I've heard my sisters' names—Astarte, Maya, Kali, Kybele—fall from temple faces and be trampled into stone. I've seen generations of goddesses and gods, so-called immortals, come and go.

I was a goddess before mountains were mountains.

That artist Phidias may carve my face as he wishes. He may make me a Gorgon for all I care, but you will hear what I know.

I love laughing. Humans shake their bellies and cry out "Baubo, Baubo," to imitate me. If you weren't my daughter, I'd laugh at what you write. If your words came from a human, I'd fall silent and watch. I've seen tribes, entire peoples, whole cities created, destroyed. I've seen them disappear. I remain. What could I possibly care for this season's philosophy?

Don't bother me with new ideas. Prometheus may call immortals enfeebled, Zeus may stumble over the new empty places on Olympus, Ares may fall from wounds in one of his fine wars. Oceanus and Artemis and Apollo and Hekate, all these and others may withdraw their powers from the universe. But I am the growing, the grain. Without me there is no worship. I remain.

Even your own grandmother, Rhea, withdraws her presence from the universe. She turns her face away from life on earth now that humans grow careless of her ways. She was the mother of us all, gave life and enjoyed every age the earth has seen. She should not go. She withdraws from the universe and I mourn her. But I came from afar. Before any, Rhea was. I am Rhea's daughter. I am my mother's daughter, and I am Persephone's mother.

At first I wanted to laugh at your letter. Then I saw you were serious. Persephone, the innocent, judging herself. Persephone, faded and guilty. My daughter, immortal innocence.

You speak of guilt. It is shame you should feel, to hear yourself worry over change. I walked the earth when the horizon first raised one eyelid. I lived on earth when it was empty.

Then humans came. We don't know how they got here, no

more than I know my beginning. Nor care. I was with the humans when they huddled in caves. I saw them wander, child and mother, child and mother. I watched them bake the first loaf, stood by as they wove a mat for the first hut. Now in that place stands the great city called Athens.

You speak of guilt and innocence. You speak of retribution and redemption. I know what they are, humans' new names for suffering. I have mourned and stumbled over earth as humans do. I have felt death. No agony can surpass it. I know the loneliness of wearing skin. Each year I walk the Sacred Way listening to every stroke a human heart beats. I know humans. They do as well as they can. I reward each one.

Don't tell me humans grow "consciences." Like a second spleen, they'll grow them. But when the hunger comes, when pain grips the belly, the spleen is worthless. It can be cut out.

If it were any but you. . . . This conscience will pass. See already, each forgets it when his belly hurts and his neighbor's granary looks full.

Even your Pythagoras, your Socrates and your Plato, three humans who thought themselves great as gods. I fed them, they took to my nipple like any.

If you want laughter, look at those three. Look at your Socrates. He amused humans in his lifetime, he amused me, saying goddesses and gods were mere illusions. He named us "fever dreams of humans' childhood" as if we had never existed. He resides with you now. Charon collected his corpse from the banks of the River Cocytus, and the coin on his lips tasted of hemlock. His own people paid him in poison for his words.

And this Plato. I laughed when he wrote Socrates' favorite sayings down for others to read. What wisdom can be babbled in a marketplace? What wisdom stays fixed on a page like a leaf fixed on a path? Like the leaf, Plato's pages will wither and fade. A leaf can't make a seed that grows another leaf.

I am the mother. I gave the grain.

And your Pythagoras, with his talk of transmigration. He

said souls return to earth in extra skins, and he believed in his geometry, his numbers. Humans chatter of his "theories." Show me a theory. Hold it up in the temple like an ear of grain. Will initiates see it? Will it make them immortal?

One human even tried to write down music in numbers so other humans could read it. Show me a number that can dance like the Muses.

Don't speak to me of philosophy. Don't speak to me of theories or numbers. I have heard it and I have heard it. Everywhere humans babble of ethics. Show an ethic to a landslide. Show a book of words, your Deuteronomy, to my brother's striking thunderbolt.

Humans chatter in a hundred tongues and I know them all. I walked earth when humans prayed to hills not to rise so steeply, prayed to rivers not to run so quickly. I've seen philosophies, seen goddesses and gods, and after all that I remain.

You tell me about new gods. I hear of them—YHWH, Allah, Elohim—all the new gods that humans in one place or another babble about. And who are these gods? Specters who hide in bushes and dust clouds and whirlwinds. Temporary gods, good for one season, like a sandal.

I laugh to hear of these gods, little gods sacred to only one people, one tiny village, one roaming tribe. Gods who hide their faces in whirlwinds or show their power to one lonely worshipper on a mountaintop. Such gods as refuse to allow their shape to be cast in bronze. Gods who fear even to be seen. Such gods call it a miracle to strike a rock and find a spring. Before me, soil had not even fertility.

Don't speak to me of these, poor immortals who refuse even to let their names be known. When earth was a child, whose name did humans learn first? Before they knew how to speak their own names, they praised mine. They see me all around them, think my name and speak it with each breath. I am the giving and the fullness of things. I am the mother, Demeter, and all know my name. I gave humans suck so they might live, so these new pathetic gods might come to carve rules in mere words on stone.

I've seen stone worn to sand.

And what do these gods do when humans disobey them? They punish. They send plagues. Thousands of humans die, their skins bruised to black. Half Athens died inside city walls and we lost Pericles. When I lost you I grieved, I mourned and was angry, but I never stooped to punish. Not even Zeus would stoop to that. Pericles fallen from the plague, and half of Athens, thousands of corpses, rotting inside the city wall. So these are the ways of their new gods, for these acts humans give them worship.

I write Pericles' name and remember your letter. You feared to return to earth after the war, afraid to rise in the middle of the rubble the Persians left.

You sounded like the returning Athenians, frightened by destruction. The Athenians are only mortal so we expect less of them, but look what happened after that war. The Athenians saw how the Persians left their great city, tumbled rock walls, burning roof beams, smoking ruins. They wailed, fell to the ground, helpless, helpless. Then a green shoot sprang forth, grew out from the olive stump, from Athena's own tree where their city once stood. The Athenians knew eternal favor when they saw it. They found strength and stones and rebuilt each wall. Every hearth went back as it was, or better.

As for our temple, Cimon rebuilt it. Then came the great Pericles, a remarkable human. Now each year you return to a temple four times as large as any ever seen, a roof so huge it needs forty pillars to rest its belly on. You feared for our temple, remember? Laugh with me. We've seen change.

Our new temple has stood for over a century now, and it will remain. If we dream of fire, if flames laugh at us, we may laugh back. Now and always. Now and always. Now and always.

* * *

I pause to dream these things, but your words come back to me. Visions come—now, the past, the urgent future. All live together as one great moving thing. How can you stay blind to these things, yet say you tell yourself the truth? I see as clearly as sunlight on cold winter days. I say what I see, nothing other. If you want philosophy, I will say what I know.

I came from afar. I know only three great things, three eternal, certain things. Two of them are greater than I am.

Of these, the lesser is Change. She abides. She lived before me, and if my power could pass, she'd plow the future after I go. She is restless, relentless as rain. She has been everyone's lover and thrown from every bed on Olympus. She's been called every name. She cares nothing for words. In this she is like her better, the second certain, eternal thing. And this one is even more beautiful.

These days I sit in our temple. The uproar on Olympus disturbs me, so I seldom go there. I join the rites every year, walk all the way from Athens to Eleusis. I cure the blind so they can see you. I laugh at the men, priests who strain to make their voices high. They took over ages ago, and still fail to imitate my priestesses satisfactorily.

These days I stay in Eleusis and I watch earth. I laugh and then I'm silent. Silence is greater than Change. It is also greater than I am.

Now a law has been written in a book, a law to forbid humans to speak of our practices in the temple. Our rites are called "mysteries," not to be spoken of. This is utterly ridiculous. No law ever was needed. A law is itself since it has to be so. It abides. But these days humans actually write laws down. They write this new law too, forgetting the real knowledge in their hearts. Our secret is utterly open, no law is needed to defend it. With law, without law, all who wish may have our knowledge, and those who have it know that it can't be expressed. Taking words to it, that's like trying to carry a song in a jar.

In ten centuries I've had time to think. When I gave humans immortality, I thought, "There's my best act." I was wrong. To be immortal is a fine thing. To be silent is better.

In the sanctuary, when the throng crowds close together,

they know suffering. What of that? When you arrive they gain immortal life. What of that? But when the gong is rung, when the Hierophant lifts the grain high overhead, they hear the last hum of the bell. Then silence returns.

That, you have to know. How many centuries did I waste learning it? Never mind, I'm old.

Let me say silence is my closest friend. Silences are my only immortal visitors these days. I can feel a silence as it approaches. It pauses on the porch of my temple, and when I am ready, the threshold is crossed.

Often I welcome a silence as blue as a Greek summer sky. It knows my name like they all do. It never speaks, but stands waiting. I crouch beside it, and it is blue and huge, more immense than this horizon. I rest inside of it. Rhea once held me like that.

Another silence seems green. She holds court far below me in sea-green depths and gleaming shallows. With her, I can hear what the wind thinks.

There is a silence, green and bright as the hard skin of an unripe plum. Animals are all proud of their noises, but my gifts, the fruit and the grasses, the grains, they never bother to speak. They are themselves, why talk about it?

I know silences of trees in forests. Each one is separate. The olive in the shade has one silence, the olive in the sunlight another. The grapevine's stillness is a noisy thing, beside a water lily's quiet.

I've seen old human women who can hear as I can, but they don't talk about it. Why bother to explain? We're busy listening. Only for you will I stoop to words. A certain silence comes in only after love, and another silence comes only before it. There's sleepy silence in sunlight. It won't lie beside the bitter silence of ice.

Among the initiates, after the bell fades away, I hear a silence that is a rainbow. It shows all these, and more. Each separate stillness, each human heart, sings differently to me.

What can I give you? I send words from afar. Each word takes away more than it tells. Using words, it's like trying to drink from a flat ladle. Now humans don't just use words, they have numbers.

Here's another way. They invented a new number called zero. They say it's nothing. Our initiates have known this nothing a thousand years or more. Zero is absence and absence is something. They call it zero now. I laughed when I heard they tried to name it.

Persephone, you'll see changes. The earth looks different each time you return, but that is only Change, a puppy tearing and chewing. Search your future-knowing and try to understand. I dream of fire too, but the future shows me more. New silences linger there, humans live there. I feel bound to them. I don't think how it will be. I never told humans how they ought to live. I give growth, they give worship, and that is enough. But there are silences in the future, and I feel, like a wind coming across time, a silence greater than all the others.

This one is tall and white, a chalk cliff sunning itself in the morning. It is warm sun-baked stone. That's enough for me to say in words. What I put here is too small.

I want to finish now. I'm not angry any more, only tired of words. When you were first taken from me, I cast away my crown. I wandered earth and became like an ignorant human, using words to still my heart. Spoken words aren't so bad. In shame at how little they tell, how they lie, they dissolve in the air. But the written words. They offend against silence and Change. I'll write no more words now.

Now I recall. I said three things were eternal and certain. I named two, and I've forgotten the third.

I'll remember it eventually. I will write to you sometime.

PART THREE

The Later Years

From around 30 years before Christ
to 395 years after Christ's death

Foolish, you mortals are, and too unwise to see the measure of good and evil as it approaches.

Homer
"Hymn to Demeter"

XVI

MOTHER,

It's impossible.

I read your letter where you tell about Change and silence and all that, but I can't believe the goddess who wrote those words is the one I left on earth. I left early, but you didn't seem to care about that. I spoke your name three times, but you didn't look up. Mother, I've never seen you despondent before.

Or perhaps. . . . This sounds silly, but—Mother was that you? Or was I tricked? Could another goddess, in disguise, some other goddess have met me at the temple? Was I fooled all summer to think I was with my very own Da? But who would deceive me so cruelly?

Wait, I think I know. It's vicious exactly like she is. How dare Aphrodite do such a thing! But if Aphrodite took your place, where were you? Called away, no doubt, by a ruse.

I see it clearly now, every detail of how Aphrodite did it. Even in the temple when I arrived, when you always run to hug me, Aphrodite, wearing your robes, barely raised one dozing eyelid. She leaned back in the throne, looking weary, waiting for me to run to her.

I know, I'll think over the entire visit and see the mistakes Aphrodite made. It's obvious. The tired hag I visited this year wasn't Da at all!

But oh dear, what if it was?

Mother, if you were really in the temple, that hag part I wrote isn't exactly right. Listen now, this is getting confusing. Will you do me a favor? If Aphrodite tricked us, I must look back over it all and see how she did it. Yet if it wasn't a trick, I might insult you by what I write.

Here's an idea. I'll imagine Aphrodite took your place and you weren't there. Let me tell you everything and exactly how it happened so you'll see what I mean. First of all, I ran to hug her, thinking I hugged you, and Brimos did the same, only slightly less fooled than I was. He kept staring up at you. I mean at Aphrodite.

The initiates watched, expecting something, so she rose from the throne. You looked fairly majestic, but awfully tired. I guessed you missed Rhea and Poseidon and the others who've withdrawn lately, all going away. That's what I told myself. We stood smiling to please the initiates, touched our hands, and waited while the temple emptied. It emptied quickly since this year's crowd wasn't as large as in some years.

When the initiates were gone, I turned, thinking that you still stood behind me, but you'd already sat down. I was too shocked to speak. Dark circles puffed under your eyes and your hands fell at your sides like empty baskets. Your crown showed tarnish, your hair was streaked and gray and hadn't been combed in a long time.

"What's the matter?" Brim finally spoke.

You waved Brim away. Your voice rasped, saying you wanted to be alone with me. After Brim ran outside, I found my voice. "Are you all right?"

You answered my question with a question. "Is that child learning New Ways?"

"Not exactly," I admitted. Of course Dis teaches Brim New Laws. Brim studies heroes, knows about military tactics, but everybody studies that now. "He adores Grandmother Da," I insisted, "and he respects goddesses. He'd never scorn the Mother Ways."

I waited for your smile, but you hadn't listened. You stood and walked to the doorway. I followed, supposing you wanted to question Brim for yourself, yet when we stood on the porch, you pointed and said, "A stupid cave."

I saw the small cave mouth in dark rock, the place where Dis leaves me each spring and comes to claim me in autumn.

"They worship at it," you said.

"They what?" Mother, you weren't making much sense.

I learned, by asking questions and being patient until you answered, that nowadays humans include Dis in our rites. They pour offerings on the ground of that cave to please him.

Well I got angry. I told you, or her—whatever goddess I was standing beside—that Dis has powers too. He lets me visit each year, he rules the underworld. He deserves to have rites of his own.

Yes, now I'm sure that Aphrodite tricked me. Mother would have gotten furious hearing me say that. But she turned away and stared at the ground, where the initiates' feet had softened and trampled the dirt. "I love that smell," she said, whatever that meant.

Then Brim came running back and asked for a grain cake. Which is odd too. He likes underworld food better than foods on earth, so he probably only asked to please you.

She smiled and took him up in her arms. I had to help, since he's heavy and strong, but holding Brim, carrying him into the temple, you looked your happiest since we arrived. Your hands moved quickly, serving cakes. In fact, I only have two pleasant memories of our entire visit, and that was one of them.

I worked awfully hard for the second happy moment, and when I won it, it was so brief. But I'm ahead of my story.

Suffice to say that you—or Aphrodite using the changing spell to look like you—grew more despondent each day. She hardly spoke except to ask questions. They came like Zeus' lightning bolts, out of the blue, but she didn't listen to my answers. Many times she wanted to know if I'd felt actual love, the laughing kind, like the love you always knew with Poseidon. I'd try to answer, since I had news to please you, but before I got started she interrupted with another question. I was going to have to leave early this year, I had reasons for wanting to get back to the underworld, but I never got to tell you that. When I'd start to explain about my new love and my joy in touching and the wonderful changes happening in the underworld these days, she cut me off.

"Temple wreckers," she kept saying. "Have you heard of the Sarmatians?"

I hadn't, but she never took time to explain. Again she'd ask if Brim learned the New Ways, or whether Dis punished converts to new religions, or if ghosts gossiped much of redemption.

Honestly Mother, Aphrodite had me frightened. I truly believed she was you, she had me fooled the whole summer. I never thought about why she would play such a trick, but now I see the whole reason. If I thought you were confused and miserable, I might stay on earth longer. My new lover would wait, lonely for me in the underworld. He would leave before I returned, and I'd get back and miss him. It's obvious Aphrodite would enjoy that.

Yet nothing could have kept me from him, so one afternoon I decided that I must tell you. I could tell my news best by the clear water sacred to women, so I said, "Let's go sit by a waterfall." I had to argue to make you leave the temple, and you demanded we go to a certain waterfall, no other. Finally, sitting on sun-warmed stone by the pounding stream, I suggested we wash our hair. I hoped the flashing shock of cold might—please don't be insulted—might wake you slightly.

"He withdrew," was your reply.

"Who?"

"His tumbling loins. By this pool, I lay resting."

We'd come to the absolutely wrong waterfall. In this very place, ages ago, you and Poseidon tumbled in love.

Then you asked, yet again, "Have you felt the laughing love, the love I meant you to have?"

I began my tale, explaining about Adonis and Aphrodite and the golden box, but before I had spoken a dozen words you interrupted.

"We're bound to them."

"Bound to whom? To those we love? Oh yes," I said, "for Adonis I feel. . . ."

But you would not listen. You talked about Zeus. "My brother wants to be the only immortal," you said. "He says humans who praise that god the father, that one and only god, praise him by another name."

I agreed, Zeus is a fool to care for silly priests' ideas. "Lots of immortals still live on Olympus," I said. "Despite those who've withdrawn, lots remain there, and some humans do remember them." Obviously I was trying to be agreeable, but it didn't work.

"I tried to explain," you said and your voice got angry. "If humans forget the Olympians, they'll forget Zeus too." You went on as if I weren't there, as if I were Zeus himself and you argued with him instead of me.

You laughed. "They call me The Mother. Go on, Brother, let them call you The Father. But don't blame me if humans want one immortal over all, if they choose between us."

I was shocked, but still tried to be polite.

Now I think again. Perhaps Da did sit by that stream. Your voice was angry, but tears filled your eyes. You looked away to hide your welling pity.

Anyway, I gave up talking of Adonis, or my new joy, or practically anything, and I felt the oddest sense. Perhaps because you weren't exactly you, I wasn't me either. Since you weren't really the mother, I didn't feel like the daughter, and instead I had to be gentle and kind.

For example, you complained of the tribal people from the East. They prophesy that their god will turn into a human and walk on earth, and that other humans will execute him like a thief.

"You mean Socrates," I said. "His people killed him, but not in the East. Here, ages ago."

"Socrates denied immortals," you answered. "He never said he was a god." You said I was too involved in the underworld, I paid no attention to living humans.

Now I admit, in a way, that's true. But the point is that I felt as if I were the mother and you were the child. I felt as if I were comforting Brimos, making excuses for little hurts, telling stories to distract him from confusing thoughts. I even ended up repeating your own words.

You were complaining of the new ideas about love, your voice hard with bitterness, saying women denied their best desires. "Men sell their daughters for gold. Men call love wrong. Women hide their desires."

I pointed out that women couldn't change that much. "Women only act ashamed because humans find it appealing," I argued. Women felt as they always had. "Touching feels wonderful, like always. I, myself, these days. . . ." I stopped because of what I saw—hardness deep in your eyes. The hollows of your cheeks gone ashen, oh Mother. Or Aphrodite? I was frightened.

Yet how could Aphrodite know? Could she repeat the words I'd written to you in a letter? You said my own words, about touching and love, said them back to me. "The women feel themselves driven down, lost underwater."

I stared at you.

You seemed lost to me. You complained on and on. Mothers no longer taught their daughters the Mother Knowing. Women thought they could be virgin only once, that then they were used up forever. You feared humans truly believed this.

You see my problem. I felt awful, but I couldn't get angry. I kept my voice cheerful and soft, like a mother teasing her child. I scoffed at the new ideas, repeating the things your own letter said, all about silence and Change, about the wonderful powers you give, the many ages humans have loved you. I even mocked my Lord Dis, trying to make you laugh.

"We celebrate the rites in the underworld now," I added.

At last, hearing that, you smiled. That was the second smile I saw cross your face, my second happy moment. It may have been briefer than the first, I'm not sure.

"Ghosts line up to greet me when I return," I said. "They all stand still and bow to me." I told all about the new rite, and then said that I had to leave early.

You didn't ask why. You accepted it like a quiet child, saying nothing to stop me. I kissed you goodbye, or maybe kissed Aphrodite. Anyway, I begged you to take some pleasure.

Did you hear?

Frankly, after all I've written, I feel as confused as ever. Some memories convince me that Aphrodite did play a trick. Others frighten me. Suppose Da is sad?

I won't pretend any more. Perhaps you were with me and already know all that happened. Never mind that I told you all over again. Whether you were with me at Eleusis or not, at least now I can tell you why I thought a certain love goddess fooled me with a changing game. You will understand why I suspected Aphrodite.

First of all, you must hear of Adonis. I feel like I've been trying to tell you this all year. There's a story to it, naturally, and it goes way back, but it comes out beautifully and I want you to know the whole thing.

You see, Mother, I've fallen in love. It began in the days since you stopped visiting Olympus for news. As you say, you seldom go there any more. It happened that a child was born. His mother's story is sordid and complicated, so I won't repeat it. Suffice to say the child was radiant, a perfect human baby. Aphrodite happened to see this Adonis being born, and she fell right in love with him. Of course the New Ways say such love is sinful, but we both know Aphrodite. Besides, what she did next was even worse.

Aphrodite wanted Adonis for herself and feared that some other immortal might seduce him first. To make sure no human got the child, Aphrodite stole him. His mother was turned into a tree so she couldn't object much. Then to keep the child away from any lusty goddesses, Aphrodite decided to hide him away until he grew into a man. That's where she made her mistake.

One day Hermes came to my realm bringing one of your letters, and he also brought me a small gold box. Hermes said Aphrodite sent it for temporary safekeeping, that I must not open it. The box was tied, not very tightly, with a gold cord. The sides were carved with flowers—lovely lapping rosebuds and twining chains of narcissus. I reasoned that a box so lovely must have wonderful contents. I did not swear I wouldn't open it. Everybody assumes that, living with Dis, I'm like human women are now, accustomed to following orders. Aphrodite must have thought that too.

All this happened back when I was fretting about so-called guilt and innocence, you recall, when I worried constantly about my powers over the dead, etcetera. A ghastly time. One day, feeling bitter and resentful, I untied the cord from around the box.

I parted its two bright sides. In that instant, my life changed.

Inside the box was a child. He had shining gold ringlets and a fat bronze belly. His petal fingers uncurled and reached for me. His eyes were blue as primula flowers. He smiled and gave a sharp happy cry.

I was astonished. My breath froze in my chest. I reached and took him up without a thought.

I felt love, that's obvious. Yet at the time, never having ever truly loved any god, or even a man, I had no idea. Aphrodite knows all there is to know about love, and she knew love had been quite awful for me. She assumed I couldn't feel it, and considered it safe to entrust the world's most lovable child to my arms.

I began caring for the child as my own. Ages passed and young Adonis grew larger, always more tall and more golden. I thought of making him immortal, but only the worst places in my realm have fire, places I shuddered to take him. He lived with us in the palace. I loved to watch him, a slender moving green stalk chasing around the palace, tossing a thistle in the fields with Brim. Brim looks so like his father, thick and dark, but Adonis looked exactly the opposite. Brim grows more serious with each age, but young Adonis loved to laugh, always starting tickling fights with Brim and sometimes with me. Adonis and I loved to sit on the cool banks of the Cocytus playing lyres and singing songs he made up all by himself. He even made up songs for me. Life in the underworld was happier than I ever remember it.

Then one day Adonis and Brim were holding races across the Elysion fields. I sat watching, my fingers crossed to hope Adonis would win, when a third figure appeared in the distance. I recognized Hermes when his swift steps brought him abreast of the runners. He reached me ahead of them both.

"Aphrodite claims her gold box," he announced.

I smiled and told him to wait while I went to get it. The empty box had sat under my gold bed all these years, and I took it out and dusted it off. I gave it to Hermes and he left carrying it, but I knew he'd soon return. I called Adonis aside and hurried him to my chambers.

"You must hide," I said. "Don't let anyone see you."

Aphrodite had sent Hermes to claim her love, but I couldn't return him. He brought joy and sunlight to me, even in the underworld. Sometimes alone with him, I felt my heart pound up in my throat, felt my breath go short as a runner's. When I was with Adonis I felt beautiful, the way I felt before I ever knew Dis.

I told Adonis he might need to hide for a long time. He nodded and didn't complain, though his gaze grew dull, puzzled and afraid. It hurt me to leave him alone, confused and fearful, so I told him the story of the box and Aphrodite.

"You're not my mother?" His eyes went wide and clear as mountain pools.

"Brimos is my only child," I assured him.

"But Hades said. . . ." He hesitated, too surprised to tell me what he knew, then the truth tumbled out. One day my clever husband had taken Adonis and Brim aside. He hadn't exactly lied, that wily Dis, but almost. Dis talked and taught them the stupid taboos they follow on earth now, how sons shouldn't love mothers in that way, touching and all. Dis didn't exactly say Adonis was my son, but he implied it.

"Yet I loved you," Adonis said, tears shining on his eyelashes. "I loved you more each day, I couldn't help that. You're graceful, and sometimes sad." His words tumbled out and tears overflowed—tears for joy because his love was not sinful, tears in sadness for the worry he'd felt.

My heart beat harder than Hephaestus' hammer. I pulled Adonis close. I felt his sadness as I used to feel my own—lost in the underworld, uncertain where his mother was, confused about love. I held him as I used to want to be held, back when I first found myself without my mother. His arms held me too. I can't remember such pleasure since being small, Da, held in your arms.

We held each other close and his tears wet my hair. I stroked his cheek a while, and he touched mine. Then other things happened, you know. To tell the truth, I'm still shy about discussing these things. You can imagine how I sit now, trying to write, crossing out words and blushing like an asparagus pea flower. Anyway, it's enough to say that before Hermes returned, I vowed never to let Adonis go. He was my lover and I was his. He swore he would always care only for his dearest Persephone. Unfortunately back then I was the only goddess he had known. He had yet to meet Aphrodite.

Around nightfall that same day Hermes returned to the underworld in a panic. Aphrodite had found only one gold ringlet in her fine box. She was furious and went into a rage, storming up one side of Olympus and down the other, her creamy skin blotched with fury. Finally she calmed down and interrogated Hermes, and he admitted seeing an unusually beautiful youth in the underworld, a tall golden boy who won races against Persephone's son. Aphrodite turned on her heel and ran straight to Zeus.

Hermes stood before me now, getting his breath back.

Finally he said, "I come from the Immortal Who Exceeds All Immortals." Zeus insists on being called that lately. "Great Zeus awaits you on Olympus."

I had to go, of course. I needn't detail what happened. You can imagine. Despite the many immortals who've withdrawn, a Boule was called and enough came to support a good bicker. Not quite a squabble, but nearly. Fortunately, Zeus felt like being fair, so he did not invite Dis. Matters got sufficiently sordid without him. Aphrodite called me every name men use for women nowadays. I countered with nasty ghost-gossip about her. Some agreed that Adonis was mine, others said Aphrodite should have him. Others argued that Adonis should go off on his own.

Finally everyone voted and the decision went three ways. Because it all came out even, I won Adonis for a third of each year and Aphrodite gets him another third. The last third he may have to himself.

By the time news of the Boule reached the underworld, Adonis was already my lover, officially. Being a stickler for law, Dis couldn't object. Except that he's become more considerate. He lets ghosts celebrate my rites in the underworld, and he strives to please me at last. Dis goes along with New Ways, and I know he's ashamed of my pleasures with Adonis. It makes him embarrassed that I feel desire beyond the call of wifely duty, so-to-speak.

But Mother I almost forgot to tell you the best part. Adonis touches me gently all over and I feel, once more, curious and eager as a maiden. I recall your letter—about the sweet burst of yielding—and truly I feel it. I wish Rhea hadn't withdrawn, I wish she could know this.

So now you see why I thought Aphrodite might have tricked us, pretending to be you at Eleusis this year. Aphrodite's dreadfully jealous of my time with Adonis. To Adonis, of course, a certain love goddess is irresistible, on the level of pure lust. For me he bears a deeper longing. But Aphrodite tells him stories, says I'm pallid and spectral and all other nasty things. She's especially jealous that he loved me first.

It would be just like Aphrodite to pull a trick like that, changing into a sad vision of you, wanting me to think my own mother had grown old and unhappy. Then I wouldn't return early to my love in the underworld.

But if it was you, Mother, oh dear, please write soon. I worry.

Please don't pay attention to all the changes, to all the humans and their politics. Rome may rule our Greeks, humans may talk of one god only, but haven't we heard such silly ideas before? Now that Poseidon has withdrawn, you must find someone new and take love with him. Trust your daughter, love can do wonders.

In the Mother Knowledge, I close.

* * *

One last thing about Adonis. After he's with Aphrodite, he gets his time alone and he's wonderfully affectionate when he comes to me. I exhaust him utterly before letting Aphrodite have him back. She must work hard to please him, so he learns new skills. He returns to my arms much improved!

Honored Queen Persephone,

Your mother called me to her temple to carry a letter to you. When I arrived she was not there. I looked for a letter, but could not find one. Instead I found this package which, as you will clearly see, she has addressed to you.

I also found many torn sections of papyrus and large leaves, each one covered with Queen Demeter's handwriting. These were blown over benches and against walls. Some were out on the porch and steps of the temple, as if a strong wind had come to visit your mother. It too was gone when I arrived.

I gathered up what I could. I will look for your mother when I return, and will let you know within the day if I was not to bring these. Until then I remain,

Your messenger in sacred trust,
Hermes

XVII

I WARM the seed in the womb. That's why women are sacred to me. That was why they worshipped me.

I warmed the seed in the soil. I pulled fruit up from earth's belly. Humans grow their food now. When the crops fail, humans believe they've sinned. They have never sinned against me. Humans are only what they are.

I had gifts. I enjoyed giving them. I had power. I was glad to give that too. Humans still worshipped me after I gave away my power, after I let them grow their own food.

We're bound to them. You must know I mean humans. You probably tire of hearing me say it. I foresaw it ages ago, so why didn't I explain? I was afraid. What's the harm if I say it now?

I gave humans life. They gave me worship. On Olympus, everybody pretends immortal strength comes from sacrifices. That's politics, pure and simple. Worship nourishes us, we grow huge and strong on belief. You already know that Grandmother Rhea heard her name said less often. So she withdrew.

As for me, humans still wanted me to pull grain up from

the ground. They spoke my name and I grew strong enough to do it. I'm not sorry that I taught them how to plant seeds. I wanted them to stop fearing me. Now they need an immortal who will give them laws.

I hear them speak the new gods' names. I hear them pray for an immortal who will tell them what is right and what is wrong. I hear the noises of all tongues—the beautiful Greek, Sea Peoples' hissing, Nile-dwellers clucking, Latin, Arabic, soft stuttering near the Amazon. I'm tired of this many-tongued place. I was always known by silence, by showing.

Humans don't fear as many monsters as they once did. Titans were once fine and terrifying. Now they only frighten children.

There are so many strange sects for worship now —Orphics, Cabiri, Marcossians, I can't remember them all. Essenes, Mithraics, Christians, Naasenes. Humans understand so little. Take that one from Nazareth, for instance. He was a better human than most, and those he cared for killed him. He reminded me of Socrates. Socrates amused me. Actually, that thoughtful Greek looks better every age.

In the new religions, they write down words about their god and study them. Fathers teach the books to their sons. They carry their books from place to place and speak the same words out loud time after time. They say their god is eternally the same, change does not touch him. Their god can stay in a book, the same each day. For my worship, books cannot serve. Knowledge of me is like a flower. Crushed between pages, it would die. A flower can't pass from father to child, the child must go and see it.

In the new religions, humans praise the line of generations through the father. Daughters command only a price. No goddesses appear with new names. Women hesitate to enter temples.

Daughter, find the part of yourself that is both a maiden and as old as Mother Rhea. It's there, inside you. The humans must see you rise from the flames— once stolen and raped, having wandered the underworld, often harassed by your dark groom's demands. Despite all this, you will appear in the temple each year, flushed after taking pleasure with that young beautiful boy.

These new priests write lies about our worship. They say we act out a rape in the temple. Now that's simply not true. Imagine a maiden harmed to entertain the faithful. What do they think we are, Romans?

In the East, angry crowds destroy goddess temples. My sisters' statues fall to stone floor. Two axe strokes and the body has no arms. Spikes of iron enter stone breasts.

* * *

I pause and look at my words. They are less than I mean to tell you. I take up a new clean sheet. You must understand. We're bound to humans. They speak our names and we grow stronger, they love us and we thrive.

In the East, a long way from Eleusis, a teacher taught in silence. He held a flower so all could see it. He knew my ways. I should go east, I should go visit there and grow stronger. Yet not all eastern teachers are so wise. Nearer, but still eastward somewhere, women's temples are burned and plundered. Stories tell of a priestess tossed to the stone floor and held down to be shared. I hear of such things. I won't witness them in my temple.

But I said we were bound to them. Now Zeus scurries from mountaintop to mountaintop, claiming the new names of new gods. He says the books tell of him and insists he is That One, by every new name. He may be right, we've all answered to lots of names. Yet I worry for Zeus.

I ruled beside gods and men all these ages. I never minded them. Ares wanted me to plot with him and I might have ruled Olympus. Now Zeus calls himself That One God All Humans Worship. My brother fears me these days.

Yet I pity my brother. He'll wait too long. They'll curse him, laugh at him. They'll forget that occasionally he was wise.

Already Hera's name is spoken only as an insult.

Aphrodite stays too long. Now she's sacred to the women who pretend to love to earn food.

I think of Hades. I understand him now, I forgave him ages ago. Zeus gave judgments. Poseidon and Demeter gave life. What did Hades give? Now there's Brimos.

I will miss that child.

Already I miss so many who are gone. Poseidon put away his staff, but the sea still tumbles. Hephaestus' hearth lies cold, but metals remain hot in the ground. Life continues. Rhea withdrew, yet life continues.

I worry for this new immortal. He's called jealous and vengeful, he's called loving and kind. How will he ever manage all that? Besides, they write about him in books and he can't slip out of it. Perhaps it's his own fault. He wanted his laws written down.

I think it's sad for humans to blame silly laws on immortals anyway. No wonder that some humans believe in nothing any more. Next, they'll start wars over which name to call an immortal. In my temple, who could argue or doubt? I'm there.

Athena speaks of withdrawing, but she stays. She finds all this amusing. I discussed my ideas with her, saying I wouldn't have a book for my worship.

"If you don't," she pointed out, "your name will pass. Fathers will have nothing to talk about with their sons." She's older now, not so arrogant, but she's still never mistaken.

"My daughter and I will write no more letters," I told her. In that moment I decided it. Now I laugh and my belly shakes. I worry about not writing more letters to you, but how can I, when I withdraw? I've never been quick as Athena, but now I become slow-witted as a Titan.

They confuse stories about me. I won't endure it.

What do I care? I won't argue with words.

* * *

I pause to read that last page and lean back laughing. It is funny, Persephone, funny. You must see it— Demeter, complaining about change, I laugh to hear myself. How ignorant, how concrete can I be? I am like a human at last.

What of change? Every year the grain is cut, seeds fall to the ground, and next year new stalks grow.

I scare easily now, also like a human. Perhaps it's my own fault because I let my heart speak to you in small marks written down. Your letters disturb me. I can't burn them, yet I know that I should.

Do you remember the night I wanted to set a hillside on fire? I never could use revenge to cure my rage. I could only withhold my gifts, hurting humans. I'm not angry now, but I'll write no more letters.

Writing was wrong. I tamed all my knowing into little marks. I cling to words now, a child's grasp, choking summer's last blossom.

Blossoms and stems are woven to make a necklace. If the stem breaks anywhere, the blossoms scatter to the ground.

Now they say a woman is a virgin only once. I'm tired of things in straight lines. Humans don't sin, they're only weak. They struggle and should be forgiven. Immortals might improve themselves, though. Perhaps I've sinned and can't take back my words.

Persephone, I'll give your letters to Hermes. You have mine, and you have fire. Do what you can. Even before you were born, I forgave you any failing.

Words are blossoms in a chain. I imagine a flame leaping up to break the chain of our letters and bring silence, and silence won't lie.

All this reminds me—Pythagoras and his theories. He tried to draw a straight line. He tried again and again, worked at it for years. I laughed so hard at that man. They hold their bellies to imitate me.

No, that too is past. These days priests write lies about me. Words. I use them too. I use them to say I'm sorry to leave you. What of that? Marks that lie still on a page. And what do I feel? A frightened bird claws at my neck and my face. Believe me, I depart because I must.

I miss Rhea. Please understand what is necessary. I long

for Rhea. You'll miss me, but I can't remain. I've absolutely decided now, this is my last letter.

Before she withdrew, Rhea came to me. She looked tired.

"What's wrong?" I said.

"I'll be sown back into stars." She met my gaze.

I felt ashamed to argue with my mother, yet I said, "But you're immortal."

"There's no help for that."

Then I asked your grandmother Rhea, my mother Rhea, "Will you be happy?"

Mother Rhea talks in riddles. She asked if I was happy.

"At times," I said.

"Are you sad?"

"At times."

"Where I go," she said, "time is one time."

"But if you leave," I said to my mother, "what will happen to life? Will it be?"

She told me a story about lovers, quite beautiful, too beautiful to put it on a page. Then she asked, "After love, when you returned to yourself, did you love Poseidon less?"

"Not less," I said, "only differently. I withdrew to myself again."

"Daughter of a mother. Mother of a daughter. Grandmother, oldest of the line."

I pulled at her skirt.

"I'm not leaving," she insisted. "I withdraw."

* * *

I've decided we should write no more letters.

I sent for Hermes to take this and the others to you.

A new flower grows. Humans call it the anemone. Did you make it?

If one day your new lover comes to you as a horse, switch your tail and offer your buttocks.

Several centuries ago, you asked whether I thought Homer might return a third time as a poet. Let me think a while before answering.

If you try to pull up a flower, if you tighten your belly and yank, if it still doesn't come, no use throwing things at it. That doesn't help.

Do you still have my crown?

* * *

Hermes will bring your letters to you. Put them with mine. And do you still have my crown, the one I threw at the flower? If you can find it, wear it.

I will not see you again. Each day I feel it more fully. But I have so much in my heart left to tell you. I read your words about Adonis and love and my heart swells with imagining.

Adonis, beautiful name. I feel joy for you both. Tumble and writhe gently with him, imagine yourself as earth under the plow. Or this: lay him under you. Tamp his shoulders into the furrow of the field.

Adonis. Somewhere in the East they praise an Adonai. Is he the same? If Aphrodite teaches him the skills of loving, he must be excellent at it. Oh well, he'd find Da too old.

Did I ever tell you about the day I tumbled with Iaison? Oh yes.

Aphrodite has a potion for the times when a lover grows tired. Ask Adonis to bring some secretly.

Another time: place him at your back. Then rear up, so your breasts jog with the pounding. I don't mean to embarrass you, but you do lack some experience. You may also wish to whinny like a mare.

But Adonis. I remember now, it's important—love him. Love Adonis. Lie with him. Your laughter, your cries, your abundant joy and your pity, pour all your plenty over him. For the sake of women, take pleasure, never bargain time against the fullness of pleasure. When the mother withdraws the daughter's duties increase.

* * *

All right then.

Before she withdrew, Rhea came and sat by me. I asked

her many questions. She told me how she would be going. She could not leave before teaching me that skill.

Perhaps I'm wrong to write of it in words, but you must know. Imagine that I sit beside you. Our skirts overlap. Our radiance combines to one brightness. We've shared a cup of wine and our foreheads are flushed with it. I speak plainly, and I stop to hear your questions.

"Like a wind," I say, because you have asked about time. "The proper moment crossed ages, flying straight at me."

"A wind?"

"Yes," I say. "But listen now. A wind that doesn't rustle a single leaf."

"A silent wind, strange." You pull at my skirt. I feel myself drawing away. The crown you wear is the perfect size. "A wind," you say again.

"Imagine time," I say. "At long last it lets out one breath before it falls asleep."

Your breasts rise as you take in the breath. I let a long breath go. My own fullness slackens, settling to my middle.

Then we both hear it, the gentle music of silence. We know its expanse, stretching ahead of us, a marble plain. I recognize it, enter it.

Where I go, as Rhea said, I'll still be myself. Pity and love will fill me, also grief and anger. Nothing will change. I'll fold back into my name. I'll simply stop talking so much.

This letter ought to end. Hermes should have come by now. He's seldom swift any more.

I fold this letter over the others and I wait for Hermes. I hope you can set this log of letters in a fire. You're accustomed to the discipline of the underworld. You have fire.

Persephone one more thing never mind
brightness on the far steps of the temple

XVIII

ARE the soft winds of spring blowing? Do gentle zephyrs blow?

I wrote that question once. Long ago I wrote it and did not know if Da ever would read it. Writing it again now makes me feel peculiar.

Do warm winds blow? If they do, I should go up to earth. I sit writing.

I doubt that Mother will ever read this. Hermes won't come to carry it to her in his pouch, I know that. I'm alone now. But I manage loneliness better. I have Brimos, and Dis of course, which I didn't have then. Still I'm back where I was, writing notes with nowhere to send them.

Could Da ever read this? My future-knowing can't tell me. I see only an open expanse. Lovely colors, blue and white, used to be there, and sometimes red joined them. Then one day they all faded, I will not try to understand it. Mother knew about future-knowing, about Change and all, about silence too. And I remember love, all the different ways she used to speak of it.

Adonis. Adonis is dead.

Will I ever get used to it? I write it again, Adonis is dead.

Mark it over and over like one of Brim's history lessons—is dead is dead Adonis is dead.

No, I will never get used to it, even though centuries have passed since that day. With each century the awful colors of it seem to draw further back, closer to shadow. At first when he died, when I knew he was here in my realm, thoughts of him fogged over every thing I did. I used to wish he'd bathe in the River Lethe. If only he'd go back up, I thought, wash away his memory, forget me, forget Aphrodite and the life he knew, if only he would go back up to earth, I wished and wished. I would not visit Elysion where he was. To see his golden body pale in mist would be too terrible.

A wild boar's tusk tore open his belly.

A century ago I could not have written those words.

The tusk ripped the soft flesh of his belly.

Perhaps I get used to it. Who was it who said, "Eternity is long?" Hephaestus, I think. Mother often repeated it. I'll teach Brimos that saying. Hephaestus. Demeter. Rhea. Poseidon. Athena. Hermes. Hera. All gone. I shouldn't pester Brimos to learn his relatives' names, yet I do.

But Adonis, dead, and not even my fault. Sometimes I wish it were my fault. Then I'd feel punished, which would be simpler.

Perhaps Aphrodite feels punished. She was careless.

Aphrodite lingers too long, I think. Her worship becomes only love spells for potions. I wonder if she has a potion to help her forget Adonis. I wonder if she uses it every day or only once a season. I wonder if it helps her forget the day Adonis died.

During his time with her, Adonis loved to hunt. I knew that and I worried, but Aphrodite swore she'd stay near him. She carried ointments to heal any wound.

Who sent the wild boar? Could Dis have done it? That's not likely. He would wish it, but he's too old. All his life has been law. Adonis was legal, after all, my lover, and Dis would not violate the Boule that gave him to me.

Who lured Aphrodite away? Only once, that afternoon?

No one, possibly. She's not as swift or as alert as she once was. She lies in her bath dreaming of the time when women took many lovers. She should not stay. Let her withdraw so love may finally become a rite recorded by human judges.

Beautiful Adonis hunting among trees in the forests. He would be tall and bright, a tree turning gold in the sunset. Ahead at the hem of a clearing, a bush trembles. A shadow breaks from green shining leaves. The boar scents, but cannot see Adonis. Adonis hears the stamp of a hoof and he looks. He sees the nostrils flare.

Golden corded muscles. Adonis' arm moves. He reaches back and a bright shaft trembles in his hand. I hear the arrow stretching the gut-thread. Adonis kneels, he takes the shape of an altar. The hooves pound earth, the shadow grows, a cord of light cuts the air of the clearing and the arrow glints and glances from the bristly back, falls away.

I hear Adonis cry out. The boar...

I will put words to it, yes

...the boar struck him.

The earth shook. I heard the cry in the underworld. Cold sweat broke out at the small of my back and raced over all my skin.

On earth, Aphrodite heard it too. She leapt on the back of the fastest wind, but it was too slow. She arrived and poured out her healing oils, oils meant to give life, and they joined the falling flow, a stream of blood so full and wet it softened the ground.

Her oils dissolved the moist soil, mixing in it to give life. Adonis was gone, but the blood-red anemone pushed its bloom from the mud. In its flower center, a dark eye accuses Aphrodite.

Anemones, ugly flowers. I stare at them, they stare back. I've cursed them. I've disowned every one. They grow wild along roadsides anyway. Humans see them and praise Persephone's art.

They grew everywhere all at once and I was angry and I wanted to curse earth. Mother was angry once and withheld her powers. I could also. I'd let no flowers grow. Yet my grief, unlike my Mother's, could change nothing. Adonis once was human, now was dead. Da often called pity better than anger. I wish I could be like her.

I had heard the cry. Earth's valleys repeated it. The few immortals left on Olympus heard it. It echoed down to the underworld, and what was my first thought? That Dis had heard. Somehow, my feet carried me through halls and across the courtyard. I pulled the tall gates aside and saw Dis. He sat on his throne in our golden room.

Change, Mother knew it. Silence also. Maybe in some future I'll be as wise as Mother was.

Change and silence. Dis had changed, Dis sat silent. Dis looked away from me. I wanted to ask if he caused it, if he killed Adonis, but I'm glad I didn't. That would have been unkind. Back then I could not see how much Dis had changed. Only lately I realize it, I see the reasons too. New human ways weaken him as much as any immortal.

I stood before him that day, seeing him somehow for the first time. How long had I given all my love to Adonis, how long had I forgotten Dis? Never mind, eternity is long. Those centuries had changed him.

Dis used to like the New Ways. I remember way back to the first day when he showed me this realm. In the thistle field how he chattered about justice, good for good, evil for evil. His hands danced in the air, he was so desperate for me to see it. Justice was beautiful.

And Necessity! I laugh to think of it, a small laugh, a brittle clicking of pebbles. No, I'll laugh bigger and make my breasts shake.

New Ways came. My Lord Hades' honors increased. His realm would punish each new sin. He gave the Judges instructions to punish the wicked, reward the good, make each judgment known and written down in careful records. Old Tantalus was condemned to hunger and thirst, insects tormented fickle Alcibiades, wealthy Croesus was so funny-looking at first, and he still darts to-and-fro, dodging showers of gold coins. All the trouble that Dis took perfecting punishments, and for what? Keeping accurate records. Of what?

Tortures. Humans scorn us now and call our realm a hell. My great King is called a demon, priests make up ugly stories against him. Humans call our fine realm a place of horrors. Dis knows, he hears ghosts' talk. Heaven has gone elsewhere, and they name My Great Lord "hell's brutal emperor." Dis hears the stories. Lord Hades, a vicious petty tempter, a sneaking demon making humans disobey laws. I see his face when he thinks about it.

Once when we lay together after the touching, Dis spoke about it. He'd only meant to be absolute, he said, "To be just."

What could I have said? I found no comforting words. He went on about how he used to feel lonely before he brought me here, those many ages ago, but now he felt a different loneliness. That first loneliness was outside, he said, "But this is in here." He pointed to his chest. "Humans never loved me, I know. And they speak of me even more often now, but I am less than I was."

I pretended I hadn't heard. I started chattering about young Brimos, how strong our son was, how rich he'd be. I bounced on the bed, all excited over how Hades and I had created a life, a young strong son and all, and wasn't it wonderful?

I still please Dis with silliness sometimes, though I'm not as good at it as I once was. We both pretend somewhat.

But on that day, when I stood facing him in the throne room and we both heard Adonis' cry still echo, I saw no point in pretending. On that wide golden floor I stood before my King. Dis sat silent, staring down at his robe. On the hem, ash had turned the black edge gray. I wouldn't flatter him, or use arguments to persuade.

"My lover is dead," I told him. "Charon will claim the body soon. Aphrodite herself put a coin on the lips."

Dis listened silently, but the strings in his neck trembled. My lips felt cold, as if I myself tasted the coin.

Then Dis spoke. "Before that ghost meets my Judges," he said, "I might arrange that he visit the palace. Only briefly, of course." He hesitated, coughed. "Adonis, your . . .friend, he spent his childhood here."

My Great Lord paused, as if unsure how to express himself. His mud-dark fingers knotted over the throne's carved arm. "I, of necessity, would go elsewhere," he finally added. "I have duties to perform. I am quite busy."

I shook my head, but I kept my chin high as a Queen must. "Send that ghost . . ." I paused, my breath caught, "Send him to Elysion. Hades' Queen makes this judgment."

My King gave a quick nod. I bowed and stepped backward out the gate.

So it was. I never saw Adonis' ghost. I kept putting it off, wishing he would discover the Lethe and float back to earth. I followed the ghosts' rumors about him. The word of my judgment spread rapidly. When I came near, ghosts would hush their whispering. I heard much more than they thought I did.

"The Queen's lover got special treatment," they'd say. "That ghost was never judged. How can that be fair?" This one injustice marred great Hades' realm. Soon everyone knew it. All ghosts' rumors get back to Dis, I know that's so.

These events happened ages ago, and in all these centuries my King and I have never spoken of them. He became solicitous to me for a time, then that also passed. I suppose, being frank about it, my care began its slow death when I saw the anemone. My sadness fades slightly every century since. Look now—I even write of it in words.

It lies there before me, told as plain events on a page. Making words of it, I don't actually feel any pain. But I can't think of anyone in the universe to send this letter to. Quite unqueenly, writing pointless letters. Warm spring winds blow and I'm expected on earth. I ought to be leaving.

I suppose matters were bound to end like this. Dis would call it a justice, each thing itself and bound by duty and law. He would call it Necessity. That idea still strikes me silly sometimes.

But what will I do with this letter? And with all our earlier notes, the rolled log of pages that Mother sent to me? I still have every one. When I received them the edges were worn from handling, and I've made them worse. Some of the script has worn away. I know what words belong there, know the letters by heart. Parts of them amuse me. I was occasionally clever, but mostly silly and young.

Da wanted me to burn our letters, that's obvious. Both of us studied our future-knowing and we always saw fire. I envy her having withdrawn, and I think she was wise. It protected her from pain, hid her away from history. She does not have to witness this life, what I am now, how we live, Dis and I in this realm, how I rise each year without even a temple.

That hurts inside, doesn't it? The humans burned the temple at Eleusis. Does that memory splinter inside my thoughts? A Queen could decide what she felt. I suppose then, it's the temple which hurts. I do feel pain at recalling it, and often I feel like mourning, but then I don't know what to mourn for.

How many times did fire confirm our prophecy? I'll count, that's it, counting gives me something to do. First the Sea Peoples came inland and burned temples. They destroyed Hera's homes and Artemis' places, but never touched ours. That perhaps doesn't count as the first fire then, since the Eleusinians had built stone around our temple to protect it.

Second, anyway, almost eight hundred years later, the first actual fire. In their retreat, Persians burned the wood and scattered the stones. When I saw it like that, I thought it's done, no sense complaining. Except I did complain, I hated to rise amid rubble.

Mother laughed at me over that. She watched Pericles rebuild it better than ever. She was right, it was huge and for centuries it welcomed swelling crowds. We watched Alexander come and go with his wars, and he never harmed our sanctuary. The rites took place year after year. That counts as fire too, I suppose. The celebration was cancelled only once in all our history, the year Alexander sacked the great city of Thebes. But our fire burned in the temple again the very next spring. Quite frankly, I began to feel safe. Alexander died not long after, but his generals were powerful all over the land and they sent troops to live in Eleusis.

Mother would have hated that if she'd noticed. In those days she seldom left the temple. I don't blame her, things had grown quite confused. At first immortals enjoyed watching Alexander's kingdom fall apart, a bicker here, a squabble there, skirmishes, skirmishes. Later it got so boring that even Ares ignored the little wars, so many and in so many different places, he could hardly attend to each one or pick winners. I myself stopped paying attention. Years later I looked around and saw all our Greeks ruled by Romans. I was surprised.

I wonder if Mother cared?

Anyway, the Eastern raiders came after that. Men burst through the gates at Eleusis and knocked stone from stone. They hooted and bellowed their rude language in the temple, they set fires, they left bodies fallen in the sanctuary. Then their fire, too, passed over Eleusis. I pity Da, having to bear that, and so tired already.

Well, I was frightened. My fear was silly too, as usual. Within a day, stonecutters came from all over Greece, and Romans came too. They worked right alongside our people. No one stood by and gave orders. The emperor in Rome decreed that no wealth would be spared in rebuilding our temple, and they worked all winter. The very next spring, Marcus Aurelius himself was initiated.

I forgot, I'm supposed to be counting. But then if I count in the yearly ritual fires. . . . I don't know my thousands well. All those zeros confuse me.

The new temple, anyway, was magnificent. Any human who wished to go around its outer walls had to spend half a day walking in the sun. Nevertheless, Mother's time arrived. She withdrew.

The temple lasted, of course, but I presided alone. A priestess served in Mother's place, and everyone was kind and pretended. Our rites welcomed all Greeks and Romans who spoke Greek, except killers of course. I rose in the midst of fire, spectacular as ever. I recalled Mother's instructions, how I'd appear flushed after love with gentle Adonis. The rites went on as usual, three whole centuries.

Then a wild boar came out of the woods. A boar's tusk ripped the soft skin. As I write that, colors swirl inside my eyes—green, gold, earth, then red. It's not so bad, though, not really. Not like it once was.

That year the initiates who met me in the temple saw me in clothes of mourning. I looked paler, slightly more thin, yet still majestic. I still brought up earth's flowers. Except the anemone. Everywhere on earth humans praised me.

Not so many initiates came any more, not like it used to be, and even in the underworld I heard what the new religions said about me. I never actually minded, at least not until the last century or so. Then Christians, lonely men wandering in the wilderness, began writing their lies about goddesses and sin. I ignored them. I felt confident. Dis and I lived quietly, performed our duties, raised Brimos. Life had settled into a peacefulness.

Occasionally, I admit, Roman emperors got strange ideas. One ruler would recognize the Christians, then Change would do her work, and the next ruler favored ancient practices. Then vice versa, age by age, with an etcetera tossed in as well. I do remember one emperor whose story amused me, except I can't keep track of Latin names.

He worshipped the male god and lived in Rome. He hated to see the crowds of humans who came from all over the world flowing to Eleusis. He did not dare forbid them to worship me, so he devised a clever edict. He prohibited all rites performed after sunset.

His edict fell as heavily as a feather on water. The Greek proconsul who received it was eating olives at the time, I recall. The page arrived, he read it, shrugged and let it fall into the pile of skins and pits by his couch. Nobody even considered holding our ritual in daylight, no human would honor such a rule. Valentinian—that's the Roman's name—soon heard the Greek's reply. Eleusis held humanity together, it was said, Eleusis' center kept the peace in the world. To neglect Mother and Daughter would make life unlivable everywhere.

So much for emperors, so much for edicts.

In short, I grew comfortable. I re-read Da's letters. She had promised that our rites would last and they did. Fires came and went, yes, but after each one the temple rose far better, more beautiful.

I talked it over with Dis once, and he agreed, based upon the evidence. Mother and I had been sacred at Eleusis for almost two thousand years. There could be nothing to fear.

Then they came, barbarians. Greeks called them Visigoths. Ugly word, ugly noise of it. And coming after them, Christian monks. The fire came so hungry, so hot, it melted mortar between the stones. It spread along the dry weeds between the floor stones. It danced like a pack of wild children in the sanctuary, and it clung to the roof, making Eleusis' winter night like day.

I felt the fire in the underworld. Something was wrong. I felt a terrible new cold, cold burning up in me, and I sensed something awful happening. I wanted to go up into the world, to stand in the midst of that fire myself, make it stop, but it was winter. I could not go. The Visigoths burned everything down, all Eleusis embers and ashes, but I finally felt them go elsewhere.

I went to my safest place in this realm, the small cave where each spring I go up. I lay there. It was cold and damp but pleasantly small, and I wanted to sleep. I lay shuddering. I saw all that happened after that.

Mother could explain why those Christians did what they did, but I still can't find words to understand it. I never will understand those people. Mother's and my ritual always celebrated growing life, but these people praise a dead memory. Yet they believe so strongly. It was like a madness, how on the heels of all the burning and plunder, even while the fires still flickered, the monks came to Eleusis.

They burned their clothes and their hands when they touched hot temple pillars, knocking them apart. They lifted glowing stones and threw them against each of our statues. Their strange faith said I was evil, was as dark and fearful as awful Dis himself. My Lord Hades, I mean. The monk men knocked the heads from the statues, beat the noses from carvings. To chase out Mother and me, those men knelt, burning their knees, and carved their sign into the floor at the gate. Two crossed sticks. And that's supposed to surpass my power. On such crossed sticks, their god, a mere mortal, died like a thief.

I don't pretend to understand. Only today, thirty winters since, do I pause to consider the meanings. We Olympians never claimed to be perfect, to be eternal. We'd never be so silly. We changed our names and our shapes, ignored contradictions, tried to live up to stories, that's all. Show any one of us who claimed she was eternal. We're only immortal, after all, in certain forces and ways. "On the individual level," as Dis says, "we're temporary."

I asked him about all this once. Actually, I agree with his explanation. He's better at understanding rhetorical, I mean political, matters. Sometimes he rambles though, talks and talks about so-called historical forces, so-called necessities. He says Christians worship the dead, whom they call martyrs. I've probably slept through many fine lectures about Christianity. I suppose I ought to care.

I find all this boring or else ugly. And the temple too. Our temple has lain in rubble thirty years now.

I feel a stone in my belly. I do feel sadness in my throat. It's been a long time, a strange time, since I felt much of anything. This feels peculiar.

I do grieve for our temple, an empty place hardly worth returning to. Besides, now the Christians plan to put one of their churches on the hill overlooking the Maiden's Well, the very place where Mother sat grieving. How sad she would be if she knew.

I'm sad. I wish I were angry. I'd like to get truly angry just once. I'd grow more furious and more furious, enough to stop this—this what? What's the name for this tepid sadness?

All right then, I'll admit it, self-pity. Should I feel shame or guilt to pity myself? No one will read this anyway. I sit here feeling sorrow for myself, yet feeling that . . .I do feel something. It is what I feel.

I wonder if Dis gets bothered by feelings any more. Probably. One day he turned to me and he said, "Here's a problem to practice your logic on."

To be kind, I looked attentive.

"If the Lord Hades withdrew," and then he pointed to himself to make it clear, "what would happen to his realm?"

I didn't pretend my shock. "But what of justice?" I blurted out. "What happens to the wicked? Who'll do the punishing?"

Dis shook his head. He's always discouraged by my lessons. "My duty," he said, "is older than I am. I do what's necessary. I'm just. I shouldn't confuse myself with justice, itself."

"You confuse me with it." I didn't understand.

He explained about the three Judges, and the many-headed Hydra down in Tartarus, and Charon the boatman. Plus that dog Cerberus I used to love, poor raggedy thing. All of them are necessary, Dis said, they're not flawed, as he is, by desire.

"The Judges invent punishments. Lord Hades only advises." He felt he had to explain it slowly. "The Lethe would still flow upward without me. Hydras make fine guards, and they breed on their own."

I interrupted. "Wouldn't our realm change at all?"

He looked away. He often liked to think it would, he said, yet he'd never figured out just how.

So much for Rhetoric. I remember studying it, and it can be made to say the worst things. I suppose I pitied myself then too, when I studied it. Of course I've been quick at rules and Boules and deals for ages now, and what use is that on an empty Olympus?

Self-pity again.

All right then, I'll pity myself. Temporarily. I'll simply say this—I mostly miss colors. I'll pity myself over that. I'll take that one thing, flowers' colors to be exact, and I'll pity myself about it, and then I will be done.

I loved flowers' colors, I loved them quite deeply. Now it's later and I'm sad. Yes I pity myself. I do. Over that. I no longer see the brightness of every flower. Has my realm's darkness hurt my eyes? I wondered that, when it first happened. I no longer wonder.

Are the warm winds of spring blowing? If warm winds blow, I have to rise. That's necessary. Flowers appear when I do, and I stare at them, their blank faces. I know they're quite as brilliant, quite as laughing as ever, but the whole world looks to me as if an artist drew it with charcoal on a page.

There, I wrote that down. The growing life looks black, shadows cast against a white shore, the sky. And there's Persephone, I see myself there. I see a shade between the light and the dark.

Well, that's disgusting all right. I add a few words, cry and spoil the page. I write a few more. Pity makes me sick inside. I'll push it back.

Then, inside my memory, I hear a voice. It whines, oh how pathetically too, like a maiden insisting, "But it is how I feel. And I do feel something."

To that, Queen Persephone, Consort in Hades' Great Realm, must reply, "What of that?"

* * *

Yes, that's finished. Organize my thoughts. What else did I intend to say? I haven't written in ages, and now I see why. My eyes burn all over again, and I must finish or I'll get all weepy and only have to face destroying this anyway.

Outside, at the furthermost gates, ghosts are whispering. I can still hear, thank you, quite well. Ghosts join their voices to make an echo down the hall, and they insist that I listen.

Gentle Mistress. Western winds blow. Springtime will be late. An old man waits at the temple and calls, ruins echo Persephone, Persephone. Earth waits for you.

I must go.

Yet why did I begin to write? Before I leave, I must decide what to do with these letters. After these many ages, I guess I know my king, and I know Dis will choose to withdraw soon. Dis will be punctual, will obey his time. I'll go with him. He'll think I go for love of him, and that's just as well. He deserves his Queen's honor.

But these letters. Hermes brought them from Da three centuries ago, and I haven't decided what to do with them. Why did I begin writing one more? Mother could have simply let go, but obviously I can't. I've always been weak, not like Mother and Dis. Da and Dis were always strong.

I've never been brave, never had courage. I'm not, actually, very wise. Yet Mother was great and there were things she did not do, could not do. She never killed anyone on purpose, she couldn't burn these pages, she couldn't ask me to swear I'd burn them.

I lack the courage to burn these rolled-up sheets. Another idea comes to mind, but it's got the same problem. Christians have their book, a Bible, and there are Sutras, there's a Torah, all sorts of books. I could carry this rolled-up bundle to earth, leave it somewhere to be found. Humans love to have books of immortals' gossip. It would be simple to do.

And I won't do it. Not because Mother would have hated it, not out of principles, not in scorn for words or books. It's all because of myself. I've never truly done anything. I don't know how to start.

Dis calls. He'll want to withdraw soon. Da calls. I should go up to earth. Dis, then Da. Dis again. Dis and Da. Dis and Da. I ran between them all these centuries, life and death handing me back and forth, like a flower.

I feel contemptible.

I have to go, the ghosts keen loudly. "Flowers," many whispers insist, "colors." Flowers, colors, brilliant, what do they want? And why do I rage against it when it's only my duty?

I should rise.

Then an idea, yes. I leave these letters here, in the middle of my gold table. Since they're left out, Dis will read them. He may burn them. He may bury them, or tear them up and scatter their leaves to float up the Lethe. Perhaps he will give them to Zeus, That One Great Immortal Over All Others. I laugh, the letters would be misplaced in his travels, never recovered.

So what of that? Then I'll place this page on top.

* * *

To my beloved King and Lord:

> I am sorry to add this burden to your many other duties.
>
> I honor whatever you do.

Ghosts are keening. Warm winds chatter my name. All right, all right, you impatient seasons, I'm coming. Vicious round, I'm coming.

> Happy is that man among men on earth who has seen these things.
>
> Homer
> "Hymn to Demeter"